THE DARK MESSIAH

THE SECOND DARK AGES

MICHAEL ANDERLE

LMBPN PUBLISHING

DEDICATION

From Michael

To Family, Friends and
Those Who Love
To Read.
May We All Enjoy Grace
To Live The Life We Are
Called.

The Dark Messiah
The Second Dark Ages 01

Beta Editor / Readers

Bree Buras (Aussie Awesomeness)
Tom Dickerson (The man)
Sf Forbes (oh yeah!)
Dorene Johnson (US Navy (Ret) & DD)
Dorothy Lloyd (Teach you to ask...Teacher!)
T S (Scott) Paul (Author)
Diane Velasquez (Chinchilla lady & DD)

JIT Beta Readers

Brent Bakken
Heath Felps
Michael Horgan
Thomas Ogden
Michael Pendergrass
Melissa Ratcliffe
Hari Rothsteni

Keith Seymour
Warren Wheeler

If I missed anyone, please let me know!

Editors
Stephen Russell
Kat Lind
EllenCampbell (Version 2.0)

**Thank you to the following Special Consultants
for The Dark Messiah**

**Jeff Morris - US Army - Asst Professor Cyber-Warfare,
Nuclear Munitions (Active)
Heath Felps - US Navy CPO (Active)**

LMBPN Publishing

PMB 196, 2540 South Maryland Pkwy

Las Vegas, NV 89109

First US edition, 2016

Version 2.00 Edited by Ellen Campbell, July 2017

Version 2.01 August 2017

The Etheric Dimension

THE NUMBNESS WAS EVER PRESENT. The darkness a cocoon of protection for Michael against the pain of remembering.

The guilt building up over the days, weeks, months, years and decades of selfishly resting in the knowledge that pleasured his soul. The time his consciousness flared to life, but his physical body was not yet complete.

She was out there.

Michael's connection to her feeding the emotional craving that his heart needed to be filled.

Until the *pain*.

The pain he felt through the connection within the womb of Etheric energy his body was using to repair itself.

His eyes snapped open to see nothing clearly. Then, the grayness, a void, as he turned his head first left, then right, as his eyes adjusted and focused. Finally, he looked down at this body. He frowned, he was naked as the day he was born.

Worse, he was hairless.

He stood slowly, feeling the little crystals that had been clinging to his back evaporate. He was, he admitted as he turned looking in all directions, clueless.

The shock of pain that had jolted him from his mental stupor was receding into the grayness itself.

Was the pain real, or had he imagined it? Michael stood in the mist and waved his hand through it. Like a fog on the New England coastline, it swirled in the light. Neither transparent nor solid, it merely created eddies of diffusion. Candy to his eyes.

He frowned. Like the calories from candy, they didn't help him one damned bit.

He turned around and considered what he remembered from the dreams, from the nightmares.

His eyebrows drew together into a mask of concentration. Piecing together the remnants of a time before his sleep, his eyes flashed once, twice, then three times red and the third time they stayed red.

Now, the fog in front of Michael swirled, the glow from his eyes merging with the space around him, pushing the new color into the gray.

He turned his head, his mind seeking back to the time, the time when life wasn't strictly Honor, Responsibility, and *Loneliness.*

The time of when his life changed because of the woman. The woman he still felt in his soul, the connection he shared with her strong here in this... He looked around, this Etheric Dimension. He had been here before.

With *her.*

She had... has, he corrected, black hair and a sharp tongue.

He smiled, the first time in how long he couldn't know. Her name would come back to him. He did remember her sarcastic, and occasionally caustic, verbal skills.

She was a fighter! She was the one... the one who had made him desire to live again, and now a second time she brought him back from being a dead man.

Michael started walking, taking determined steps unerringly towards where he needed to get out of this dimension and return to Earth.

He had a promise to keep. While he might not remember the details, he was sure he wasn't going to fulfill his promise in this place.

No, he needed to step out into the world of the humans again and find her.

His sense of honor demanded it.

Michael slowed his walk, feeling the rightness of the location he had come upon as being the entrance he had used so long ago to escape the pain. Now, he needed to figure out how to leave this dimension.

His eyes flashed brightly a fourth time, glee written in the shadows that fell on his face.

Her name was Bethany Anne.

SOUTH OF DOUGLAS MOUNTAIN, Old Colorado (United States Post-Apoc)

JEREMIAH KICKED THE HORSE. "Ktch ktch, let's go, Black," he said as the horse left the shallow stream and climbed up out of its bed to the rise above.

It was just twelve feet up.

It hadn't been much cover, but it had been enough to hide Jeremiah as he and Black walked down the streambed, so it had been enough for him. Better to be proactive than dodging gunfire from those here in the Fallen Lands.

Five minutes later, he pulled on the reins and put a hand on the horse's shoulder. "Still, stay still." He had finally caught on to why Black had been nervous for the last minute.

He loosened the gun in its holster, but he was pretty sure this wasn't a shooting discussion. "You know," he said conversationally, throwing his voice out ahead of him. "If you want to talk, let's talk. It's damned hot out here."

He looked east and could see the eastbound dirigible rising over the remains of old Denver, heading God knows where and taking God knew who out of these Fallen Lands.

Even a century and a half after the world went to shit, protecting yourself first was the rule of the day. Justice hadn't made its face known again, at least not out here.

Five seconds later, two horses and their riders broke from cover about a hundred feet ahead of him on the trail.

One of the guys, black hair and a scar across his nose, spit to the side as he and his partner rode towards Jeremiah.

"Plenty close," Jeremiah commented, and the two pulled up ten yards away. "Can I help you?" he asked, eyeing each of them.

Scar-nose rested both hands on his pommel as he looked around, the sun beating down. He turned back to Jeremiah. "We've been told to deliver a message from the boss, so we're here delivering it."

Jeremiah nodded for him to continue. He watched the talking man's partner, a thin and wiry guy, eyes darting about the area. He was the one who would possibly fly off the handle and just start shooting.

"The boss is tired of Sarah Jennifer telling him to take a hike," Scar-nose said. "So tell her she's got one week to reconsider either selling or bedding. Each day she continues to be obstinate?" He shrugged and spit again. "Well, the price goes down, and the pleasure is decreased. At some point, even gentlemen don't give a rat's ass anymore, and the boss will stop trying to be civil in this godforsaken uncivilized land."

Jeremiah understood.

The two turned, with Scar-nose looking over his shoulder to give a parting shot, "You might mention to the other guys she's got helping her on her land, those that don't fire on us? We won't fire on them."

This time, it was Jeremiah's turn to make a face of disgust and spit into the weeds.

Sarah Jennifer had fourteen hands helping her with the land. There were only three others—including himself—he was positive would be willing to shoot back in her defense.

Jack "the Boss" Childers had thirty-two.

Even with Sarah Jennifer's mercenary skills and weapons from her time before, that still left them outgunned at least two to one, and that was the best case.

"Ktch Ktch," he called to Black, pulling on the reins to go to their right. "Let's get home, I've got to report back to the lady."

The two started moving off into the brush.

He ducked under a tree limb. "Cause shit just got too damned real," he murmured.

THE ETHERIC DIMENSION

STUMPED.

Michael was frustrated, his lips compressed into a tiny line cutting across the horizontal plane of a face irritated with itself.

"How does she do this?" he mumbled for the hundredth time, if he had mumbled it once.

Michael had been standing there for what seemed like forever. He knew he merely needed to take a step and he should be on the other side. He should be... He took another testing step, and dropped out of the grayness into nighttime on the side of a hill, falling through limbs, as he slipped and tumbled twice ass over head.

"Gott Verdammt!" he cursed before his legs hit a low-hanging branch that twisted him him around sadistically, turning him over to land hard. His breath exploded out of his mouth, his eyes wide in surprise and pain.

He was now on the ground, lying on his back, looking up into the branches of a tree above him. Silvery moonlight caressed its branches.

"Oooouuuch," he moaned, lying there a moment to collect his thoughts.

Michael reached towards his back and rolled to his left. His right hand grabbed a small rock and yanked it out from underneath him. He pulled it up in front of him and looked at it in the moonlight. He opened his mouth to say something, but then shook his head and tossed the rock away to land in the bushes.

He listened for a second, not hearing or feeling anything dangerous. Twenty feet above him, something silvery and translucent seemed to close slowly.

The silver expanse, he would later swear, snickered at him when it closed, and the tree limbs behind it were all he now saw.

He was losing it. He rolled forward and stood up, brushing pine needles and other dirt and detritus from his body.

He looked around, snatches of memory of a run coming back. He had a bag, a package. NO! He had a bomb. He had been running to return it to someone who had attacked the...

Michael turned, looking up the mountain. He had been running away from the base.

Michael took his first step in the moonlight, up towards the location where there should be a base.

A base... and answers.

SOUTH OF DOUGLAS MOUNTAIN, **Old Colorado (United States Post-Apoc)**

JEREMIAH RODE into the main yard about two hours before sunset. He pulled off the saddle and rubbed down his horse. He put Black in a stall and stuffed some oats into the feedbag, then dug around in a sand filled tub to find a carrot.

He nodded towards Jake, one of the men who, in his opinion, was a question mark, and headed towards the back of the house.

Towards the office.

Sarah Jennifer wasn't some old woman willing to take in just anyone. No, she was an ex-tactical member of the FDG—the Force de Guerre. Still young, she had suffered some neurological damage during a mission, and they couldn't get her back to prime reaction speed again. She wasn't willing to be dead weight on the tactical teams and refused to take an office job.

It reminded her too much of what she couldn't do anymore.

Jeremiah arrived at the back and pulled the string that rang a bell inside her office. Soon enough, her voice came out of a tube next to the door. "You got my attention, who is this and what do you need?"

He was pretty sure she knew exactly who was standing there, but her ability to keep secrets was legendary. For example, none of them knew how many weapons she kept as an ex-merc. To keep that a secret this long? Pretty damned impressive.

He grinned for anyone who might see him talking. "It's Jeremiah, SJ." He lowered his voice. "I got a message from TB's goons to relay to you."

Her voice, confused, came back through the tube, "TB...? Oh, that jackass." Jeremiah could almost picture her blue eyes rolling under her blond hair. "Come in, let's discuss scuzzbucket's latest threat." With a clunk, the door unlocked, and Jeremiah pulled it open and walked in. The door closed, and a small bar automatically locked into place behind him.

The hallway was only ten feet long, with a door at the end that opened into the house proper. He took two steps and turned right. Inside the room was a small round table with three chairs for meetings. Sarah Jennifer, a pencil in her right hand, was tap-tap-tapping the desk as he walked in.

She noticed his sand and sweat covered body and got to the point. "Okay, what's bull-shittiest-maximus want this time?"

"Your ass, or your land, probably both," Jeremiah told her. He grabbed one of the two chairs in front of her desk and pulled it back to sit down. "Sucks to be you!"

She snorted. "I understand it used to be that women wanted men to appreciate them for their intellect, not their tits. Now, my intellect is third string behind my land."

Jeremiah kept his mouth shut.

The tap-tap-tap of the pencil continued. "That's not all, is it?" she asked, watching his fidgeting hands. "You got something you don't want to say. What's asshat got planned now?"

Jeremiah looked up at the ceiling and then back to Sarah Jennifer. "The two heavies told me you got a little time to make a decision, one week. You either decide to marry him, or sell to him. If you go past that, then he reduces what he's willing to pay, and the insinuation is... it won't be a wedding bed at the end of the deal, but there will be a physical consummation." Jeremiah looked pissed that he even had to pass on such a despicable threat.

Sarah Jennifer's eyes narrowed. "So, sell or rape?" Jeremiah returned her gaze and nodded. "Well, at least the disgusting pig is finally showing his true colors." She blew out a breath. "He's got about thirty in his crew?"

"Last I heard, it was thirty-two. But if he decides that isn't enough he could get some cheap hands willing to pull a trigger and maybe get ten more from closer to old Denver. That is, if he

decides it's going to be a pain in the ass to root us out. But..."
Jeremiah turned to look in the direction of the hands' sleeping
quarters. "I can't promise you more than three for damned sure,
and five if I'm giving a couple the benefit of the doubt."

Her lips pressed together and she followed his gaze where
it led.

Out toward the building where her hands slept at night.

2

Outside an Old Military Base, West of Old Denver, Colorado (United States Post-Apoc)

CONFUSION WAS HIS FIRST REACTION.

Michael looked around and considered confusion to be his second, third and damn near the fourth reaction as well.

What happened?

He walked, bare ass naked, through a base that had seen better days. When he pulled open a door, and it dropped off of its hinges, he had to admit it had seen better years and most likely decades.

Perhaps a better century?

Michael walked into the old command center. It was dusty, a broken window in the front allowing the weather in. A few leaves were lodged in crevices.

Empty.

He moved further into the base inside the mountain, trying to understand what was going on. Each office he checked was cleared of anything relevant. He found no computer equipment and more than that, he found none of the lights to be in working order.

It was chilly, so the time of year had to be fall, at least. It took him a while and the only thing he ran across was a small supply room. He did find clothes of a sort. They were old work clothes, a single suit. He snagged an available tan pair but made a face.

They weren't his preferred style. But he was clothed, and that had to be worth something at the moment.

He walked across the base, the parking lot empty, and went to where he had lived with Bethany Anne. The building was not only empty, it was boarded up. Not a type of boarding because windows were busted, no, this was boarded up to keep people from going through something important inside.

This was professional, and it had the faintest marks that showed warnings about radioactivity. Which seemed ludicrous. His time in the Etheric enhanced his ability to discern energy, and there was no radiation that he could feel.

Well, he hoped there wasn't. His lack of hair was bothering him, and all he needed to do was get a fresh dose of radiation to screw any chance of his hair growing back. He could still regenerate from wounds, that he had figured out after falling out of the Etheric and using the limbs of a tree to slow his rapid descent.

He willed himself to turn to Myst, that amorphous state that allowed him to disappear and fly, moving through gaps that only air could flow through.

Except he was still standing right in front of the boarded up living quarters, looking stupid.

He turned to look around, but there was nothing but the old, rundown base and a bird flying overhead about a quarter-mile to the north.

And, he wasn't in his Myst form at all.

"Okay, something broke that used to work," he muttered. "Like my hair growing."

He made a fist and tapped on the board where the door

should be. The noise from his knock confirmed his guess, it was hollow behind there.

He made a fast, sharp punch and the board cracked. He did this twice more and reached in with his left hand, pulling out pieces and noticing the thickness of the wood.

They really didn't want anyone in here.

Tossing the chunks of wood behind him, he grabbed a few more pieces and pulled, yanking them off. He found a metal crossbeam and smiled. Something he could really get a grip on. He set his feet, his eyes glowed red, and he pulled, the strain on his muscles felt good, felt warm, felt like...

CRACK!

A massive, ten foot high by a four foot wide chunk of the wood was breaking out of the protective surrounding. Michael frowned. He felt both stronger and weaker at the same time. It was as if his energy was deeper, like his connection to the Etheric was beyond his previous ability.

But his muscles didn't work nearly as well. He flexed his arms, rolling his shoulders to test his body.

"Now, this is damned embarrassing." He was out of shape for the first time in over a thousand years. "Can't let Bethany Anne see me like this. I'm hairless, and in desperate need of some serious exercise," he huffed in exasperation.

He took a step to the side and yanked three more times on the steel beam, and finally, a huge chunk of the wall cracked, and he tossed it to the side, dust coming up from the ground where it made a resounding crash.

Behind the opening was the door that led into their apartment.

"Nothing ventured, nothing gained." he checked the door-knob, and it was locked. "Of course it is," he kicked it open. What was inside surprised him.

The living room had the couches removed. There was a round table, with two chairs.

The table stood in the center, a piece of paper in the middle. Michael walked past the table and went to the bedroom.

It held their bed, made up. He looked around, but there was nothing else in the room. It seemed an empty room one might find at an old motel, it was so devoid of anything personal. He opened the closet, but it was empty.

"No clothes. Couldn't you have at least left behind some clothes, baby?" he muttered. He stepped into the bathroom.

Clean.

He stepped out and made his way into the brighter main room, heading straight for the table and the note. It was time to see what this was about.

"Dearest Michael,

Your clothes, if you should need them, are in the locked area near the Team BMW workshop. You should be able to Myst through the opening we left you at the top. I didn't know what you would want to wear, so I left you everything from suits to jeans and a few items in between.

John and the team left you a surprise.

There are weapons for you as well.

I leave you these things because you made me a promise, one I expect you to fulfill.

You had better return to me, or when I am done with the Kurtherians, I will figure out how to go back in time and kick your ass.

All my love and my heart,

Bethany Anne."

Michael stood there for minutes, reading and re-reading the note. She expected him to return and she was waiting. He folded the note and put it in the pocket on his chest. The outfit he had on might be ugly, but it had a lot of pockets.

He turned and walked out of the suite and took a slight left. He needed to go about a half mile around the front and to the other side of the airplane hangars where Team BMW's garage used to be. Apparently, his love had taken the fight out into space. And by the look of things, something must have happened here on Earth either before or after she left.

Something that had caused them to leave Earth, and apparently for her to lock up their base and make it look like it was dangerous to explore. He suspected they had washed it down with radioactivity sometime in the past.

Nothing he could feel, anyway. He sure hoped he wasn't wrong and didn't glow in the dark. That's all he needed to see in the mirror.

A bald head that reminded him of a light bulb at night.

South of Douglas Mountain, Old Colorado (United States Post-Apoc)

The seven men decided to camp away from the main house that evening. Two of them nodded to each other and the first, the one with dark hair, walked out away from the fire to guard against the chance of someone trying to sneak up on them.

It wasn't likely to happen, but this evening, it was as much to protect against those from their own people coming up to the fire and listening to the talk as it was to protect from others who might wish them ill.

The second man, David Tellison, waited ten minutes to make sure his friend was properly down the path. Once the time was up, he walked beside the fire that the other five guys were sitting around, drinking a form of coffee that they made out of bark off some tree and clapped his hands to get their attention.

He looked around at the men eyeing him. "Okay, I know the rumors have been heard by everyone. So, I'm here to figure out what you guys are going to do when Boss Childers' men attack Sarah Jennifer. I'll tell you this straight up. She's been good to me, but she ain't been good enough to me so that I take bullets for her. I ain't waiting to be stuck there, guns in front and guns in the back of me."

Jackson spit behind the log he was sitting on. "I figure he has what, forty guns?"

David nodded. "That's the low count, he can afford more."

Jackson chewed on a bit of jerky. "Wouldn't be right to leave Sarah Jennifer and run over to Childers' group."

"I'm not suggesting we go join Childers, even I know that would be a dick move," David retorted.

"Dick move or not," Buddy spoke up from his log next to Jackson, "it'd be easy money."

David nodded to Buddy. The man was strictly out for himself, and David figured if the best he could do was make sure six out of the seven here didn't join Childers, then that was something for Sarah Jennifer.

That night, five more decided to leave the employ of Sarah Jennifer and seek their fortune somewhere else.

Somewhere that didn't have thirty or forty men gunning for them.

—

The small town was less town as much as it was a stronghold. Men and women came in—some left again, others stayed. Either they were persuaded this was a safe location… or they remained, as slaves.

The young woman, attractive, used her sense of touch to grab the next plate.

Others asked the boss why he kept an obviously deficient girl in the camp.

Too many thought that a blind girl couldn't listen and think for herself. But in that, they would be wrong. She hadn't always been blind, that was a new development that had happened when her people had been attacked. She had left her pack against her dad's wishes and decided to travel the Fallen Lands. Seeking her fortune, he told her, was a damned fool's journey.

She had yelled back that she would just be a damned fool then.

Now, she couldn't see. For her kind, it was almost unheard of. She should have healed from the damage by now, or died.

She wasn't dead. The hours in front of a tub of water washing dishes and occasionally in front of a tub washing clothes, was proof she was still alive.

But she could hear, much better than normal humans, and she had heard the boss's answer.

He was just waiting until she was old enough so he could bed her. Didn't the rest of them see how beautiful she was going to be? He was waiting, he told the men, for the flower to be as beautiful as she would ever be before plucking it.

Jacqueline always kept a knife secreted on her body.

This flower, she had decided, was going to have thorns.

Deep Under the Base

The E.I. woke up.

It had been in a passive mode for almost eighty-two years, by the records it kept. The typical intrusions into the base had been logged, and it had obediently uploaded the information to the E.I. resources in outer space, placed there by TQB Enterprises when they had used this base.

Well over a hundred and fifty years before.

The base E.I. was hidden behind tons of rock that had been dropped before the old government could try to force their way into this hidden server room.

But the E.I. was still connected, still recording, and still updating the files to the E.I.s in outer space.

It logged the human who had found the supply closet. Then, the person left for a couple of hours before it triggered the alarms that brought the E.I. online.

It was in front of Storage Location D.D.2. The E.I. watched, patiently, as the human stayed in front of the door for three hours before it seemed to disappear off of its sensors.

The E.I. remained on full alert for another twelve minutes, then it changed its parameters required to wake up and went back to sleep.

Never realizing the human had gotten inside a secured room within the base.

3

South of Douglas Mountain, Old Colorado (United States Post-Apoc)

THE THREE MEN ate sitting around a small fire. It was a little chilly, but they dared not build anything larger. The stress up at the main house was tense.

The size of the fire matched the size of their spirits. Small and not much help warming them up.

Jeremiah looked out at the landscape and blew out a heavy breath. He turned back and nodded to the others. "Todd, Dirk, I got to ask, and I'm going to lay it out right up front, I'm staying."

Todd, about six foot two inches and thin as a sapling tree snorted. "You know it's our deaths, right? Sarah Jennifer ain't going to go down for any man. She'll take her size whatever the hell they are boots and shove them up Childers' ass, guns blazing before she takes any of his deals."

"Seven," Dirk answered. Both men looked at him. "What?" He shrugged. "Common size for women, it isn't strange or anything."

"She had you clean them, right?" Todd asked. "Caught you cussin' around her?"

"Damn right she caught me cussing," Dirk admitted, smiling at the memory. "I slipped and popped myself in the mouth trying to pull some leather. It hurt. So, I go off and say shit or something like that. I turn around and there she is, glaring at me like my mom or something. I figured, what the hell, so I went ahead and let loose with everything I could remember."

"Got them all out of your system?" Jeremiah asked.

"Yeah," Dirk said.

"So, did you screw up again?" Todd asked. "Just curious, took me three times to start looking around, myself."

Dirk smirked. "One other time."

Todd turned to Jeremiah. "You?"

"Oh, no." Jeremiah shook his head. "My mom was hell on wheels about cussing. So I learned early to treat all women as ladies."

Todd nodded in the direction of the house. "That why we all making our last stand?"

Jeremiah turned in the direction of the house. "No, not for me. Sometimes you realize that when civilization cratered, morality took a beating. Justice died, and ethics took a sabbatical." He turned back to the two men with him. "Ain't ever gonna come back unless someone is willing to take a stand."

Dirk pointed to Todd and then Jeremiah and finally at himself. "So, the three of us against thirty... or more right?"

"Well, say it like that, and you make me want to tell Childers he needs to bring another twenty or so. Don't forget Sarah Jennifer is worth probably ten of those sad sacks."

"And her armament."

"Have you ever seen it?" Dirk asked.

"Her guns?" Jeremiah asked.

He never got to answer, a call came out of the night.

—

Michael had been walking for a day already. It had taken him three solid hours to figure out how to Myst again and go through the damned hole up at the old base.

At least he had decent clothes again.

Bethany Anne had left money. While he kept some, he figured it would probably be useless. He had on jeans, a black shirt, and for some insane reason, her guards had left him a black leather trench coat.

It did help hide his two pistols, apparently Jean Dukes Specials. He read the instructions carefully before locking them to his palm print. With over five thousand rounds, he figured he would be good for a while. But he had no idea how often this new world would require... attitude adjustments.

He practiced with the pistol, turning up the kinetic kick from one to ten and back down. Ten had impressive destruction. John's note to him explained how the gun used Etheric generated magnetic something or other and how the rounds were made to replace them.

Basically, he realized, he had a tiny railgun in his hand. Technology ahead of its time and probably still ahead of this period, as well.

Well, he sure hoped so. He was sure that railgun technology would be pretty nasty stuff to deal with if it was pointed at him.

Finally, she left two Wakizashis and one Katana. He left the Katana behind as being too impractical and kept one Wakizashi, the two pistols, two sets of clothes and scrounged for soap and other stuff, pushing it into a leather bag he slung over his shoulder.

He had no shampoo. He spent an extra hour looking for any damned shampoo, but the base was dry. He passed a mirror at the hour mark and saw his reflection.

Making a face, he realized the soap was sufficient. He still had no damn hair.

It took him another two hours to once again attain his Myst

form and make it back up and out of the base. He was pushing himself, flying fast, and had made it halfway down the mountain when he suddenly dropped out of Myst form. This resulted in an ass over appetite, arms and legs flailing, tumble down the slope. He traveled more than a hundred yards, introducing himself to hundreds of small rocks and stones and bouncing off of one damned large rock in the process.

He lay for a minute, just muttering "OOOOwwwww" over and over again.

Finally, he turned over and stood up, trudging back up the hill, grabbing his bag and thinking about why he was having trouble with skills he had honed over a thousand years.

"Focus," he muttered. "It's got to be the focus." Some time later, he saw the campsite, the tiny fire burning like a lighthouse beacon for him.

—

"Helloooo the fire!" a strange voice called out.

Jeremiah, Dirk, and Todd all turned towards the voice, Dirk sliding out about twenty feet into the trees off to the side.

"Not looking for trouble, guys," the voice called to them. "Just looking to make a difference and get some questions answered. May I approach?"

Jeremiah called back, "Who you with, stranger?"

"Just myself, I recently landed in these parts," the voice replied.

"C'mon in, but behave yourself," Jeremiah allowed. "We ain't got much, but what we got, we'll share."

The man entered the dim light of the fire, and Jeremiah's eyebrows went up. He was damned handsome, even though didn't have a lick of hair on his head. Nor could he see any scars on the man.

And he carried himself like a warrior.

"You can come out of the trees, Dirk," Jeremiah called out. "If he was here to harm us, I imagine he would have already done it."

Todd looked over at his friend. "And you say this because why, the black coat?" He turned back to the stranger. "No offense, the black leather is impressive. But Jeremiah here," he threw a thumb back at his friend, "is way too impressed with clothes. He was indeed born in the wrong age."

"No, jackass," Jeremiah replied, and pointed at the stranger. "Because he balances like a cat, he's got at least one pistol I've seen and something else underneath that coat. I'd guess a sword. He knew where," he pointed to the trees where Dirk was just appearing, "Dirk went, and he wasn't bothered by coming right up to us. So," he turned back to the stranger, "is it just you, or do you have another out there waiting to come in?"

"No," the stranger said, "it's just me. I overheard what you were talking about, so I have a basic understanding of what you're up against. So... I thought I might see if it's a fight I care to join."

"Let me get this right." Dirk scratched his nose. "You, mister, want to join the three of us," he pointed to his friends, "and one lady you haven't met against thirty to forty guns?"

"You said she was worth ten herself, right? Doesn't that leave, at best, ten for each of us?" the stranger asked in a no-nonsense voice. "I don't know about you guys, but in my time, we tended to pride ourselves on being better than the ladies."

Todd's mouth dropped open and he butted into the conversation. "Stranger, you got a name?"

He turned towards the man, his calm eyes seeming to bring the temperature down a moment. "Yes. It's Michael."

"Well, Michael," Todd said, a little less boisterous, "unless you've been in the FDG, you might have a small problem with Sarah Jennifer. I'll be willing to bet you a boot cleaning..."

"Excuse me, a what?" Michael interrupted. "A boot cleaning?"

"Ahhh," Jeremiah tried to explain. "It has less to do with money and more to do with embarrassment. No one likes to lose a bet and be made to clean boots, it's humiliating."

"And the FDG?" Michael prompted.

"You from another country?" Dirk asked. "You never heard of the FDG?"

"Can we pretend I'm from another time and leave the real history out of it?" Michael asked, pushing a little soft velvet over steel tones into his voice.

All the men agreed that was a splendid idea.

Michael mumbled as he looked around the campsite, "Glad to know one damned thing still works."

"The FDG," Dirk answered, "is Force de Guerre. They started over a century ago. They come in, they kick ass, they leave. Made up of a lot of damned impressive people. Many are really strong, or really fast. They try and keep a little normalcy out here in the Fallen Lands."

Michael bit his tongue, he would follow up on that later. "So, they're the police force?"

Todd and Jeremiah both snorted. "I wish," Jeremiah answered. "If we had a police force, the three of us wouldn't be rushing forward to die."

Michael's eyes narrowed. "And why do you think you're going to die?"

"Because chivalry," Todd answered, eyeing his friend, "makes us dead."

Michael raised an eyebrow. "Oh, then I definitely want in on this."

"Why, you have a death wish?" Dirk asked, amusement coloring his voice.

"No," Michael said, his voice going cold. "I just have something against those who would wish a woman dead."

—

Sarah Jennifer looked out over her yard, her dark, vacant yard, and snorted.

Not one.

Not one damned man decided to stick with her. Well, except

for Jeremiah, Todd, and Dirk. She knew why the guys actually stepped off the property here by the house. It was easier for the other dickless dirtbags to put their tail in between their legs and run away.

She turned and entered the house. What was done was done. She wasn't going to change anything by screaming in annoyance when it was her feelings that were hurt, not her concern with dying.

Her old merc leader, TH, had told her one time, you do what you got to do. Most of the time, it will come out all right. Occasionally? Well sometimes it might come up snake eyes, and you just hope that when you close your eyes a final time, you can be proud of yourself.

That was over ten years ago. She considered what she had built out here in the Fallen Lands and found it good. She'd helped over a hundred souls through the years and pulled a few out of a bad future. Now, she had three who were willing to walk into purgatory with her.

She stopped in the kitchen and started the coffee water to boiling on the old pot-bellied wood stove. It helped heat the house and warm the body.

And hopefully, the soul, when all of this was done.

"Hellooo the house?" a strange voice called.

Sarah Jennifer turned towards the door leading outside. She pushed the coffee pot off and walked towards the back of the house, grabbing a rifle on her way.

It would be stupid not to be careful.

She took a sidestep into the viewing room beside the door and looked out. In the faint light, she could see her three guys up on their horses, surrounding a tall man in a black trench coat, the light reflecting off his bald head. He was looking at the yard and the apparent lack of activity for such large buildings, the stables mostly empty.

Bastards had even taken the horses she had provided them.

With her men behind him, she considered it safe enough. She set the rifle down and walked around to the door, opening it and stepping outside.

—

Michael looked around, his lip twitching. He could see the signs that there should be at least another fifteen people minimum here right now.

All this woman had was the three guys behind him and now, him.

Seemed like the other side might need to bring another thousand if they wanted a shot at this.

His cold eyes turned back towards the house when he heard the slight grating of wood on wood. He caught the motion and saw the concealed place she was using to check him out.

Him and his bald head, he frowned. How very Yul Brynner of himself.

Fortunately, the bastard nanocytes that had his hair wrong didn't consider his eyebrows too. He was having enough of a problem dealing with his chrome dome up top. If he didn't have his eyebrows, he might decide it just wasn't worth living any longer.

He snorted, perhaps Bethany Anne was right. Just a little.

He *could* be rather vain.

He could hear her close the viewing door and move around. The main door opened up a second later, and an attractive, slightly older woman stepped out. Her figure cast shadows from the lights around the yard.

She nodded to the men behind him and then spoke to him.

—

"Mister, can I ask why my guys here are bringing you around? I can only trust that these miscreants informed you we expect to be attacked tomorrow?"

"Blunt," Michael replied.

She raised an eyebrow. "Do you have a problem with blunt?" His little smirk annoyed her. "Do you?"

Michael pursed his lips. "I don't. I doubt you can be blunter than a couple of women I know." He thumbed at the guys behind him. "And, these men did inform me that there was going to be a little activity here tomorrow."

She threw an annoyed glance over at Jeremiah.

Jeremiah put up his hands. "Hey! I told him the details. He said he wanted to come along."

Sarah Jennifer stepped off the porch and started her way towards Michael. "And what details would those be, Jeremiah?"

Before Jeremiah could answer, Michael replied, "Probably forty, maybe fifty guys coming here to burn down the place, take you whether you like it or not and the expectation they'll all end up dead."

Sarah Jennifer threw a glance at the guys. Dirk leaned forward as he sat on his horse and hissed quietly towards Michael, "Way to go get her pissed off!"

Sarah Jennifer pointed to the men. "That's going to be boot washing for all of you, bad attitude!"

"How about..." Michael interrupted, drawing her ire as he put his hands behind his back, and started circling Sarah Jennifer. He looked her up and down.

"What are you doing?" she asked, but quickly countered his walk, keeping him ten feet away, and now focused on this stranger.

He nodded towards her. "You are favoring your left leg, be careful when you announce that."

Her eyebrows raised in surprise. "How about I use my supposedly weak right leg and kick your ass with it?"

"Well, if you're just going to be angry," Michael said, his hands still behind his back. "I'd still suggest using your left leg, more power."

Her eyes narrowed. "What was your suggestion going to be?"

"I understand from Jeremiah that if I cuss around you, it might be a boot washing if you can best me in a fight?"

"Or soap in your mouth, but we happen to be out of soap, so maybe horse dung instead?" she said, the thrill of a good fight already loosening up her muscles.

"Oh, I'm not worried about horse dung ever reaching this mouth," he told her, his right hand coming around and pointing at his face. "But how about we agree if you can't take me, then these guys are absolved from any punishment?"

"You are a cocky one, aren't you?" she proclaimed. Good, she liked them cocky.

"No, you mistake confidence for cocky," he said.

"What weapons?" she asked. "I see a sword and a couple of pistols if I'm not mistaken."

Michael stopped and cocked his head. "You aren't, but if you want weapons, feel free to go get some."

She stopped circling as well. "I always enjoy feeding a cocky person their foot to chew on."

"Well..." He reached into his jacket and pulled out the Wakizashi. Her eyes widened a little.

That was a beautiful piece of work, and it had been taken care of very nicely. She couldn't spot any dirt on the scabbard, at least not in the dark.

"Jeremiah?" Michael said, and when he knew he had the man's attention, he tossed the sword in its scabbard to him. "I'll expect that back in a moment."

"Wow, let me change that to super cocky," Sarah Jennifer said.

Michael turned to look at her and smirked. "Oh, I'm just getting started." At that comment, she raised her own eyebrows in surprise before they narrowed with purpose.

No one pushed her buttons and got away with it.

He reached under his jacket and pulled out two pistols. Todd whistled. "These are locked to me, you try to use them? Well, this Boss Childers won't need to worry about this place as we'll all be blown to kingdom come. So, if it's all the same to you, I'm putting these back in the holsters, and you have my word I won't draw them." He turned his right pistol and held a small button above the trigger.

All four heard a click.

"Turned off," he said and did the same for the second. "Now both are turned off."

"Or on," Jeremiah said.

Michael snorted. "So, this whole time I've been with you guys, I had my pistols off? I don't think so, and neither do you."

Sarah Jennifer's eyes narrowed. What kind of technology and guns did this guy have? Was he a plant from Childers?

He holstered the two pistols, and they heard the snap as he placed the leather back over them in the holster. The guys figured they had him if he played foul, they could take him with enough time to spare.

"Now, it's time for you to learn why chivalry was needed in the first place, Sarah Jennifer," he said. "Because, in my day, a woman understood why attacking a man was a poor idea."

The FDG or Force de Guerre never understood why Sarah Jennifer was faster than almost everyone in the group, except TH.

He knew, but he never shared the reason with anyone.

All Sarah Jennifer knew was she could kick ass. Men, women, it didn't matter. She didn't like being told she was about to be put in her little woman's place by a smirking man in her own yard.

But she wasn't a fool, either.

She cracked her neck and assumed a position with her right leg behind, only half her body now facing the guy. "Whenever you're ready to feel my size sevens up your ass," she said. "Bring it."

"Why is it," Michael asked as he started walking towards her, "that after so long being absent, I have to hear about size seven shoes coming from a female's mouth again?"

4

"Boss" Childers' Town, West of Denver, Colorado (United States Post-Apoc)

"HAVE YOU EVER," Jack Childers asked his second in command as the two of them walked through the small fortified town, "wondered how men dealt with having to turn the other cheek before the apocalypse?"

The two men topped over six feet tall. But Jack was at least thirty pounds of hard muscle larger than his hatchet man, Russell Wood. They stopped walking and looked around. "Seems to me," Russell turned away to spit into the dirt, "without that damned bitch for some of the slaves to run to for protection..."

"Or even giving them ideas," Jack interrupted.

"Point, giving them ideas," Russell agreed. "Life will be a little easier to deal with around here." Russell nodded towards the mess building. "You going to pop the cork over there?"

Jack turned around to see where Russell was nodding. "Jacqueline?" he asked as he turned back around to his partner.

"Yeah," he agreed. "Got to say, you called it on that one. She turned into a real beauty. Might be something to get ready for tomorrow night's festivities."

"Huh," Jack turned back around and started rubbing his chin. "That might not be a bad idea. Damn, I could go with getting a little pre-victory slash before..." the two men turned towards the front gates when the clanging started.

It was the signal for visitors, not a danger signal.

Although visitors could be a danger, as well.

Russell started walking towards the gate, Jack only half a step behind him. He looked over his shoulder at the Boss. "No rest, or sex, for the wicked, eh?"

Jack chuckled. "Maybe not tonight, but that wine only gets better with time."

They laughed as they approached the gate to find out two men from Sarah Jennifer's had arrived, wondering if they needed an extra hand or two?

SOUTH OF DOUGLAS MOUNTAIN, **Old Colorado (United States Post-Apoc)**

THE FOOL WAS WALKING RIGHT at her, not even trying to set up.

This man was stupid. She would spell it out in capitals for damned sure. What a world class shithead.

She darted forward, using the strength from her back leg to come at him faster than most anyone she had ever fought before. She tossed a right, a left and then followed it up with an uppercut.

CRACK!

Sarah Jennifer hit the dirt to her right and rolled twice before coming up eyes blazing, eyeing the man who had just casually knocked her ass silly. She put up a hand to feel if her burning cheek, and her teeth, were still a part of her body.

Behind them, Todd leaned towards Dirk. "Did he just block both of her punches, catch her fist and backhand the shit out of her?"

"Shhh!" Dirk answered in reply, then, "Yeah, I think so. It went so damned fast I'm not sure."

Michael turned to face the woman. "Not bad, but it's going to take a lot more to get those," he pointed at her feet, "anywhere near my ass."

Sarah Jennifer's eyes narrowed. "You surprised me."

"No, you're cocky," he replied. "Too much time being top bitch."

"Fuck…" She started towards him. "You!"

"Oh God," Jeremiah whispered, "She really, really hates to be called a bitch."

"Ready for your spanking?" Michael asked her. Her eyes, almost flaming mad, opened wide. Then she ran at him, ready to pound the smirk off his perfect face and make him swallow his damned teeth.

Using her momentum, she jumped, kicking out at him.

The pain, when it hit, was intense. He pivoted too fast. He used his left arm to stop her kick cold. Then he hit her in the shin with power she wasn't expecting. His right arm was out, and he let her momentum carry her right onto his fist, knocking the breath out of her. She damn near bounced off of him to slam into the ground, dirt and dust billowing away as she rolled over painfully a few times, making sure she didn't get kicked easily.

She couldn't breathe in enough at the moment to curse him out. Her shin, however, was cussing the shit out of her.

"So," he asked the woman lying on the ground, trying to find enough breath to struggle to get back up, hopping on her left leg due to the pain in her right. "Now we get to the point where you decide if you want to accept reality or allow your pride to put you right back there," he looked at the ground. "Again."

Her eyes darted to the three men on horses, all of them wide eyed at the spectacle.

"You should always believe," Michael said in a calm voice, a teaching voice, "there could be someone out there who can take you. Just because you might never have experienced it, doesn't make the reality an impossibility."

Sarah Jennifer, able to breathe again, spit out, "I've been bested once, but not by anyone not in the FDG."

"So, my lack of pedigree is the problem?" he asked, his eyes questioning. "I was told I had to prove myself to you to be included in teaching what the term chivalry really means."

"You, however," he continued, "need to prove to me that a lady is inside that body for chivalry to have any meaning." He turned to look around. "Obviously, the original meaning of chivalry is absent." He turned back towards her. "I'm referring to the more modern version of chivalry including manners, especially to the weaker, or fairer, sex." He nodded in her direction.

"And if I tell you to get the fuck off my land?" she asked him.

Jeremiah heard Todd whispering, "Please don't do that, oh please oh please oh please oh *please* don't do that…"

"This is your land because of what?" he asked.

"Hard work, and a willingness to keep it," she answered.

"Then you would be a fool to turn away an offer to help," Michael said. "And I've not been accustomed to helping idiots."

Sarah Jennifer was trying to figure out the man's meaning. His abrupt answers took a second for her to parse. "So, you're saying you would leave because telling you to leave is foolish."

"Indeed," he answered.

She gritted her teeth. Why the hell couldn't he just answer 'yes' like everyone else? She used her hands to start knocking the dirt and dust off of her clothes. It irritated her to know he didn't need to dust off at all. "Fair enough." She jerked her head towards her guys. "I'm too prideful for myself to keep you here, but I've been told that as a leader, your pride is what you swallow most."

Michael nodded his agreement.

She turned towards Jeremiah and started walking towards him, calling out over her shoulder, "You got a last name?" She reached out for Michael's sword, Jeremiah handed it down to her. She started back towards the man.

He reached out and accepted the sword, sliding it inside his jacket and connecting it somehow underneath it.

"Yes," he replied, his eyes looking out into the dark.

She put her hand on her waist. "Okay, thanks for making me play twenty questions, what is it?"

"Nacht."

"Good to know," she said, stepping around him and heading into the house. "Place to sleep is that way." She pointed towards the crew house.

None of the men noticed the fear in her eyes as she walked up the stairs to the porch.

—

Michael accepted the bowl of stew Jeremiah offered. He deflected their questions about his martial skills and speed.

"Don't you think not cleaning boots is enough for tonight?" he answered Todd. "Otherwise, you and I can have a physical discussion where you're too busy to ask me questions I obviously don't care to answer."

Todd stopped bugging him after that.

Michael stepped out of the crew house about midnight. A minute later, Jeremiah stepped out behind him.

"Hey," Jeremiah said.

"Good evening, Jeremiah." he replied.

"Don't be too hard on Sarah Jennifer. My family would say 'she's good people.'"

Michael grinned. "Anytime three men are willing to die to protect a woman?" he said, still looking into the night as if he actually saw something in the dark. "The woman is good people."

"I'm not sure how much you can help, Michael." Jeremiah chose to look into the dark as well. Why the hell not? "We need a damned savior for this to go in our favor tomorrow."

Michael chuckled, the sound wasn't peaceful. "I'm not an angel, nor a saint, Jeremiah," he said. "And certainly not a savior. Someone I love very dearly would tell you I'm just a stubborn, obstinate, pain in her ass."

"Where is she?" he asked. "Sorry if you've lost her."

Michael looked up at the stars, eyes flitting from one to the next wondering which one she might be fighting around right now. "Oh, I might have misplaced her for a while, but I haven't lost her."

—

Michael was leaning against that same post the next morning when Sarah Jennifer came out of the house. She eyed him, then set her shoulders and stepped off the porch, heading in his direction.

He raised an eyebrow at her in question.

"Firewood," she told him. "We need some. You willing?"

"Of course," Michael answered. "Which direction are you clearing?"

"Huh, hadn't expected you to know that." she turned and pointed to Michael's right. "About half a mile that way. You'll find a small hut with the tools in it. I'll send a lunch and one of the guys about noon to grab what you got so far." She turned back to him. "Be back here by dark. I think I know Jack Childers well enough to know he likes using the dark to ramp up the fear."

"I'll be here in time," he promised, then started walking in the direction she had indicated.

—

"You did *WHAT*?" Jeremiah, usually pretty quiet, hissed in anger at Sarah Jennifer.

The two of them were in her office, and it was late afternoon. Dirk and Todd had come back with two loads of firewood. More than they would need for days.

"I told him Jack wouldn't be here until dark," she replied, only slightly annoyed with him for getting angry at her.

"Help me understand, SJ," he said, his false calm evident. "Why you sent our one seriously badass guy away? He's going to get caught outside of the fight and not be able to help us. If he was to do anything, they'll just track his ass down and kill him."

"Look, I don't expect you to understand," she replied. "But there were a few stories that the FDG whispered, and they all came from Terry Henry."

"God!" Jeremiah burst out. "That man was not a god! Not everything that came from his mouth was Gospel!"

She leaned across her desk, finger pointed, eyes angry. "Then you tell me how many times you've heard 'Nacht' as a name before?"

"WHAAAT?" Jeremiah said, not following her logic at all. Typical female argument tactic. "The hell does Nacht have anything to do with this?"

She leaned back with a thump. "Because TH always said that if you should ever, ever meet someone that seemed too good to be true, with the last name Nacht, to leave them the fuck alone."

"We ARE leaving him alone!" Jeremiah argued. Then he pointed back towards the north. "The PLAN is we're not going to tell *Childers* to leave him alone!"

"Doesn't matter," she replied, her voice growing tired. "He's gone. He can't get back."

He shook his head in frustration. "You just screwed our best chance of living through this, SJ." Jeremiah stood up, pushing the chair back. He eyed her, the anger that wasn't in his voice clearly in his eyes. "The best chance for a savior of this colossal fuck up and you just pissed him away."

"He's no savior, no messiah, Jeremiah," she whispered to the empty room—he had already left her office fuming. She looked out, seeing the darkness coming in the sky, the shakes taking her.

"He's a dark messiah," she finished pronouncing to an empty house.

5

Michael had used the axe for his morning of wood chopping, enjoying the use of his muscles for an action he hadn't done for hundreds of years.

His skill was coming back like an old friend.

Todd and Dirk had joined him at noon, just like Sarah Jennifer had promised. They had been shocked at the amount of wood he had cut.

He had tried to be slow, but even going slow, it was obvious he was more than normal. So be it, some things he just didn't care if they figured out.

He had read her mind this morning. He knew she had intended to keep him out of the fight. But, in her own mind, it was honorable. She expected him to leave once he heard the gunshots, not come running in. No matter what she believed, she wasn't going to try and kill him.

Or let him die for her.

After Todd and Dirk had left, Michael started working on bringing back some skills. Namely the ability to create a thin micro-sized, incredibly sharp, Etheric edge along his arms. He practiced by cutting wood.

After a couple hours of practice, he looked around and rolled his eyes. He had over twenty trees all chopped up, with pristine cuts across every one of them. It was such a joy to use a skill that had been a part of him for so long and actually have it work, that he hadn't considered the results.

Well, Bethany Anne had taken over the responsibility for the strictures from him. If she was going to be upset, she could come down here and spank him...

Oh yes, he smiled, she could sure try. Then, he lost his smile. Without his Myst ability, was he still up to taking her?

"Oh... shit." he murmured, realizing he needed to get back into fighting form damned fast. His luck, she would show up and immediately decide she wanted a sparring partner.

Then, she would hand him his ass.

He turned towards the camp and started walking. "Time to get back into fighting shape."

—

"Todd," Sarah Jennifer nodded to the first man inside the door. "Dirk, Jeremiah." She shut the door, locked it and then Dirk and Jeremiah lifted the hardwood protection and placed it next to the door. Using a bar, they wedged it into place. All afternoon, they had prepared as best they could.

They had food, water, ammunition, and a shit-ton of wood. They used the extra to put against a couple of windows for more weight.

"Hell," Sarah Jennifer had said, when the guys got back with the wood. "I'd almost ask him back just to cut the wood for us."

Jeremiah eyed her, annoyance written plainly on his face. Dirk and Todd took the news that Michael was being left out of this fight without too much comment. A shrug from each.

It took about three more hours, an hour after sunset, for the first call to be heard.

—

"Go on," Jack pointed towards the house. "You wanted to join us, Buddy, so go do what I'm telling you."

The man nodded and kicked his horse a little to get it moving. The horse, knowing this was home, gladly headed towards the back of the house.

He paused outside of the main buildings. He suspected they were all in the house, but that Todd could be a sneaky ass. He shifted in the saddle, and shouted, "Sarah! Sarah Jennifer!" He waited a couple of moments. "The boss is ready to hear your reply. Are you going to give up your land and take his hand or..."

BAM!

Jack and Russell both snickered when Buddy's head exploded from a gunshot.

Russell leaned over his horse and spit out on the ground. Leaning back up he said, "I guess we got her answer."

Jack turned in his saddle. "Okay boys, circle the house. It's three nights in Denver on me for the one who kills her." There was a lot of whoops and yelling when he told them of this reward. When they died down, he added, "But... it's *TEN* nights if you bring her to me alive!"

—

In the trees a quarter way around the house, Michael watched the beginning of the altercation and smiled with the simplicity of the response Sarah Jennifer made. Michael had noticed how the horse only spooked a little when the body fell off. Then it walked into the barn.

Nice to know Sarah Jennifer didn't have much of a problem dealing with the riffraff.

—

"I figured Buddy might be one of the few that went to the other side," she said, ejecting the spent cartridge from the rifle. "I never could get him out of his selfish focus."

"You can't save everyone," Jeremiah commented from a room away.

—

Jack waited patiently as the fight started. He hoped they didn't have to set fire to her place. It was a nice home, well built and had a field of fire cleared for a hundred paces all the way around, offering the occupants a really good defensive position.

The pistol and rifle shots started cracking faster as the men found suitable locations to hide.

"I think we're going to have to burn her out," Russell said.

"You got the dynamite?" Jack asked.

"Yeah, but it'll be a bitch to get close enough to get it in place without getting shot."

"That's why I'm paying for nights in Denver. They have a couple o' good places for the men to get laid and taken care of. They won't remember a damned thing, but I'm sure they'll have fun."

"Speaking of Denver," Russell started.

"Give me time, Russell," Jack stopped him cold. "That's a bit of a bigger nut to crack. My people inside the city are making a few alliances to let us take over the West side if we move Kraven out. Once he's out of the way, we have West Denver and the Fallen Lands out this way."

"Well," Russell replied. "What I think is…"

He never finished his comment when the first scream came from the left of the house somewhere. It stopped… abruptly.

"The hell?" Russell stood up in his stirrups to look around and then sat back down again. "Can't see shit," he said.

"One of those assholes must be outside. Well, that's why…"

Then, a second and a third cry were heard. The guns slowed their fire at the house as those outside realized someone, or something, was hunting them.

That was when their horses started acting spooked.

—

"So," Jeremiah said. He stroked the trigger of the rifle Sarah

Jennifer lent him. The butt of the gun kicked him in the shoulder. "Damn, only made him duck."

"Did you guys hear a scream?" Dirk called out from the front of the house.

"No!" Sarah Jennifer replied, trying to find a new target. Her last one was either dead or had moved position when she got too close.

Moments later, she did hear a scream in the night. Then another. The bullets hitting the house slowed down.

The next, blood curdling, soul-shredding scream caused bumps to form on her arm.

"What... the... hell... is... that?" Todd asked.

"He's here," she whispered.

"Who's here?" Dirk asked as he walked into the room.

Jeremiah yelled, "Get back to your room, Dirk! If they think being in here is the safest, we can't let any make it in here!"

Dirk's eyes got big, and he turned, darting out the door, his feet clopping down the hallway back to his assigned location.

—

"Jack," Russell had turned his horse around, so the two were side-by-side but looking opposite directions. "That's the fifteenth scream."

"Tell me," Jack grated under his breath, "something I don't know! I can count past twenty, Russell."

"Well, we can't run afraid back to our town until our guys are all dead, or we have to kill them on the way back to town."

"Another unnecessary observation, Russell," Jack said.

Then, both turned their heads toward the east when a man yelled, "No... NO!... Oh God NOOOOooooooo!" his voice stopped as if someone had cut off his head.

—

"Sixteen," Jeremiah said inside the house.

The butt of Sarah Jennifer's rifle touched the floor. She turned and walked to the couch she had moved over from Denver herself to help furnish the place.

"The hell?" Jeremiah, sticking his head into her room, giving her a funny look.

She glanced at him. "Don't worry, you got your wish," she said.

"What wish is that?" he asked, wondering if he should call Dirk to take her position.

"The Dark Messiah," she pointed at the location of the last scream.

"He's here."

—

Michael was enjoying himself. He heard a total of forty-seven heartbeats he could send to hell with a good conscience tonight.

Provided they all stayed put.

This sixteenth one must have caught sight of his glowing red eyes.

He could hear five heartbeats, running about as fast as they could without exploding to his left. Tonight was a very good night for killing.

—

"Twenty-one," Dirk said. The four of them were in the same room as Sarah Jennifer now. There were random shots fired, but none in the direction of the house.

"You don't think they're going to get here, do you," Jeremiah asked, and she shook her head.

"No," she exhaled loudly. "A lot of the stories coming from TH, I thought, were bullshit. But in all the years I knew him, he never, ever joked about that. Now..." she stopped as Dirk interrupted.

"Twenty-two."

She continued, "Now we know why."

That was when the fear hit.

—

Michael got clipped by a bullet, grazing his skull. He lost his amusement at the situation and fear exploded out of him, horses bolted, men dropped and scrunched up in fetal positions and others cried.

His eyes were blazing red in the night. He went from location to location, killing any he could still find in the vicinity.

He looked towards the north, still able to hear multiple horses rushing in that direction. He looked towards the house and dipped his head before turning towards the north and starting to jog.

—

The fear receded.

"Is it," Dirk gasped out, his hands covering his ears, "is it over?"

Sarah Jennifer leaned against Jeremiah who had sat down beside her, allowing her to squeeze his hand in her fear.

Now, he was busy shaking it, trying to get the feeling back, out of her sight.

She nodded. "Yeah." Her voice squeaked. She cleared her throat and worked to get her sense of leadership back. "Yes, it's over. All except the burying."

"You think he got everybody?" Todd asked, walking towards the viewing hole.

Jeremiah answered, "No, I heard horses spook. I bet some are heading back to their town."

Sarah Jennifer, her eyes not focused, said aloud what all of them were thinking. "Wrong move, assholes."

—

In the morning, the woman and three men ventured out, finding thirty-three dead men. Two had their hearts ripped out of their chests, two more, their heads cut clean from their bodies. Multiple corpses had slashes from a sword. Probably what caused the screaming before he killed them.

Jeremiah was looking down at the second man he had seen

with his heart punched out of his body. He looked up when Sarah Jennifer came out of the trees and stood next to him, looking down at the corpse.

"Dark Messiah, indeed," he said, his voice low. "You were right."

"And so were you," she said, looking down at the body. "He was our savior." She turned and snapped her fingers in front of Jeremiah's face to get his attention. "I've already apologized to Dirk and Todd for being a stupid bitch to all of you, trying to throw around my ability to fight."

Jeremiah was about to speak when she put two fingers on his mouth. "Shh, please. I'm not done yet, Jeremiah." Surprised by her touch, he nodded his head.

She blushed and looked down for a second, before looking back up. "Jeremiah, you've been my rock, and I've known it for three years. I knew, no matter what happened, you would be there for me. I never allowed myself to appreciate you for being you. I was too busy being full of myself."

She looked down another time before looking off to the right and then back into his face.

"Sometimes it takes something like staring death in the face to realize what a fool one can be. I know this is horrible from the standpoint of tradition," she said, then reached out and took his hand in hers. His eyes were captured by the emotions she was displaying. He had never, ever, expected to see something like this from her.

"Jeremiah Kaye, would you take Sarah Jennifer Walton to be your wife? Will you marry me?" she asked, tears streaming down her face.

BOSS CHILDERS' Town, West of Denver, Colorado (United States Post-Apoc)

JACQUELINE PUT the next plate up on the drying rack, her hands all shriveled up from being in the water all night.

The men, partying earlier in their excitement to undertake the great attack on Sarah Jennifer's house, had made a mess. It took the slaves who had been tasked with cleaning the mess room over an hour to get it cleaned up.

The only one still working was her. The other two women who were responsible for cleaning the kitchen were a little looser with their nighttime activities and weren't required to stay late.

They had other tasks.

Jacqueline didn't care. As far as she could tell, it was by choice, not force. That it caused her more work was a byproduct. It kept her busy, and tired, but it gave her some level of exercise.

So, she was up when she heard the clang-clang-clang of the gate's bell. Then, the sound of men getting up, some cursing freely. They were either waking up or having to stop their own physical activities. This bell meant serious business. It was rarely ever rung, and only for practice in Jacqueline's experience.

They were under attack.

Jacqueline grabbed the rag and dried off her hands. She confirmed her knife's location and caught up a six foot stick she had been practicing with. Her hearing was good enough that if someone came for her, she had a chance to fend for herself.

If she could see, she would have already been heading for the town's walls to see if she could get over and get lost before anyone noticed.

The screams and the fear hit at almost the same time. She stumbled back, hitting the cupboard hard enough that some of the dishes crashed to the floor.

She put her hands over her ears. The screams coming out of the night caused her blood to run cold. She knew that men she would have gleefully killed moments ago were dying out there, but it brought her no happiness.

Then there was a pause in the screaming, and the fear

receded. She listened, her Were senses straining to hear anything, to give her any sort of information on the outcome.

That's when she heard Jack Childers start screaming in pain.

—

Jack and his posse came riding hard into the town. "Stanton!" he yelled up at the gate guard as he rode past. "Ring the alarm bell!"

The bell's ringing caused another ten men to come out of the buildings. The riders dismounted, and the horses were gathered up and taken to the stable. The men formed in the middle of the street, Jack looking around, ready to pull together his defenses.

"Men!" Jack called out. "We've been attacked by something evil in the Fallen Lands. We have..."

A voice, dark and malicious, cut through the night, stopping Jack's speech cold. "How nice of you to gather everyone in one place."

The men, some pulling out their pistols, looked around in alarm. The voice seemed to be coming from everywhere, even from inside their damned heads!

The voice continued, "So, this is how evil perseveres? Men who are willing to follow the decrepit in spirit, the weak in heart, for selfish gain. Allowing the soul that should be free, subjugated? *Where is the honor in that?*"

Jack, looking around, couldn't find where the voice was coming from. "Show yourself!"

"Why, Jack?" the voice whispered. "I'm right here!"

All of them turned to see two red eyes. The fear hit them at the same second, and most of them lost their ability to stand.

Tony stumbled to the left, retaining enough muscle control to raise his pistol. The evil demon turned and walked toward him. He slid his hand over Tony's gun hand and helped Tony point his own pistol at his own head.

The man in black spoke. "There you go, pull the trigger, and the fear will go away," he said, his voice velvet over steel.

BAM!

Jack and Russell, both fighting the fear from the ground had to watch the scene play out as Tony shot himself, the brains from his head spraying the side of the building.

The demon turned towards them and reached under his coat. He pulled out a short sword. The metal gleamed in the moonlight, the lanterns around the town reflecting from the glinting silver steel.

"You see, your sins give you away."

He stopped in front of Earl Withers and knelt down. "You cut off the fingers of those who upset you?" He stood up and stepped on Earl's wrist. "Eenie, meenie... screw it." Earl screamed in pain.

"That's one finger for each time you did it, Earl." He started walking around the group again, eyeing Jack and Russell and pointing at them with his sword. "I'll get to you two in a moment."

It took Michael five minutes to dispatch them. Then Russell and Jack faced him. His eyes weren't glowing anymore.

But they were...

Alone.

6

"What the fuck has that bitch ever done for you?" Jack grated out. "You killed over forty men."

"Fifty," Russell spat, still fighting the fear racking his body.

"What the fuck ever, Russell." Jack snapped. "Why is one slut worth fifty men to you?"

Michael looked down at the two men. "You're asking me why I kill your people? When you intended to kill the four in the house, especially the woman?" He got no response. "Then, you want to argue with me that perhaps I went overboard with killing fifty people to your planned four?"

"Fuck... you..." Russell cursed at him.

"My my my." Michael walked over to stand above the large man. "Here, let me help you focus." Michael reached inside his coat and pulled out a pistol. One Jack didn't recognize. "Now, I don't know that you have ever heard this speech before, so you probably won't know how I changed it, Jack..." he nodded to the other man. "... or you, Russell."

The gun had something glowing on the side, and Michael pointed it down at Russell. "This is a Jean Dukes' special, or so the note informed me. It's the most powerful handgun on this planet at the moment. In fact, I have a version that goes to eleven." He turned the pistol in his hand and admired it. "I'm not really into guns myself. I prefer swords, or just claws usually. However..." he turned the gun back, once again pointing it at Russell. "I think this is an appropriate use for the gun, right? You shoot others, the death by the weapon is appropriate, right Russell?" The man's eyes went wide as the pistol aimed at him. "You will notice the gun barrel hole is rather tiny. The reason I'm not asking you, 'how many shots have I fired, punk,' is that this baby will shoot about five thousand."

Michael smirked. "And there is no way I'm wasting that many shots to make the conversation fit the movie I'm stealing this from. So..." Michael depressed the trigger and Russell's head exploded, disintegrating into mist, his body twitching for a second before it stilled.

Michael returned the pistol to his holster, and the fear receded. Jack was able to turn and see the destruction of his friend.

When he turned back around to face the stranger, he saw the man had red eyes and fangs. In fact, he had also grown two-inch nails on his right hand.

Jack started screaming and continued crying after Michael plunged his hand into his chest. Breaking through his rib cage easily, he tore through the blood vessels holding the heart and pulled it out. Jack had just enough life in him to hear Michael's whispered statement.

"I'm being called a Messiah, Jack," Michael said as he watched the life leave Jack's eyes.

"Just not yours," he finished and dropped the heart beside the dead man and stood up, and sniffed the wind.

His eyes narrowed, and he turned in the street before walking towards a scent he hadn't expected to smell.

The scent of Were.

—

Jacqueline could hear the pain, the questions, the violence outside.

And her body trembled.

This man wasn't just any killer. He was someone from her world, the UnknownWorld, and he wasn't a Were. He had to be a vampire, and her father had warned her many, many times that she needed to get ahold of her anger over her mother dying. Because one day, she might run into a vampire and if she didn't know how to keep her anger in check?

Well, vampires often had a no second chances policy.

A tear traced its way down her face. Thinking about her father, whom she had left so many years before to walk the Fallen Lands, caused her to revisit the guilt she felt in her soul. He had been right. She had been wrong, and now there was a vampire killing the men in this town.

Correction, she thought as she heard the door to the mess open. He was here with her, not out in the town.

She opened her hand and let the stick drop. It didn't matter, she couldn't see. What was she going to do, swing wildly at him? Hope to connect her stick to his head and then do what? He would just heal, and come find her.

His voice, when he spoke, was gentle. "I smell you, and you hear me. So let's talk."

Jacqueline wiped the tear off of her cheek and stood up. She reached out with her left hand to grab the wall to feel exactly where she was.

About to die or not, she wasn't going to go out like those two assholes out in the street, crying like the little bitches they were.

She heard him laugh softly.

"I'm coming," she told him when her hand reached the door opening. She opened the door and stepped out, cocking her ear to find his heartbeat. Then she turned her head towards the door he had come through.

He started tapping, allowing her to find his position accurately. She had deftly passed three of the tables when he commanded, "Stop!"

She stopped in place.

"One moment," he said. She could hear him pull something from his coat and then a very tiny, high-pitched noise followed by a huge CRACK. A man cursed outside, then a body lurched off the porch to land in the street.

He started walking towards her. "My apologies, they thought to intrude on our conversation." She heard him pick up a chair. "This would have been in your way. If you turn around, you can sit down."

Her hands trembling, Jacqueline turned around to feel one of the chairs gently bump up against the back of her legs. "It has armrests, use them to sit."

She reached back and found the armrests he was talking about. It took but a second for her to sit. He walked to stand in front of her. "Name?"

"Jacqueline."

"Pleased to meet you, Jacqueline, my name is Michael," he replied. "I can smell Were on you, but don't understand why you can't see." His pause was short. "How did this happen?"

"I was in the F-Fallen La... Lands..." she stuttered before taking a moment for a couple of calming breaths, and starting again. "I was in the Fallen Lands, seeking my fortune when the people I was with was attacked. I was shot, but not killed. I look young for my age."

"Yes, good genetics," he agreed.

"Well, not so good at the moment. I was sold to that bastard you killed outside."

"Jack?" he asked her. "Sorry, there are so many bastards dead out in the street, I'm just making sure I know which one."

She nodded. "He thought to keep me until I matured so he could... well, so he would be my first."

"Well, he would have been disappointed," Michael

commented. Her lips compressed and her face went from scared to annoyed.

She was actually working on trying not to piss off the killer.

She heard a dark chuckle. "No need to be annoyed. I don't know your sexual status. But my experiences with Weres indicates that you're a randy bunch, and your age isn't anywhere near your looks. So, I guess he wouldn't have been your first."

She shook her head. "Known many Weres, have you?"

"Thousands," he murmured, his attention somewhere else.

Thousands? How could he have known thousands? She was the daughter of a very, very old and important Were and if she knew just ONE thousand, she would be shocked. She probably knew of less than three hundred.

Seven of those were killed when she was captured.

"I see," his hand touched her face. No matter how gentle it was, she had to resist the desire to bite it.

He said, in a normal speaking voice, "You try to bite me, and I will slap your mouth into tomorrow. It would not be nice to attempt to bite the hand that is going to return your sight to you." His voice brooked no argument. "Now, grab the armrests, this will probably hurt for a second. I'll try to do something that takes your mind off of it."

Jacqueline put her hands around the armrests and gripped hard. Not sure what the man was expecting to do, or how he was going to...

OH... M... *GOD*!

She felt like she was going to fall apart, the pleasure centers of her body were flooding as intensely as the fear aspect that had hit her earlier.

She swore she heard women, screaming in pleasure, from the next building over. She bit down hard, trying to make sure she didn't say, moan, or do anything she would be flaming embarrassed about later.

She felt pain near her eye, but frankly, the overwhelming pleasure was making it hard to care about.

In a few seconds, the pleasure started to recede, and she was left hyperventilating in the chair. She turned towards him, noticing that she saw an outline.

AN OUTLINE!

"Oh my God," she choked out, her hands coming up to her eyes. "You've healed me." She turned her head and could start to see the round blobs of tables. Turning back, she saw his face was becoming clear for her.

"Oh... damn. You are fucking beautiful." She just stopped her hands from reaching out to touch his face.

"Well, thank you," he answered.

Her face blushed crimson. "I did NOT just say that out loud, did I?" Then something behind her eyes popped and everything was in focus. "What happened to your hair?" was the next thing to come out of her mouth.

He rolled his eyes up to the ceiling, his voice gruff. "Nanocytes are a four-letter word, that's all I'm explaining."

"Oh, sorry!" She put a hand to her face. "I can't believe I can see." She started to get up, and he stepped back. "Although, the hairless look is very good on you." She turned to look around the room. "How did you do it?"

"This," he answered, and she turned back around to see him holding up his index finger for her to look at. She moved closer to look at what he was showing her.

There was a blood-covered silver fragment on the tip of his finger.

"I was shot with silver?" She looked up at him for confirmation.

He nodded. "I imagine that's how they killed the others of your group." He aimed his hand away from her and flicked the silver away.

She turned towards the door. "There are visitors." She stepped around him to grab her stick and came back. "I've been waiting to get a bit of my own back."

"You plan on hitting women?" Michael asked her.

Her brows drew together and she sniffed the air and looked at him quizzically.

"I think, perhaps, the effort to make you more comfortable when I had to find the silver was a little too strong?" he asked.

She turned around, ripping off the apron and tossing it on a chair as she walked back to the kitchen. "Back door."

Michael raised an eyebrow as he looked at the front door and then turned to follow the Were woman.

"Good plan."

—

Michael made sure Jacqueline had supplies and two horses.

She would head towards Denver first, then try to meet back up with him, perhaps to move on to Chicago where her father lived if Michael wasn't available.

Since the Apoc, the temperatures had risen all over the land, and Denver had no major source of water. She would warn the local Were pack of the hunters using silver and then return to catch up to him inside Denver to help him understand how things worked these days.

She was shocked to learn he didn't know about how to get around the Fallen Lands at all.

"How are you alive?" she muttered and then realized how it sounded. "Sorry."

She needed to see her father one more time if only to tell him that she loved him and that he was right. She really needed to work on her anger and how the hell was she supposed to know daywalking vampires existed?

Michael was able to grab some food and other supplies. He stashed them on the handful of horses he was leading. He camped out for the night and part of the morning before he continued back towards Sarah Jennifer's home.

He could hear some muffled cursing as he came over a small rise. He stopped, allowing those at the house to see him and confirm he wasn't an enemy, before casually walking down the rise towards the house.

Breaking out of the trees into the area cleared around the house, he walked the horses into the stable. Dirk and Todd came over and helped him.

"Take the supplies up to the house, I'm leaving shortly," he told them before hearing the back door slam.

"Well," Todd smirked, "seems like the two rabbits are coming out of their hole."

Michael turned to him, confusion on his face. "Rabbits?"

Todd said no more but pointed towards the house. "A dead man would be able to tell."

Michael stepped out of the stables and saw Jeremiah, a huge grin on his face, followed by Sarah Jennifer, a look of passion clearly written on hers as she tucked in her shirt.

"Indeed," Michael said over his shoulder to Todd.

"Damned good to see you again, Michael!" Jeremiah held out his hand, but when Michael took it, he wrapped Michael up in a hug. "No handshakes for someone like you!"

He stepped back and rubbed under his left arm. "Please tell me that's a sword, and you're not just happy to see me? Because if you're happy to see me then I am going to go cry at my inferiority."

Sarah Jennifer slapped him on his arm. "Oh My God!" She stepped around and stopped before Michael, looking up in his face. "Michael Nacht, I owe you an apology... and a promise."

Michael raised an eyebrow. "I'm sorry, I was expecting Sarah Jennifer. Who are you and what have you done with her?" He made a point of looking at the woman who stepped into his personal space.

She poked him in the middle of his chest. "I'm her, you dick!"

Then she rested her forehead slowly down on Michael's chest and started crying.

Michael's eyes opened wide in alarm and he looked at Jeremiah, confused. Jeremiah pantomimed patting her on the back, so Michael did so, being gentle. The woman started talking as she tried to clear her teardrops.

"I was a bitch, ok? I was a kickass female who took no shit from anyone and GOD what a mistake." She stepped back, into Jeremiah who wrapped her up in his arms. She cuddled against him for a second, composing herself. "Not no shit from no one. But the bitch part." She wiped at her face. "Someone taught me that you can be gentle, and still not take any shit from anyone." She looked up and kissed Jeremiah on the cheek before turning back to Michael. " And I love him. So... I promise not to be that person again."

Michael, poleaxed, turned to Todd and Dirk who just smiled and shrugged their shoulders as if to say, 'who knew?'

"Well, you have more work ahead of you," Michael started to explain but Jeremiah interrupted.

"Boss Childers?" he asked.

"Dead," Michael confirmed.

"Russell?" Todd asked from behind him.

Michael turned to look at the man. "Very dead."

"What about his other guys?" Dirk kicked in.

He shrugged. "Not sorry to say, no longer with us," he answered.

"What about all of the women over there?" Sarah Jennifer asked.

"Free to be who they want to be. Anyone Jack used to attack me, plus one other, is dead," he answered.

"That's the work we have ahead of us, helping them?" Jeremiah asked.

Michael smiled at the man and turned to grab the one packhorse that he was keeping. "No," he answered and stepped up into the saddle and turned towards the east. "I'm talking about your child. Sarah Jennifer is pregnant." He touched his nose and gently popped the reins of the horse, which started trotting out of the yard.

All of the men stared at Sarah Jennifer, who was looking down at her own stomach in surprise, holding it with her hands.

7

South of Old Denver (United States Post-Apoc)

JACQUELINE RODE into the area south of Denver with the horses. She didn't need the animals so much as she needed something to trade with.

The Weres had taken over a couple of large buildings. One of them was a huge warehouse. It was so big it could cover their little encampment with room to spare. By using found scrap, and some judicial use of muscle, the families had built a nice fence between the buildings.

She rode up and waited for the...

A male voice called out, "I see you, what do you want?"

"Name's Jacqueline. I was here a while back with seven of my friends before we went out into the Fallen Lands. We traded then, would like to trade now."

"Don't remember you, where are you from?" the male voice called back.

"Pack in Chicago," she replied.

"Oh, a rich bitch," he retorted.

She briefly frowned. With patience she hadn't had last time she was here, she answered, "No, that's the pack to the east of Chicago. Rich and righteous, all of them. Act like they can walk on water, and their shit don't stink."

She heard the laughter from her talker and… yup, a couple of others.

"All right, you know the secret password," he replied and then the screech of metal and wheels needing lubrication hit her ears as she watched the massive door open a few feet. Enough for her and the two horses to get through.

It took her three hours to find someone to trade the horses for a couple of weapons and some local money. They recognized she didn't have the feed to keep them inside for more than two days, tops. They used it for bargaining power, not knowing she wanted to be out of there by the morning.

It took another two hours for her to see the Alpha.

He told her in no uncertain terms, she would meet with him again the next night. Using what felt like the last of the patience she had found when encountering Michael, she nodded her acceptance and left his quarters. She stepped outside the main building and walked around the grounds, wondering if Michael would come here, or if he would leave her behind.

Well, shit. Now she was stuck in another camp.

She turned to look into the shadows when she heard the noise. A mess of old blankets moved and then a voice, ragged with age called out, "Hello."

She looked around then stepped towards the voice, only getting close enough so their conversation had a chance of being private. "Yes?"

"You look like you aren't from here, are you child?"

Jacqueline looked around. No one was close to them. There were people with rifles up on the roofs of the two buildings, but none close enough to hear her. "No, Chicago."

"Recent?" came the old man's voice, a cough racking him. He

had to be close to death, this old man. Most Weres stayed in good shape.

"No," she looked around one more time and chose to step a couple of feet closer.

"I ain't going to bite, young lady. Even were I young enough, I was taught honor."

She snorted. "Honor, now there's a word I hadn't believed in." She spoke as much to herself as him.

Another couple of coughs before the pile of blankets asked, "Why not?"

Jacqueline considered her response and finally just walked about ten feet along the darkened wall. She came to a stop then and, back against the wall, slid down and sat on the concrete. The covers the old man was using were old and full of dirt, sweat, and a little sickness. She couldn't smell him over the putridness, and she was thankful for that.

She stared out across to the other building but kept her voice low. "Because being told I need to have honor came from my Dad. He was always so upright like he had a stick up his butt when I was growing up. He kept preaching and preaching and preaching at me. It felt like nothing I did could get a compliment without a warning. Finally, I figured I knew enough and decided that searching out the Fallen Lands with my close friends was the way to a better life. Come out here, find some technology that could be used again and my life would be set."

"Didn't happen that way?" he asked, softly.

"No, it didn't," she admitted. "We made it here to Denver and just one day north of the city we got attacked by hunters who used silver. Seven of my friends were killed, and I was blinded."

Worry came from the old man. "You healed, right? You seem like you can see now."

She nodded. "I can see now, but that was because I was healed by a man. I spent a long time as a slave to a human, hearing him tell others he was just waiting for me to get old enough so he could be the first to rape me."

"Rape you?" the man cried out in alarm before his coughing took over.

"Didn't happen," she replied, her voice calm.

"What did?" he asked once his coughing subsided.

"The Dark Messiah did, just like the stories my dad told me when I was but a little girl on his lap. Like the vampires of old, before the apocalypse."

"Who," the old man asked, his voice a little stronger.

"What?" she turned to him.

"His name,"

"Michael," she replied.

"Oh my God," the old man whispered. "He actually came back. She was right."

"Who was right?"

There was a long pause from the old man. "Didn't you listen to your dad's stories?" he asked her gently. "Michael has a woman in his life. He was killed, so we thought, by a nuclear weapon out west of here. But his love, Bethany Anne, always said he would come back for her. Now, you're telling me he's back?"

"Well, if you mean the Michael that can walk in the sun, cause men and women to feel so much fear all they can do is lie on the ground and piss themselves, then yes... he's back." she agreed.

"I'll be damned, we have a shot to get you out of here, Jacqueline," he said in awe.

The old man told her a few more things, and twenty minutes later, he left her crying silently, holding on to his covers as her tears fell freely into them. Now that she had the covers next to her body, she could smell her father.

—

It took Michael a little while, and a couple of backtracks, to finally locate the old road that he could follow to Denver. This time, he didn't Myst or use any extra abilities.

He just enjoyed the ride with his horse, Tabby. On more than one occasion, the horse tried to do the exact opposite of what he wanted. So, he named the horse after the one person he remembered causing him such trouble.

And Tabitha was her name.

He considered calling the horse BA, after Bethany Anne but figured he might feel a little weird leaving the horse behind. He sure as hell wouldn't have the same emotional connection with one named Tabby. Not that he didn't love Tabitha in his own way, but leaving behind an annoying and petulant horse named Tabby?

He could manage that.

Michael rode into Denver, a city rising up out of grass and weeds. He stopped Tabby and looked at the outline of a city in ruin.

Mother Earth reclaiming her materials, one year at a time.

He noticed that only a small portion of the city was actually being used or even had some electricity. Most of the outskirts he had ridden through were shades of their former selves if they even existed any longer. There had been a fair number of wooden structures, but now all that was left were areas of grass and dirt, the cement foundations succumbing to the years with no humans present.

It was certainly hotter than he was expecting. He popped the reins and Tabby started walking again, heading into a town that most, it looked like, had forgotten.

—

Juliana had been on her feet for seven hours already. As the main waitress in this bar for the last eighteen months, she had seen a lot. Been pitched job offers, proselytized to by men who needed to feel good about drinking, and had enough men leer at her that she had two designations for men. One was scumbags.

The other was dead.

So, if they walked in under their own power, then scumbag it was. That was okay, she got paid well by scumbags. She knew how to use her assets.

For whatever reason, her hair was so black it seemed to have blue highlights when the sun caught it just right. The simple outfit of jeans and an old, men's dress shirt that she wore untucked, was the only uniform she ever used.

"Juliana," old man Milton called out from table ten back in the corner. He had made it to his fourth decade and actually survived over twenty years mining. Now, he invested in the younger guys and made sure they treated him fair in their agreements. Well, his knee-breaker and life-taker, Kent who always stood behind him, made sure they were as honest as they needed to be.

She turned toward him. "Another moonie, Mr. Milton?" He picked up and showed her his empty glass and she gave him a thumbs up and walked towards the bar. The door into the building opened behind her, but she ignored it. "Jimmie," she called to him, "we need a clear Moonie for Mr. Milton." She pointed down to the open tabs on the desk behind the bar counter. "That's him third from the top. Make sure we have..." She looked up to find Jimmie was looking behind her. "Dammit, Jimmie! Listen to me, Mr. Milton..."

But, Jimmie wasn't paying any attention to her. She turned to see what he was watching, and that's when she saw the man in black, his head as bare as a baby's behind. As he was looking around the room, she checked his shoes. He didn't have cowboy boots like most travelers. No, his looked black.

Like combat boots.

And he radiated danger.

"Here, Juliana," she turned around to see Jimmie offering her the drink. "I wrote it down on his tab." She nodded and put it on her tray. She turned back around and headed toward Mr. Milton's table, sneaking another glance at the stranger.

—

"Can I get you something?" she asked him.

"Don't know, what do you have, and can you let me know if you've seen a young looking woman in here?"

"Except myself?" she answered. It wasn't often she had to work a flirt with any guy. But he certainly wasn't paying any attention to her, and he wasn't dead. He didn't radiate the feeling that he batted for the other team either.

"Yes, of course." He glanced up at her, his blue eyes taking her in, but she merely felt he was now aware of what she looked like. She couldn't get upset for being judged because he obviously didn't judge her.

He was dead to other women. She already hated this other bitch. Juliana might not like most guys, but she liked even less it when other women could hold a man's attention when she was right in front of them.

"We have local moonshine and three kinds of beer, all locally brewed. We don't have a large enough population out here to import any special beers for general sale. We have some beef either ground up for burgers or cut up in a stew with leeks and potatoes."

"I'll try your moonshine, thank you," Michael answered.

She took his order and left to go to the bar.

Behind him, the door opened and three toughs entered. He considered moving tables based on the thoughts he could pick up from the first man's mind, but he really needed the practice.

Or at least that was what he was telling himself.

The waitress returned with his glass, but he waved her off. "Keep it, or it will just get spilled."

She looked at him strangely, and then at the three men coming up behind him and turned around and headed back towards the bar.

"You're in my seat," the man growled behind him.

"Your point?" Michael asked, not bothering to look behind him.

"My point is, you need to move," he replied.

"I'm comfortable here. But to prove I can be magnanimous," he pointed to the three empty chairs at the table, "You can sit with me. I won't even charge you for the opportunity."

"Listen, last time it cost me a half day's wages when we busted up Kraven's bar."

Michael turned in his chair and looked up at the tough. "Kraven, really?" his look of wonder caught the tough by surprise.

"Yeah, Kraven. He runs Denver and owns this bar. Me and the boys here work for him. So, we're important, as well."

"No, I think you misunderstand," Michael replied. "I'm asking because that has to be one of the top twenty stupidest names I've heard someone call themselves. Let me ask, is he a hunter?"

"Mr. Kraven isn't going to like someone disrespecting his name, Robert," the guy in the back on the right piped up. "He probably would be okay with a little destruction before we take it out into the street and beat the shit out of him."

"Yeah, good point," Robert said and threw a sucker punch at Michael, trying to hit him in the jaw. Michael kicked his chair back into Robert as he ducked back to allow the punch to pass by.

"Here," Michael said as he raised the chair up to catch Robert under his chin, breaking a couple of teeth in the process. "Why don't you take this seat?" He flipped the chair so the four legs were aimed at Robert who had stumbled backward, grabbing his mouth.

He stabbed out with the chair, breaking one of Robert's ribs. He tossed it to the guy on the left and fairly blurred towards the other guy and punched him.

Once.

By the time the third man had caught the chair, Michael had grabbed Robert's shirt. He yanked the chair back and set it down on the floor. He popped Robert on the side of the head. He slumped down into the seat, and Michael looked at the third guy.

"Now," he pointed to Robert, "you can tell him I let him sit in his chair. You got a chair you want, too?"

He looked at Robert, then down to the floor at his friend who was out cold. He turned to Michael and shook his head in the negative.

"Good, now leave me alone." He turned and headed to the bar. Pulling money out of Robert's wallet, which he had grabbed during the fight, he asked the bartender, "How much?"

Juliana watched with awe as Jimmie told him the price. Michael pulled out two silver pieces. "Two of these?" Jimmie nodded. Michael grabbed the moonshine and drank it in one gulp. He slapped the two pieces of silver on the table, then tossed Jimmie the wallet. "You can return it to him when he wakes up."

Michael nodded to the waitress and made his way out of the bar.

"God," Jimmie said when Michael left. "I want to be like him when I grow up."

"Hell, if you are half him when you grow up, Jimmie, I'll take you home all night, every night," Juliana murmured.

Jimmie glanced at Juliana to see she wasn't paying him any attention.

Challenge accepted, he thought to himself.

8

***

Old Denver (United States Post-Apoc)

THE OLD WERE was able to leave the pack's area easily. The local Alpha didn't care what one old man did. He had come here months before, looking for someone.

A girl.

Now, he had found the one he'd been looking for. Found his daughter once again and his heart was a little lighter. But with his new knowledge of the local situation, he wasn't sure how they would make it out of Old Denver. He was pretty sure the two of them could make it out of the pack's little fort. But once they were known to be gone, there would be a pack hunt, and he wasn't the man he used to be.

Now he knew exactly how he could see his daughter safe again. Unfortunately, he didn't tell Jacqueline how bad he was.

But, he had told her he loved her, was proud of her, and had never been upset with her decision to leave.

When she told him of the Dark Messiah?

Well, then he needed to go see the man one more time to ask a personal favor.

God willing, he would accept.

New York City State, Upper East Coast (United States Post-Apoc)

"There are rumors," the fat man said speaking around a cigar he had firmly planted between his teeth, "that we have figured out the problem with keeping vampire blood fresh."

There were two men in the room. It was nicely appointed and had that rare feature only available to a few cities across the world.

It had electricity.

The fat man looked at his law enforcement representative. "I don't remember wanting this information to be public. Are we clear?"

The other man nodded, turned and left the room.

Old Denver (United States Post-Apoc)

It seemed like everywhere Michael went, people had degenerated to the Dark Ages again. Lack of fresh building activity, everyone just reusing the plentiful old buildings from Earth's past.

Like they had decided to move into old Egyptian pyramids to live.

Further, mankind had moved into a dark time ethically. Here, so far as he had seen, everyone thought might made right.

The problem with that? When Honor's Champion decided

that Justice had been absent for too long, and was seeking to balance the scales, it was going to get ugly.

He kept his hands in his pockets, the coat flapping in the wind as he walked down the street towards the location he had pulled from Robert's head.

Kraven? Michael snorted. Who kept a name like Kraven?

It took him five minutes to walk the necessary blocks, having to backtrack one time when he came upon a building that had collapsed. He didn't care to jump over the rubble and have people realize just how different he was.

Michael stopped in front of the forted up area and studied it.

It wasn't bad, he had to admit. He wasn't sure where they got the materials, but the walls were well built and twenty feet high. Some sort of wire on the top, and a guard station overlooking the roads in multiple directions with a large building in the center.

Which was lit up with electricity?

Interesting.

The gatehouse door was open, and there was a guard there, so Michael decided to see if walking in was an option. No need to make this harder than he thought it should be.

—

The old Were passed the old tenements and then the buildings and another three miles beyond. He headed towards the place Jacqueline had explained she had described to *him*.

The West Side bars.

He visited two before coming to Kraven's joint. He heard the commotion before he walked inside. Straightening his clothes as best he could, he opened the door and stepped in, immediately taking a step to the right and checking out what was going on.

It wasn't much.

There was some guy off in the corner, with his guard standing behind him and three toughs sitting at a table in front of him. One was fine, one had a towel with ice to his head, and the last was awake, but groaning with his head lying on the table.

Now that, he thought, just might be Michael's work.

He stepped over towards the end of the bar, catching the bartender's attention who walked the ten feet down the bar to ask him, "Liquor or beer?"

The old man reached into his pockets and pulled a small amount of change. "Beer, the cheapest that isn't vile," his gravelly voice said to the young barkeep, "and a story of what happened to the youngster back there, he drink too much?"

The barkeep swiped the change into his hand while shaking his head. He grabbed a mug and pulled the beer from a keg before turning around and placing it on the bar. "No," he inclined his head towards the three men. His voice was low and close to whispering as he answered, "Those three came in twenty minutes ago and tried to take a chair away from a new guy in town. The new guy doesn't know who Kraven is, so he took offense to someone pushing him."

The barkeeper, who glanced to make sure the three men weren't paying them any attention continued, "You should have seen it! The guy gets up, tosses the chair to one of them, lays out one and pops the one with his head on the table. Before he could collapse, he grabbed the chair for the dude to fall into. He asks the third if he wants a chair, but he was smart enough to shake his head. Then, he comes over here and grabs some money out of the one guy's wallet. Pays me, just downs a shot of our moonshine and drops the glass back on the table like it was water. Then, he walks out like it wasn't any big thing to beat the shit out of two guys."

The old Were took the beer and lifted it up, taking a long swig. He didn't say aloud what he was thinking...

What's two when you have killed two hundred at a time without breaking a sweat?

—

Michael was surprised. They let him keep his weapons and once inside, he understood why.

This was a tiny little town within a larger town. The large building had bars, restaurants and other businesses all set up inside as well. There were a lot of men who looked like they had been mining out in the mountains, and a few businessmen as well.

This was the local seat of power, he figured.

The sun was getting lower in the sky, and with the buildings around plus the tall wall, it was getting darker inside what was probably a three block area. He could hear a fight going on around the other side of the building. Seemed like it was strength that ruled inside these walls.

Michael grinned, that was the way he liked it.

"You!" a voice called out and Michael glanced to his left. "Oh, sorry!" It was a guy in clothes that were better suited out in the country. "Thought you were someone else."

Michael nodded and then wondered how many people went around with bald heads?

There were additional stalls set up outside the walls on the sidewalk surrounding the fifteen... he glanced up, no—twenty story building. Considering how many people he had seen so far in this town, this could easily house a quarter of the total population. Probably the top quarter if electricity was as rare as he had seen so far.

The hustle and bustle of getting through the crowds as he reached the main doors into the building were a little surprising. So far, even in that small town with Childers, there hadn't been thirty to forty people in a space this size.

This building had eight doors leading in and out. All of the doors were braced open. There was enough heat in the building that the cool night supplemented the straining fans. No air conditioning in this place, it seemed.

Michael chose to take the second door on the right, and the person in front of him suddenly darted out of the line. Michael looked ahead and could see a couple of men heading out of the building, aiming for the obvious entrances.

Might makes right, indeed.

Michael kept his hands in his pockets and kept walking. He acted like he wasn't aware of the two men, nor the smirk on the one in front. That was okay. Michael sped up just a bit to make sure he would go through the door first. When he came out, he led with his shoulder against the other's shoulder.

Michael's shoulder won.

The man bounced off Michael, spun rapidly counterclockwise and tripped over another person coming in the other door. Michael was fifteen feet away as the man, cursing a storm, got up.

His partner helped him stand up, Michael could hear his comment, "Fuck' em Darren, c'mon. Kraven wants us to check out where the hell Robert and those pricks are."

Michael smirked, Robert should still be nursing a headache back in the bar he had just left.

Inside the building, he paused to realize this was designed to have stores on the first three levels before the offices, or apartments, started above. He walked towards the stairs to go up a flight to the bar level. Businesses were on first, bars and restaurants on the second. Other services, it seemed, were on three.

Taking the stairs up, he arrived on the second floor and turned right to walk towards the 'Corner Bar.' It was appropriately named because it took up the whole corner on this floor. There was no door, just an opening that looked to have had two doors sometime in the past.

He nodded to a waitress as he took a table near the wall in the back, allowing him to sit with his back mostly to a wall and watch everyone. The bar was over his right shoulder so he couldn't see very well in that direction. However, the far wall was mirrored, and it allowed him to keep an eye on it.

"Liquor or beer?" The waitress asked. Michael looked over, the brunette was wearing an old style dress. It didn't quite cover her knees, and frankly, she looked like she would rather burn it than wear it.

"Water, if you have it?" Michael asked.

"It's still a dime out here, even for water, stranger," she told him, smacking the gum she was chewing. "The gum is natural beeswax." Michael raised an eyebrow. "Everyone asks how I got it. We sell it three for a dime."

"A dime is fine," he said. "I've had the liquor."

"Water it is," she turned and walked away, but Michael had already read her mind.

She had tagged him as someone to set up. Michael closed his eyes and his shoulders dropped, just a little.

I'm trying, Bethany Anne, to remember that everyone here doesn't deserve to die. But if you were here, you would realize this is damned hard. He looked around at the patrons in the place, probably about twenty. *When you are surrounded by so many that deserve punishment.*

The waitress came back, set the drink down on the table and picked up the dime Michael had set there. He had retained some more of Robert's money earlier and probably needed to figure out how to acquire more. Nothing would point him out as a stranger faster than being someone who had no money.

Which he had plenty of back in his New York home. He had a lot, actually, back in his New York home.

She stepped next to him and bent down, kissing him on the cheek.

"And that's for what?" Michael asked.

"Sometimes mister, you shouldn't go where you aren't known," she said and then left, leaving him with a glass of water, no ice.

He wasn't particularly bothered by cold, and while the heat wasn't a big deal, he didn't really like it. He should probably figure out a way to handle modifications to his body. He had more reacted to the situations he was thrown into rather than thinking...

The light from the door was blocked, and Michael turned, sizing up his next interruption and shook his head.

This asshole had a sword.

"Flirting with my woman, stranger?" This guy was easily six foot and probably pushing two hundred thirty pounds. Some of that weight, though, was definitely fat. He had suntanned dark skin and dirty blond hair and frankly smelled like the woman.

"Why, isn't she your sister?" Michael asked, loudly. A few of the tables had already noticed the altercation and were turning in their chairs to see what would happen. None of the people seemed bothered. "So, is this some sort of racket you and her are running?" Michael continued before big and beefy got another word in. "She fake kisses me, you come along to do something? Maybe try to shake me down for a little money?"

"What I'm going to do," he said to Michael, pulling out his sword. It was easily three feet long and gleamed in the light. "Is allow you to leave after paying a toll."

"Is that right?" Michael asked. While he was carrying on a conversation externally, Michael was weighing the pros and cons of taking out the leadership. They were taking advantage of people and frankly, they lacked something that had been annoying the hell out of him.

They lacked Honor.

"That's right," he said. "See, if you don't, I get charged for getting the floor all bloody... again." He held the sword out, its point just a foot in front of Michael's chest. "And that upsets a few people who can't have their..."

Judgment Complete.

Michael sped up, reaching under his jacket for the Wakizashi. He unsnapped the scabbard and yanked out the sword, easily parrying the one in front of him to his right. He kicked back his chair to bounce off the one behind him and pivoted on his right leg, kicking out with his left and catching the man in his stomach, knocking him flying. The big man's feet caught the table behind him, dragging him down, but his body landed with a crash on the table one behind that.

"You know," Michael's voice went cold. "You've taken advantage of strangers for the last time." He walked to the table between them, grabbed it with his left hand and flung it through the air behind him.

Cursing erupted, and chairs and tables were quickly evacuated. This wasn't going according to the script they'd seen before.

"BILLY!" the waitress screamed from the bar as she realized the stranger wasn't going to pay the toll and leave. This had worked every time they had tried it so far.

Billy, quick for his size, got up and held up his sword.

"You're holding that wrong," Michael said. "That type of sword is best with two hands, not one. Unless, of course, you have phenomenal strength." He darted forward and cut down, catching the sword as Billy screamed, his forearm spewing blood where Michael had severed his hand from his arm.

Michael ignored the screams as he unwrapped the hand still clutching the sword and let it drop to the floor.

"You bastard!" the waitress screamed and turned to reach behind the bar, coming back around with a shotgun.

Michael turned towards her, flinging the sword. It stabbed through her stomach, embedding its point into the wall in front of the bar.

She looked shocked, staring at the sword that now pinned her to the bar like a butterfly on an entomologist's display board. The gun dropped from her fingers when she grabbed the sword and tried to pull it free, each tug had less strength as she slowly bled out.

Michael turned away from her to look the other way. He spoke to the man who was reaching for his gun, "You pull it, you will die."

"I pull it, I ain't the only one who's going to go down fighting," he growled. "You just killed a lady."

"One that set me up to die, yes I did. I don't think you did anything to stop that, now did you?" Michael asked as he walked over to Billy, who had been trying to wrap his shirt around his bleeding stump. "Judged," Michael spat out and slit his throat. When he reached down to clean his sword on Billy's shirt, Michael reached under his jacket with his left hand. Standing up, he aimed the Jean Dukes special he had pulled and shot the man who was still pulling his pistol up.

The man fell backward, his body crashing over his chair.

"You see," Michael told the group casually, "Injustice only survives when justice allows it to continue. When those who won't shy away from violence are determined to see justice served? Then opposites attract, and only one, justice, or injustice, can continue. So, I'm going to go see Kraven and have this confrontation."

During his conversation, Michael had placed his sword back in the scabbard and then pulled his other gun. Another seven men had come to stand in the doorway to see what caused all of the noise. Michael could smell perfume, so he suspected another woman or two must also be in the group.

He looked around the room, his pistols down by his side. "Now, I've tried this once before, so I'll just say that I'm leaving and it can be with, or without you dead. Which is it going to be?"

No one wanted to be the first to pull their gun at the moment.

"Well, that's rather disheartening, folks. I was rather looking forward to seeing what these completely unique pistols could do." Michael pulled one to look at it, giving everyone a chance to see that it was, in fact, unique. No one had seen one before. "It's a shame, really. Because with these pistols, a man," he looked out at the crowd in the front, "or woman might rule."

Someone in the doorway yelled, "Kraven says fifty bucks in coin for each pistol!"

Now, Bethany Anne might not approve of Michael's baiting the people around him, but her lawyer Jakob Yadav would appreciate the gambit. He didn't randomly shoot people, and those who had evil in their heart went for their weapons.

Those that didn't want to be a part of it were running, ducking, or jumping out of the way.

They say that there is a certain enjoyment in being in one's element. Michael wasn't normally someone who enjoyed guns. However, these were beautiful weapons and made with exquisite care.

Who was he not to use them appropriately?

At least, that was his story for Bethany Anne, he decided, and he was going to stick to it.

The first shot at Michael missed since he had already ducked and rolled out of the way, to pop up ten feet away from where everyone else was aiming.

9

It was a beautiful symphony of destruction.

Michael stood up, his pistols aimed in opposing directions, each turned to eleven on the knobs. Then he became a blur of action.

He would shoot from both guns, turn and roll backwards, popping back up five to fifteen feet away. Keeping the people aiming at him guessing.

Twice, instead of shooting people, he shot the wall they were hiding behind. With a Jean Dukes special, walls weren't that much of a concern. Most died immediately, it was a rather pass/fail pop quiz.

When the last person who had been trying to shoot him was down, Michael looked around, making sure he had no one else to worry about, and reached out to feel the intent of any minds near him.

Huh, one around the corner.

Michael holstered his pistols and walked over to the woman, now dead, who was pinned by the sword. He grabbed the hilt and yanked, the dead body falling into the pool of blood congealing on the floor.

Walking back through the wreckage of the room, he went to the wall and tapped on it with the sword. Moving down away from the door opening, he tapped again, and smiled.

He took another step further down and tapped once. Using his vampiric speed, he rammed the sword through the wall. A scream erupting from the other side confirmed he had guessed very well.

"One shouldn't expect an ambush to work every time," he said. He yanked the two pistols back out of their holsters and mentally listened for anyone.

It was quiet, except for some movement where he had stabbed, what sounded like a woman.

He stepped around the corner, noticing the ambusher on the side of the walkway, a few feet from where the sword had erupted out of the wall.

Michael turned and walked towards the stairs.

The person he wanted to talk to was up on the top floor. Why is it they were always on the top floor?

With his enhanced connection to the Etheric, Michael did not feel like his energy had diminished so he felt no need to feed. Not having to ever drink from a neck again? Under normal conditions he would think that priceless, then he rubbed the top of his head and the payment was obvious.

Again.

His priorities, he decided, were first, figure out how to follow Bethany Anne into space. Second, have her put him into the Pod-doc so that they could figure out why the hair that should be on his head wasn't growing.

And, for dessert, kill Kraven.

Bethany Anne had told him one time he needed to save the dessert for after he ate his dinner.

Well, what she didn't know, wouldn't get him into trouble.

Gerry made it to Kraven's fortress and he could tell, based on all of the people running around, that Michael was still here.

He smirked. The general chaos of people trying to carve out their own kingdoms in the Fallen Lands, or power in the City-States through economic means, was more dangerous for those alive now than before the fall. But what they believed was power was a mere pittance of what had been wielded centuries before.

Michael and Bethany Anne had taken out the worst of the most powerful. For those in the UnknownWorld, the stories Gerry told of the times before were met with skepticism.

He had his life enhanced and cleaned up by Bethany Anne before she left. He had taken on another wife after the fall. Then, later, they had a child. A daughter, one who didn't believe his stories until now.

Now, she was not only a believer, she was damn near an apostle.

Unfortunately, Gerry's time was up. Even with Bethany Anne's enhancements, he was fading, fast. That Michael rescued his daughter was something he never would have thought a possibility. Unfortunately, he needed to ask that he do it one more time.

—

Michael was enjoying the hell out of himself. This building was like those video games he had heard about from the guys around Bethany Anne. He hadn't played them, and hadn't cared to learn about them. But he could understand the attraction at the moment. For each floor he climbed, the challenges went up. By the fifteenth, he had someone throw a grenade down at him.

He Mysted and floated up.

Puzzled, he thought about his success as he left the stairway and solidified behind those who were watching it. Michael holstered one pistol and grabbed his sword. The first figured out where the stranger was when a sword tip erupted from his stomach and he looked down, surprised. The sword pulled back out and he didn't register that the man next to him had his neck sliced open.

Because he was on his knees, his hands failing to hold in the blood spurting out of his body.

The third, turning around when he heard the commotion, had his brain splattered across the wall, a round from Michael's gun exploding out the back of his skull.

The fourth died when Michael kicked him into the stairway, where he failed to catch the metal railing before falling over the side, screaming on his way down. He hit the railing on the third floor with his forehead and died instantly.

His body, corpse really, made a disgusting sort of splat when it impacted on the ground floor a fraction of a second later.

The fifth had his eyes wide open, staring at the barrel of Michael's gun, which was pressed against his forehead.

"Now, I can be a conversational person," Michael explained, "and I'm sure you understand I might be a little twitchy at the moment." The guy, his eyes still on the barrel of Michael's pistol, nodded minutely. "Good, that makes this conversation easier. Is Kraven an honest leader?"

Michael allowed the man to answer, but he trusted what he took from his mind. The man licked his lips. "Yeah, honest... He uh, he uh, he tells it like it is."

"And what does he tell most people?" Michael continued.

"He tells them..." The man started trying to concoct another lie when Michael heard three sets of footsteps come out and start rapidly jumping down the stairs from above. Michael reached up and grabbed the man. Aiming his gun, he shot into the wall parallel to the stairs going up, blasting concrete chips up the stairway. A long string of cursing occurred and Michael threw the man he was holding, into the stairway heading up as he heard a pair of boots coming around the final corner.

"No, It's MEEE!!!" Too late... the man was shot three times before the one coming down realized he was shooting his own man. His mistake was short lived, as Michael, stepping around the corner, shot him between the eyes before resuming his climb up the stairs.

Step... step... step...

Michael could see a man leaning over the rail trying to get a clue. So he shot through the railing then watched as the man fell screaming past him.

Step... step... step...

The third man had turned, retreating back up the steps.

Step... step... step...

Michael looked at the count on both of his pistols. He reduced his loadout about seventy-five shots in one, eighty-two in the other.

Step... step... step...

He wasn't attacked again as his final step took him to the door on the twentieth level.

If those waiting on the other side thought he was just going to walk on through those doors, they were insane.

—

Gerry watched the confusion on the second level from his position on the first floor. Looking around, he also noticed the group of people around the stairway. It was too clogged up to use so Gerry decided he would wait for Michael to come back down. If he chose to come back down, that was. He could always Myst out of the building.

But that didn't seem to be what he was doing. Assuming he could Myst, he obviously wasn't doing it. Not based on...

Gerry heard a very weak scream that was escalating in loudness, and closeness. People started rushing away from the open doorway to the stairs and Gerry heard a THUD as a body landed on the bottom floor. The guy's head, did a good imitation of a dropped egg, exploding on impact.

Seemed Michael was still busy up top, he mused. Gerry turned and looked around, finding a niche in the wall near the exit. It would allow him to see what was going on, while still being out of the middle of the floor. No telling how Michael would come back down and he would prefer not to be killed by friendly fire.

—

Michael tried to Myst again, and it didn't happen. His lips compressed in annoyance.

Apparently, some of his abilities worked on instinct and need. He needed to get past whatever block was happening. It was almost like his mind associated the pain of Mysting and the explosion, and didn't like going back into that state because of negative associations.

Well, there was always one talent that worked every time he tried it.

—

Alvin Sudacki sucked on his lower lip, looking to his left and his right. There had to be... seven, eight, nine. He turned to look on his right and finished his count. Plus himself, that made seventeen men aiming guns at the doorway to the stairwell. This guy might be a badass, he thought to himself, but he can't dodge seventeen guns all aiming at him.

A sudden pulse of fear went through him. He clenched up on his pistol and let his eyes dart to his left and right. He wasn't the only person who felt that!

At least four turned their heads, questions written on their faces.

"Don't let that bastard in here!" Kraven ordered from behind them. He was in the back, so technically there were eighteen men.

And Kraven counted for two, easily.

Alvin was there because his usual post, two floors down, had been called to come up top for the ambush.

Another flash of fear ran through the group and two men shot into the closed door.

"Stop!" Kraven called. Another three started firing before Kraven was able to get them to stop wasting ammunition. "I don't know what's happening, but we're just wasting our ammunition. Wait until..."

That's when the real fear hit and the men ignored Kraven. Guns started blasting at the door. It was an old door. An original for this building from so many years before. It was made of metal, but holes were being punched into it, some bullets getting lodged in the door, most moving on to pepper the stairwell beyond.

A few men, bullets spent, grabbed another magazine and reloaded.

"SSTTOP!" Kraven was yelling, but his commands were being ignored.

—

Kraven was frustrated. He hadn't had his command authority ever tested like this. The fear was real, palpable. He had a slight idea what might be on the other side of that door and, as far as he knew, it shouldn't be there.

The men were gone, mentally. He stepped backwards, turning finally and entering his office. He moved with purpose to his armory and opened the door, reaching in to grab his M1911 with silver ammunition. He checked the magazine, made sure the ammunition was silver like it was supposed to be, and stuck it in his waistband.

He turned back towards the firing and was almost to his office suite door when the third wave of fear elevated, and he dropped to his knees in pain and fear. He turned slowly and looked at his window, the external staircase was just outside.

—

Michael waited, his guns holstered for the moment, he was looking at his nails wondering where he was going to find a pair of nail clippers. Was he going to have to raid an old drugstore?

The metal wouldn't degenerate over time, but were they all stripped bare over the years?

He sighed and pulsed another level of fear, amping it up this time and the gunfire ratcheted up. The wall across from the door one floor above was getting peppered by the gunfire. He imagined no one up there could hear anything.

Awwww, dammit! Michael could sense Kraven leaving the group. He grabbed his pistols and started for the steps, his coat fluttering behind him.

He pushed out his fear, turning it up to eleven, as Bethany Anne would say, and the gunfire stopped.

Step... step... step...

He made it to the final landing and walked to the door, kicking it off its hinges and stepped into the hallway, both guns out in front of him.

—

Kraven had fallen down the second set of stairs, but the fear level was decreasing the farther away he got.

Then, the fear stopped and his eyes widened in surprise and his body straightened. He got himself up, ignoring the pain in his arms and legs and made his way to the next set of stairs down. He went down as quickly as he could possibly go.

—

Michael shot two men in their heads as soon as he could find targets. The door was still in the process of slamming into a couple... or three... people who had been in front, throwing them back as the door rotated above them, slamming into and rebounding off the wall behind them.

Michael's arms spread, as he continued down the line on both sides, shooting the men in the head, and a couple in their chests when their heads were blocked.

One he double tapped for having been smart enough to try and dodge behind another person.

"You messed up my perfect score, jackass," he murmured. And

then he looked back and forth, and nodded his head as he walked into the office behind them. He holstered his weapons as he got to the open window and looked down.

A man was halfway to the ground, racing down, trying to reach the level beneath him as fast as possible.

Disgusted at the cowardice, Michael stepped out and walked onto the fire escape. Jumping down the flight he landed with a BANG on the next turn around, the reverberation carrying through the metal down to the bottom.

BANG, one more floor down.

Far below him, Kraven Cochrel looked up and his eyes opened wide...

—

Bang!

Gerry's head twitched.

BANG!

The *bangs* were getting louder, so he started watching outside, and noticed one person looking up, and then pointing.

He looked around inside the building and decided that maybe the fun had moved outside.

He left his little hiding place, walked back through the doors and kept his head down, not acting like he had any suspicion something was going on behind him until he was across the street from the building. Then, he turned around, looked up and smirked.

Some guy had just shot a couple of rounds from an old M1911 at a figure that was rapidly descending. The person was wearing a black trench coat that flared out every time he jumped down a flight of steps.

BANG! Hitting the next landing below.

The lower man, who Gerry assumed was Kraven, turned and quickly, almost without worry for his own safety, started his own process of jumping down the next level. Recover and run to the next set of stairs to jump again. He was definitely going to make it to the sliding ladder before Michael.

Then Gerry looked close at the figure. His eyes, not as sharp as they used to be but still good enough, yeah, that was Michael… but he had no hair?

—

Kraven, his breath reduced to erratic gasps, was finally at the slide down ladder. He stepped over the railing and grabbed the ladder, his weight dropping him down rapidly. It hit with a CLANG on the sidewalk. People were watching, but staying out of his way.

Two shots fired from his guards on the walls, then two screams and Kraven saw one blasted off the wall.

Then, the stranger jumped the last three flights of stairs to land on the ground right in front of him.

—

The first bullet from the guards on the wall hit just beside his face as he landed. The fragments from the wall peppered his skin.

Michael's eyes narrowed and he reached into his jacket. He had dialed down the destruction capability of the pistols. His hand had actually started hurting. Something John had mentioned in the instructions that came with the pistols. At the time he had smirked, thinking maybe John had been getting soft.

Apparently not.

He casually aimed and took out the two guards that had guns up, and found two more who had turned to watch what was going on.

He shot them both in the shoulders. They wouldn't be shooting anything today.

He looked down to see Kraven had made it down the sliding ladder. So, he grabbed the railing and jumped over it.

—

Gerry shook his head in wonder. The calm assurance of this Michael was apparent. But he wasn't fighting like Gerry thought he would have a couple of hundred years ago. He had followed the man down the steps instead of Mysting. He hadn't killed all four of the guards on the wall. Two of those Michael had shot received definitely survivable wounds, provided they got medical help soon enough.

—

Kraven brought his pistol up, but the stranger merely swatted it out of his hand so fast he hadn't seen the movement. Kraven had, however, felt his trigger finger break as the pistol left his hand, bouncing off the sidewalk and clattering down the street.

"It seems," the stranger said, his voice calm and deadly, "that you have not governed for the benefit of the people, Kraven."

"Who the URGHG," Kraven grabbed the arm that was holding him up in the air, his feet dangling, the hand clenched around his neck.

"My name," the stranger said, as Kraven beat on his arm and then tried to kick him, "is irrelevant."

Across the street, Gerry heard the crack of Kraven's neck before Michael tossed the now dead man off to the side. He snorted. By now, everyone realized that there was a new man in town, who had just personally decimated everyone he had come across.

"Just like old times, eh, Michael?" Gerry said.

The stranger turned quickly, his eyes sharp as he recognised Gerry. His nostrils flared and then he started walking towards him, looking across the street like he expected cars to be coming before turning back to Gerry.

"What the hell," Michael asked as he got closer, holding his hand out to shake Gerry's, "happened to this world, Gerry?"

10

Gerry reached out to shake the vampire's hand. Normally, back when he was the American Council's Alpha, he had let Nathan deal with vampires.

Nathan had a way of keeping his head on his shoulders. The secret, Nathan explained, was keeping one's mouth shut and only answering questions.

And being polite… very, very polite.

"Ah," Gerry looked around as he put his hand up to his mouth and coughed. "Love to answer your question but I don't suppose we can go to a safer location to chat?"

Michael looked around and then raised an eyebrow. It seemed the two toughs from earlier, and the three from the bar had come back, and were racing through the door.

"You going to talk with them?" Gerry asked, surprised that Michael hadn't just killed them.

He shrugged. "I'm tempted to ease my headache."

"You get headaches now?" Gerry asked, surprised.

"What?" Michael glanced in his direction before looking back towards the five men. One of those on the outskirts were talking with the lead guy, and pointing towards Michael. "No, figure of speech. In the older times, I would have just killed them. There was no thinking involved. No concern that they were someone's son or daughter."

"That sounds like Bethany Anne," Gerry ventured.

"That's because it is." Michael agreed before starting towards the men, calling back over his shoulder, "but unfortunately for these five, she isn't anywhere near here at the moment."

Gerry started walking to catch up to Michael.

—

Jimmie followed the five toughs, wondering what they were going to do. One of the members of Kraven's group had run into the bar, and yelled that the fort was under attack before running back out. The five men left, quickly. Jimmie, thinking it had to be the stranger, tossed off his bar apron and told Juliana he was taking a break.

Keeping his pace so that he stayed a block behind them, he kept looking behind him.

He had seen the pistols, all it would take would be one, or both, of those and he would be half the man the stranger was.

And Juliana would be *his*.

—

Michael walked towards the toughs.

Yessss, these five were part of Kraven's inner circle. They had dishonor flowing through their blood like silt in the Mississippi.

"You stole my money!" Robert yelled at him.

Michael said, "I took it as punishment for your poor manners. I didn't kill you, so I believe you received the better part of the bargain."

Michael stopped twenty feet away. "Apparently, you're going to make this easy for me."

"We aren't making anything easy, shithead," The lead guy reached for his shirt. "Looks like it's going to be you and me, man-to—"

Michael sped up, reached into his jacket, and pulled out his pistol, shooting the man in the chest. His body twisted in the air twice before he could finish the next word.

"I despise showboating," Michael said as the other four men started grabbing for their own guns and trying to separate.

Michael turned and shot, turned and shot...

One...

Two...

Three...

"Dammit!" He was annoyed, the fourth was able to get behind a small cinderblock structure. He started walking towards the building, focusing his hearing on whether the man was going to come out the left or the...

"DOWN!" Gerry pushed Michael out of the way as another shot blasted.

Michael, his eyes going red, twisted in the air like a cat that had been dropped. His pistol aimed backwards to find the bartender from the first bar, his eyes wide, standing in the gateway to the fortress. The man was grasping a still smoking pistol.

Michael shot him between the eyes.

Michael landed, rolled backwards and came back up. Jumping backwards, he flew up in the air, his dive turned into a flip as he came over the top of the small building. He saw the final tough coming around the left side of the building.

He shot him, the small pellet driving through the top of his head, through his neck and cracking his pelvic bone. Not that his inability to walk any more was a problem.

Michael finished his flip and landed on his feet, one hand down to help his balance, the other prepared for more attacks.

He ran back around the small block building to find Gerry on the ground holding his side, blood soaking his hands.

"I never thought I would see the day," Gerry grated out, wheezing for breath. "That I would help you stay alive."

Michael pushed his senses out, making sure he wouldn't be

taken by surprise like he had been again. He ripped Gerry's shirt off. "The slug is in there pretty good, and thank you," he murmured as he grew long nails on his hands. "This might hurt a bit. I don't think you want me to help you like I did the last time I helped someone."

"Yeah..." Gerry gritted his teeth as Michael's nails pierced his skin and went deeper into his side, "About thaaaAAAAAAAT!" Gerry's breath was coming quick as Michael pulled the bullet out of his body and tossed it to the side. Then Michael reached up and grew his fangs a touch, enough to use them to slice open his wrist.

"What are you doing, Michael?" Gerry looked nervously as Michael moved his bleeding wrist over his wound, allowing the blood to drip around and on it. He licked his lips. "I thought we weren't supposed to cross the streams here, ArchAngel."

"Dark Messiah," Michael grated out as he started pushing Etheric Energy towards Gerry, hoping the nanocytes would grab hold of the energy and use it instead of the energy from Gerry's body. Otherwise, Gerry was going to die much more quickly.

"Come again?" Gerry asked, a warming feeling going through his whole body. "What are you doing? I can feel energy everywhere."

"Pushing out what energy I can, old wolf," Michael told him. "The nanocytes need energy to help you physically. If this doesn't take, you're going to die, quickly."

Gerry looked up at the vampire. "Michael, I need you to help me one more time."

"Working on it, Gerry," he replied, still trying to feel the nanocytes.

"The girl you helped, the blind one?" he said softly

"Yes?" Michael replied.

"She's my daughter, Michael."

Michael smiled. "Huh, didn't realize that when I helped her."

Gerry grunted. "Would you have left her there?"

"What?" Michael turned to face him. "No. I would have made sure she stayed with me. People who helped Bethany Anne are special, Gerry. Even their children."

That encouraged Gerry. "Well, I need to ask you a favor. I need to ask if you would go rescue her again, Michael." Gerry reached up, holding Michael's arm. "Please. I don't want her left alone without protection again. I made that mistake once."

"Gerry," Michael answered. "I'll help you. But I'm not ready for a kid yet, it's a big responsibility and... and..." Michael watched as the wound closed, the healing taking over. "Annnnddd, you are healed."

"What?" Gerry looked back at him, confused.

Michael stood up, reaching down to grab Gerry's hand and pull him up. "You're healed, Gerry."

Gerry looked down at his side, his skin, his younger looking skin, was in fact healed. It had a few black and blue marks, but... "Damn..." He rubbed it back and forth before turning towards Michael. "How?"

Michael was searching the people, listening, feeling for problems.

None... *yet*.

He whispered, "My nanocytes have been modified. I'm basically O negative now as a blood type, Gerry." Michael said.

A young woman broke from the group watching the two men. "Sir?"

Michael looked over at her raising his eyebrow. "Yes?"

She pointed to Gerry. "Did you just heal him of a gunshot?"

Michael looked at Gerry, who shrugged. He turned back towards the young woman. "Yes."

"Are you magical? An angel?" she questioned.

Michael looked at all of the people surrounding them and pursed his lips. He pushed Gerry towards the gate leading out of the fortress before speaking. "I'm not an angel, far from it." He pointed towards the building. "Angels aren't known for that much killing. I didn't come for peace, or prosperity. No, I came to deliver Justice for the iniquities of the men who were running this town, subjugating all of you under their thumb. Using the men and women willing to be his little army of thugs. The problem with those who would prey on the weaker, is," he pointed to himself, "They eventually run into someone like me."

Michael turned and started walking towards the gate.

"And who are you?" she cried out.

Michael paused and turned to look her in the eye.

His voice, gentle but firm, answered her, "Young Tamara, some call me the Dark Messiah. What you choose to call me is up to you."

He nodded his head in their direction and turned to continue walking out of the gate, people stepping rapidly out of his way as he exited.

The people milled around. "Have you talked to him before?" an older woman asked the young one, who was still staring at the gate used by the stranger a moment before.

She shook her head.

"Then how," the older asked, "did he know your name?"

—

"Three years?" Michael asked as the two men walked along a street. They weren't heading directly towards the pack enclosure yet.

"Yes, as best as I was ever able to understand, China started a virtual war, releasing code to take over stuff. Before you knew it, we were blind here in America, other nations were blind. Some country threw the first nuke, some say Pakistan, some say Israel. Then a huge EMP burst happened over the central United States, frying all of the electronics. At least, that's the working theory. Power went out all over the world, and we dropped back into the second dark ages. Sicknesses we thought were beat came back and kicked our ass. Not so much the Weres or the vampires, obviously. But they really messed up the normal humans."

The two men stepped across the road to go down a side street. "In about twenty years or so, something like eighty-seven percent of the world's population had died."

Michael looked around at the empty city, the many buildings, some collapsed, in the distance. "So, Bethany Anne left Earth and they committed suicide?"

"I wouldn't think Bethany Anne had anything to do with it, Michael. She was gone three years already when it went down."

"How long ago, again?" Michael asked.

"A hundred and fifty years, Michael."

"My God," he murmured.

"Yes, temperatures went up all over the world. I understand you don't want to try and live near the equator, it's a death sentence. Hell, even here in Denver it gets way hotter than it used to. The food belt, isn't."

"Isn't what?" Michael asked.

"Isn't a food belt. At least, not anymore. The only way they could grow the crops they did was because they pulled water out of the ground. No power? No water. Plus, with the temperatures rising, most of civilization is going back to locations by bodies of water. Chicago and that area around the Great Lakes is pretty advanced, and New York is a big deal."

"New York is good?" Michael asked. "I wonder if my home is still standing."

"Probably?" Gerry answered. "We had moved out of New York before the apocalypse, but unless someone built right on the water, it's probably still there. I've spoken with some people who have flown in from that area."

"Flown?" Michael interrupted. "What are they using to fly, airplanes, jets?"

"No, anti-gravitic based dirigibles," Gerry informed him.

Michael shook his head. "So, they did get Bethany Anne's technology?"

"No, believe it or not, they're using technology that can be traced back to World War II and the Nazis."

Michael turned to look at Gerry. "I assume you aren't pulling my leg, but Nazis?"

Gerry shrugged. "Three guesses who found a group of ex-Nazis, or Germans or Germans who didn't want to be Nazis and helped them. Hell if I know what the whole story is there and frankly I'm a little fuzzy on the details after all of these years. So, three guesses and the first two don't count."

Michael looked up to the sky. "How does she get involved in all of these events? Is the woman blessed, or cursed?"

"Yes," Gerry answered diplomatically.

"Nice answer," Michael replied.

"I thought so."

"So, we have Nazi or World War II Germans who had technology and the anti-gravitic capabilities?"

"Yes," Gerry confirmed. "The technology works, but it's very power hungry and the world doesn't have awesome battery manufacturing capabilities built up. Plus, our nuclear capabilities are substantially burdened. If a scientist was found for many years after the fall, they would be grabbed by powerful people and bartered to others. Now, practically anyone with high technology skills needs to be careful, or they end up kidnapped."

Michael thought about Gerry's statement. "Knowledge really is power, isn't it."

"Yup," Gerry said. "One of the reasons I feared for Jacqueline."

"She's smart?" Michael asked.

"Very, gets it from her mother, before you ask."

Michael grunted. "And her trip out into these Fallen Lands?"

"Headstrong, looking for technology she could rebuild and sell." Gerry shrugged. "My portion of her DNA."

"I gathered," Michael replied drily.

Gerry shot him a look, but bit his tongue. This wasn't the Michael from two hundred years ago, but you were never careless around a wild animal that had been caged. Especially when you were witness to the destruction of just half an hour ago.

Michael continued, "She's attractive from her mother as well."

"May I say, you can be an ass?" Gerry muttered.

"You can, because you have earned it." Michael agreed. "But I wouldn't suggest you do it too often."

"Yeah, figured it was like a coupon system," Gerry put out a hand. "Slow down, we can peek around the corner to see the pack's compound. It's about five blocks away, but they have scouts three blocks out from the fence."

The two men came to a stop behind the corner of the building. Michael looked around to see the pack's location, with the two buildings inside the walls.

He leaned back and looked at Gerry. "Okay, a couple of questions before we stroll over there."

South of Old Denver (United States Post-Apoc)

"Sir, our spies are saying that a stranger is killing Kraven's men," the young black man reported to the pack Alpha.

Joshua Timmons was unusually short for an Alpha. But what he didn't have in height, he had in width. The man was huge and muscular from side to side. One of the funnier assholes in the group had once asked 'why does the sun go around the Earth? Because it's easier than going around Joshua's shoulders!'

Dumbass didn't think about the orbit at all. Joke would have worked if it was the Moon. Joshua thought it was a clever way to talk about how wide his shoulders were.

It took brown-nosing to a new level completely.

Joshua's eye's narrowed. Right now, he was responsible for his pack and while he might do a few things that weren't entirely fair to others, it was always *pack first* with him.

"No idea who, Kent?" Joshua asked.

The man shrugged. "Whispers are about a stranger in a coat. Went into a bar on the west side, one of Kraven's. His thugs went in and messed with him. He knocks two out cold and heads up the street and goes into another bar inside of Kraven's building."

Joshua put a hand over his face. "Did they try to shake him down?"

Kent nodded his head.

"Well, how many before they got him?" Joshua asked.

"Sir," Kent answered, "he's still at it."

"Still killing?" Joshua asked and Kent nodded. "That ain't human." Kent shrugged while Joshua thought. He knew that Kraven had a couple of Weres in his employ. Either they were out on an operation for Kraven, or they were dead. It was daylight and Joshua closed his eyes for a second then looked at Kent. "Okay, tell the guys to tighten up security, bring anyone not from our pack in here, I want to know what they know."

He waited a second, his eyes narrowed. "Now, Kent! I've got to make a phone call."

Kent turned and walked out, doing his dead level best to go as slow as he could without upsetting his Alpha. Joshua asked Kent one time point-blank why he left so slowly and Kent had laughed as he pointed to himself, "Spy, remember?"

Kent's role wasn't just a spy, it was his personality. There was no information he didn't want to know. The more secret it was, the more he wanted to know it.

Joshua, knowing Kent's temperament, waited for him to leave before he reached over and picked up a phone. One of the few benefits from his behind the scenes help for Kraven had been to get connected up to the phone lines that were still working.

When you had only a few people in your pack, and the humans had some serious firepower, you made alliances even if you hated the bastards.

Especially if they hunted vampires as their business.

—

"Looks like they're closing down the place," Michael murmured and Gerry poked his head around the corner.

"Probably got a runner from Kraven's earlier," Gerry whispered. "The Alpha here is a world class dick, but he does try to protect his people."

Michael turned to look at Gerry. "But not Jacqueline?"

Gerry shook his head. "She ain't pack. Her being a Were is just an annoyance to him. It's like people from any other pack are second class citizens."

The creak from Michael's leather coat sounded loud as he turned back to look around the corner. "Well, there goes talking our way in."

"You were going to go talk to them?" Gerry asked, Michael turned back to look at him and raised his eyebrow.

Gerry put up his hands. "Sorry, but your reputation is more of a show up, kill them all and let God sort them out."

"I'm trying to rehabilitate myself here, Gerry." Michael explained. "It's like being put on a diet by your girlfriend before she becomes your wife."

"What was all that you did over at Kraven's?" Gerry asked, confusion flavoring his question.

"Long overdue," Michael replied and turned back to view the corner. "Not to mention since I've returned, a few skills are a little rusty, I don't have all of my previous skills back yet."

"Like growing hair?" Gerry asked, his mouth close to Michael's head as he looked around the corner. He noticed Michael had turned and was looking back at him.

Annoyed as hell.

"Oh, don't mention the hair?" Michael shook his head. "Okay, good to know." Gerry had to bite down on his next comment. He didn't want Michael slipping back into 'old Michael' and apologizing to his dead body afterward.

No matter how much goodwill Gerry had earned, he didn't care to test him.

Michael pulled back. "Let's walk to the other walls, I want to see them, too."

Gerry looked up. "How far can you jump?"

—

A phone rang a few miles away. The man, blond hair with two scars down the left side of his face turned from his workbench and walked over to the table. The large warehouse where he was working had been converted into their living and working quarters while the team was out this far west. Except for the major Were ambush a while back, his team of three hadn't had much in the way of vampire hits in this area.

Were blood, so far, had been damned useless for the underground blood trade. He had enough to hold twenty-five large vials of blood in stasis and the only good shit was vampire blood.

Depending on the quality of the blood they put in the vials, that would be enough for the three of them to live off for five years. Even when they paid off their silent partner, they were all good for three good years if they wanted to be fair and square with him.

Hank picked up the phone. Calvin and Izzy wouldn't have heard anything from outside. "Yeah?"

"It's Joshua," the male baritone voice said. "I have a tip."

"What's it going to cost, Were?" Hank asked. "The last tip wasn't so good. We were barely able to break even after selling the slave."

"Yeah, but he took her, didn't he? You were responsible for blinding her."

"Weres heal," Hank replied.

"Not from fucking silver, *Hank*," Joshua replied.

Hank, annoyance coloring his voice, said, "Well, we ain't got time to go around killing a bunch of Weres, Joshua."

Joshua reined back his temper. "Good, cause if I'm not mistaken, you are about to get the fucking mother lode, Hank."

"Vampire?"

"Yes."

"Why do you think this guy is hot shit?" Hank asked as Calvin and Izzy came walking in from outside. He put a finger to his lips to tell the guys to keep their talking down.

They had phones, not great phones.

"Two reasons. The first is that I'm getting the news he's killing everyone over at Kraven's," Joshua told him.

"How the fuck is he doing that?" Hank asked.

"That's the second reason. I'm guessing he's a sunwalker, Hank." Joshua dropped the obvious answer and Hank's eyes narrowed.

"Dangerous," Hank finally replied.

"And imagine what his blood must be worth, Hank?"

Hank tapped his fingers on the table. "Why are you telling me this, Joshua?"

"Because I know where he's going to be, most likely," he answered.

"Where is that?"

"Right fucking here," Joshua said. "So, if you want to know where he is, I'd suggest coming and bagging his ass before he splits. Come in the lower tunnel and we'll open it up."

"It's going to take us twenty minutes at least," Hank said but made hand signals to his two partners to go suit up.

"It's not like we're going anywhere, but whether he's still around is your problem. If he's been here, I'll have either killed him, or I'll have been killed. Either way, the blood ain't going to be worth shit to you."

"Fifteen," Hank told Joshua and slammed the door down. "Load up the heavy stuff!" he yelled out and ran to his own locker.

A daywalker was a myth, a legend.

But, if he was really a daywalker, his blood would set him, and all his guys, up for life.

Hank met Izzy and Calvin as they finished suiting up.

"I think this is the big one, guys," Hank told them.

"Like the last one was?" Calvin kicked in, laughing.

Hank gave Calvin an annoyed look. "Hey, she was hot, no doubt," Izzy jumped in. "But we got ripped up pretty bad, silver or no silver."

"Yeah, that was stupid not taking the blood first," Calvin added. "We had to take it when we came back."

"Each time we use the blood, we hurt our chances of gaining a profit," Hank countered.

"Dead ain't a profit, Hank," Izzy reminded him. "And how much do you believe this is the big one?"

Hank thought about his second phone call as he strapped on his neck protection. "Yeah, okay. Somebody totally fucked up Kraven's place and Joshua is thinking he's going after his location next. We might be late, but better to be prepared than dead." he slapped the wall next to him. "But GOD I hate wasting good product."

Two minutes later, all three men had finished getting ready for battle and their feet clump-clump-clumped down the steps into the dark basement.

"Ohhhh…" a voice, a sibilant whisper, eerie in its weakness greeted them. "So, you grace me with your unholy presence again."

"Come on Daniel," Calvin lit an oil lamp and turned it up. He turned towards the emaciated late teen laying on the table, strapped down, his skin a pasty white. "You should be honored you are so valued."

An angry, weak laugh turned into racking coughing. "You kill my mom, my dad and steal me away in the night for what? To drain me dry of blood, night after night, seeing how long you can keep me both weak, and producing?"

"Wow," Hank walked over to look at the machine, seeing how much blood it had drawn from the young man. "You know how long it took me to get Izzy to understand just that much of the manufacturing process, Daniel? If I could, I'd switch you and Izzy in a heartbeat." He shook his head, but pulled the latest vial from the machine and plugged in a fresh one. "But you have the stuff in your blood that keeps the money flowing, and Izzy doesn't. So, sucks to be you. Your parents were killed on the altar of social progress and medical necessity. So, have a little spine and stop your crying. Out of the tens of thousands of people here in the Fallen Lands, we chose you."

"Yeah," Izzy confirmed the liquids going back into Daniel's body were still dripping correctly. "We drag your ass all over this land each time we move, you should feel important."

Hank stopped playing with the vials to look over at the vampire as he started laughing.

It was a dark laugh. "You have no idea who comes, who is here! I feel him, feel his energy. Power like you have never encountered and he will save us, save those who you hunt in the day."

"Well, certainly we hunt in the day," Calvin quipped. "You fuckers are a lot scarier at night."

Izzy pointed out the window. "It's turning night outside now, asshole."

Hank grumped, "Don't let him scare you, guys. He's just mind fucking you." Hank looked at the amount of blood they had pulled in the last two days. "He's about done, guys." He turned back to look Daniel in the face. "Boy, you're talking like you think there's some sort of vampire messiah. Well, that's a crock of shit, you fucking devil in a human body. You aren't even human, so trust me, I'm not worried about one of your messiahs."

"Okay then." Calvin came over and took two of the vials Hank had just pulled and passed one over the table to Izzy, the three men watching the youth on the table, his eyes withdrawn into his skull. "Cheers to a very good producer, sorry you have come to an end!"

The three men clicked the vials and then each tossed their vial back, drinking the contents before they turned and tossed the vials into the sink. Hank headed for the stairs, calling over his shoulder.

"Calvin, get the light. Izzy, turn off the machine. No need to pay to keep deadweight around."

The room darkened and the men closed the door and locked it at the top of the stairs. Daniel's eyes lit up one more time.

"Burn motherfuckers… buuuuurrrrnnnnn…"

Moments later, his breathing stopped and there was silence in the room.

—

Michael sprinted up the fire escape. The setting sun cast shadows across the city. His time of day, quite frankly.

"Remember," Gerry called out from below him, "they'll have people on the rooftops about three blocks out."

Gerry was like a damned wife, constantly reminding him to eat his vegetables or chew with his mouth closed, Michael thought.

Michael came over the side, low and quick. Staying low, he made it to the side nearest the pack encampment.

Which is to say, their buildings.

Michael lifted his head and looked. His vision, certainly superior to the Weres, easily picked them out. There was movement on three of the four buildings that he'd expect to see sentries on. As Gerry made his way up behind him, he found the fourth.

Asleep.

"What do you see?" Gerry asked.

"A challenge," Michael answered.

"You aren't sure if you can get in there?" Gerry asked.

"Of course I can get in there," Michael answered. "I'm talking about whether I can jump over the third building, or if I should jump one to the left and then back again."

Gerry lifted his head up over the lip of the building. "The hell…you're thinking you might be able to just jump over the brown one?"

Michael nodded.

"Okay, I'm impressed," Gerry admitted.

"Oh, I used to do this for fun, Gerry," Michael said. "Back in the American Revolutionary war, I would go hunting the Redcoats for kicks every once in awhile. I had to make sure it looked like a sneaky Colonial bastard, by stabbing their men in the dark. Otherwise I might have had the whole *monster* issue from Europe creep up again."

"Weren't you just a sneaky Colonial bastard?" Gerry asked.

"No," Michael answered, "I was a sneaky Colonial *Vampire* bastard."

Gerry just shook his head.

—

Down in the sewer entrance, there was a knock and Joshua nodded his head. He had Kent, Donovan who was unlocking the door, the female that had come earlier and two more of his men.

Hank was first through the door, an AR-15 on a quick sling, but a shotgun probably loaded with silver shot in his hands.

While his two buddies came in behind him, he looked at the new face. "What happened to her?"

Joshua turned. "Oh, let me introduce Jacqueline to you. You might remember her. Well," Joshua reached out and grabbed the woman by her chin and moved it left, then right. "Perhaps after she heals, you might remember her. She didn't want to admit she knew anything." He dropped his hand, and turned back to Hank. "So, I explained the local pack rules."

Hank swung the shotgun to rest on his shoulder and scratched his chin. "Isn't the rule that there is only the local pack?"

"Precisely," Joshua agreed. "She had this silly concept that Weres stuck together."

Hank shrugged. "Beats the fuck out of me. All sorts of fights in New York, so don't have a clue about Weres being civilized with each other." He looked around. "So, what's the news? None of you guys look like you're hurting too much." Hank turned back to Joshua. "Is this a false alarm, Joshua?"

Joshua shook his head. "No, no false alarm. It seems this one." He pointed to the beat up girl, "is the same one that you sold a while back. She's met the..." he turned to her, "what did you call him?"

Jacqueline glared out of her one open eye at him. Before Hank could say anything, Joshua turned and slammed a fist into her stomach, causing her to collapse to the floor in pain. Joshua looked up at Hank. "She's still not submissive enough. If I keep her around, I'll have to work on breaking her more."

Hank shrugged. "Pack politics, whatever floats your boat."

Joshua turned to look back down at Jacqueline on the floor. "Name or I start stomping on your fingers."

"Dark... Messiah..." she spit out, trying to catch her breath.

Izzy and Calvin glanced at each other, but said nothing.

"Yeah, I see the training works, eventually," Hank agreed and then looked down the hallway, pulling his shotgun off of his shoulder. "Shall we?"

Joshua nodded to Donovan who locked the door.

The nine of them left the little landing. Two of the Weres grabbed Jacqueline, who left a trail of puke as they dragged her along with them.

Now, Hank thought, it was time to figure out how to safely catch the biggest, baddest vampire anyone had so far.

His head, he figured, would look good stuffed and on his wall.

Or, maybe pickled in a big jar.

1 2

Europe

DONOVAN STRODE through the large castle, a building the Duke preferred to reside in when he was visiting the Fallen Lands outside of the City-States of Europe. Having left his lackeys outside, Donovan was careful not to suggest he was trying to compensate for the Duke's innate power.

Walking to the library, Donovan rapped on the door as he strode in, announcing his presence as a sign of respect, not that his father needed warning that anyone was near him.

The Duke heard everything.

He was old, older than the Apocalypse and old beyond that. Unfortunately, at least in Donovan's opinion, he was also ignorant. Having been trapped in the far past inside a crypt he couldn't escape from, he had slept the centuries away knowing nothing about the technologies that made the world great before the fall.

Many decades after the world self-destructed, grave robbers broke into the long-forgotten crypt, seeking jewelry, weapons, or some sort of treasure. They had ignored the signs and warning chiseled into the rock.

They couldn't read.

What they found instead of gems, was the Duke. The poor grave robbers woke him up and unfortunately, became his first feeding in centuries. This helped rejuvenate the old vampire. Their bodies reduced to shriveled husks left behind as the Duke stepped out into the night to find a new world.

A fallen world.

A world without his father David, or David's father Michael. A ripe world, the world that was now prepared for a true Forsaken King.

—

"I cannot feel the energy of your sister, Donovan." His voice, a mix of ageless gravity and youth, wasn't accusing, but was demanding to hear an answer.

Donovan found he was telling the truth, despite his earlier decision to hide it from his father.

He flipped a hand out. "She failed when we hit the small town, Father. She got soft when seeing a small human child cut down and left the attack, walking out on us."

The Duke turned, raising his eyebrow to the second child he had created once he left the tomb. "And you did what, exactly?"

"Left her in the street to either toughen up, or suffer the punishment of lying there in the sun."

The Duke pursed his lips, thinking.

Donovan waited, he was either going to die in moments, or his effort was... Well, he didn't know. Nothing he told his father was untruthful, it just wasn't the whole truth. Donovan hadn't schemed for the past three years to set up his sister to fail so dramatically, without plans in place.

He might be slow in thinking, certainly not as intelligent as his sister, but he was thorough.

"She caved when seeing the killing of the human child?" the Duke asked again.

"Yes," Donovan replied. "Her eyes opened, she looked around at the attack and subjugation efforts and then ran off the field of battle."

The Duke turned back to the chessboard he had been studying. "Pity, I had such plans for a female vampire, they are so very rare."

Donovan let out the breath he had been holding in.

The Duke made a move on the chessboard and then turned towards the large table, maps of Europe and the world spread across it. "Come Donovan, I have plans here in Europe, but I want to discuss my plans for taking the New World."

On Top of a Building, **Old Denver**

Two figures sat, their backs against a small lip on the top of the building. "You want to fight?" Michael asked again and Gerry nodded. "Why?"

"I'll not have you saving my daughter while I stay outside," Gerry replied. "There's no honor in that."

A small smile played on Michael's lips. "You are sneaky old Were." He lifted up to look over his shoulder at the pack's fortress. "That means I'll have to help you get in, unless you can jump over the fence?"

Gerry shook his head. "Only in my youth, with a boost, could I have accomplished that, Michael. I'd need something soft to land on to try it now. The benefits you gave me are great, but... well..."

Michael shook his head. "Say no more, I know how Weres age," he answered, coming up with a new plan that didn't have him jumping across to the final building and fighting his way down from the top.

"What about bait?" Michael asked, looking at the nearest sentry walking across a roof a couple of blocks away.

Gerry's turned his head to look at Michael, his eyes wide. "You want to use me as bait?"

"Not you," Michael replied, pointing. "Him!"

—

"Stupid ass duty for a stupid ass reason!"

Kevin was a twenty-seven year old who was tall and lean with red hair and he hated sentry duty. Probably because he hated heights. Anytime he looked over a side down to the street, he suffered vertigo and anxiety. His heart raced, and he had to step back from the edge and calm himself down.

The bastards who pulled gate duty had the best job. Let someone in, refuse to let someone in. The power and the occasional female they got to mess with would be enough for him.

This standing duty on the top of a building sucked caterpillar balls.

He considered looking over to see what was going on. The news was to expect an attack at any time.

With the follow-up command from Joshua—the pack comes first.

—

Timothy could almost hear Kevin's complaining. Oh, he was too far up and away for even Timothy's superior hearing to catch any of his words, but he had been around Kevin for more than ten years and he knew how much he hated heights.

He chuckled, a word in the right place and all of Kevin's worst fears were realized. Now, his friend was stuck up there for at least another month before coming down here to guard at the gate.

The door behind Timothy opened and Alphonse came in, closing the door behind him. "Word is to keep ourselves..."

The very audible scream and sudden, and disgusting, sound of a body hitting the street outside the gate had both men rushing to the small viewing window.

"Get the fuck outta the way, Alphonse!" Timothy yelled, boxing the other guy in the ears.

That scream, that voice, had sounded familiar.

"No no no no NO!" Timothy yelled. He hit the button to unlock the door and ran over to yank it open. "I'll just be a minute, don't you dare lock me out!"

The door slammed as Alphonse went back to the small window, seeing Timothy's dead friend's eyes staring at him in the moonlight.

—

Gerry took the screaming to be the signal Michael said to wait for, and got his multi-century old body moving.

It was five blocks away, and he had three blocks to go when he saw the guarded gate door open and a guard rush out, running towards a body lying in the street.

He was just two blocks away when a figure seemed to float down from above, landing behind the guard, next to the gate. Two eyes glowing red in the darkness.

He was one block away when he heard a scream quickly silenced.

He ran through the open door, it shutting behind him. He stopped just inside, breathing hard and asked the man coming out of the guardhouse, "What…" pant, gasp, "what about..." Pant, pant, gasp…

"Stop asking, I took care of the other sentries before the last came down as bait," Michael said as he looked around.

"Random choice who got thrown off?" Gerry finally got out.

"No, he had wanted to violate Jacqueline," Michael answered. Then, after a moment, "I had other plans that would have kept him alive, but changed them at the last moment," he admitted.

Gerry turned, imagining the body behind the gate and how he would have liked to go back and kick it, at least once.

"The fight, Gerry, is this way." Michael pointed away from where Gerry was looking.

Gerry spat in the direction of the corpse and turned to walk with Michael. He looked off to a far corner and closed his eyes for a second, before focusing on the direction Michael was taking them. He had hoped his daughter was still safely hidden in the shadows, but that wasn't to be.

Then, someone starting ringing a damn bell.

—

"Remember, we want this vampire alive," Hank told his partners, both leaning their heads in with him as the Weres rushed ahead, a clanging bell calling them to danger. "Pepper with silver if we have to, and nail this bastard to the wall at times, but we can grab a few humans after we lock his ass down." He popped Izzy on his shoulder. "You ready to send some hot lead out to fuck up another demon?"

Izzy snarled, eyes glowing faintly from the vampiric blood. Hank turned to Calvin, but he was already showing the middle finger. "Fuck em all up," he growled. "Go humans!"

Hank winked and leaned in, voice soft as he spoke quietly to both men, first looking at Calvin before turning to Izzy. "Don't hit too many Weres if you can help it. We might need them in a few years, so says the boss, k?"

The three men chuckled as Hank pulled back into the shadows and away from any openings so no stray shots would hit them. "Now, let's let the Weres soak up some damage first."

—

The glory of battle was rising in Michael's chest. He could hear the heartbeats racing as at least a dozen headed in their direction. He had three more pegged, watching from windows but none had aimed anything in his direction.

Yet.

Michael pulled his sword out. Gerry was agitated, angry, hostile…

All the anger he had inside, pent up with the months, and years of worry.

Michael looked at the building maybe forty yards ahead, then back at his companion, when a growl erupted out of Gerry's throat. A desire to rip apart all that stood between him and his daughter. They could see Jacqueline, her body being dragged out of the building right after the pack Alpha stepped out into the street. She was awake, but was healing and in no shape to do much.

Michael's eyes narrowed, and he listened to the heart's desire of the man, no—the father next to him.

"Fuck it…" he murmured and switched the sword to his left hand.

Michael turned and pushed his palm against Gerry's shoulder. "Take, Gerry, Alpha of the North American Council," he hissed, his eyes blazing red. "Ravage those ahead of you, protect one last time that which you love more than any other here on this Earth."

Michael pushed energy, a conduit from the Etheric through him and into Gerry, the nanocytes inside Gerry feeding in a frenzy on the power of Michael's gift…

And merging it with the fury of the father they were housed within.

Then, those Weres who could see the two men, mouths dropped open as the roar of battle echoed one more time from the fables, from the myths…

From a Pricolici.

"YOUUUEEEEE DIIIIEEEEE TOONNIIIGHGTTT!" Gerry screamed, fully eight feet tall, eyes blazing yellow orange as he ripped the rags of his clothes off his body. He started running, careless of the danger, straight towards Joshua.

Jacqueline, ignored when the other Weres saw the vampire,

crawled against the wall of the building. Her eyes, one good and one half-healed, saw the Dark Messiah and then the man beside him.

Her father, and she felt shame. Her father had come to the Fallen Lands and left everything behind to find his lost daughter. He had searched until old age had almost taken him. Standing beside the Dark Messiah himself, attacking Weres to save her.

Then he changed. Her father wasn't the Alpha from the past, but rather he was one of the stories he had told. He was Nathan Lowell, he was Peter, he was...

Coming for her!

His eyes blazed in anger, in power, in retribution and the destruction of violence he was unleashing fed her soul as the first Weres who had changed were torn apart as easily as wolf cubs might if they got in the way of a mother grizzly bear.

—

Michael, sword still in his left hand, pulled out a pistol with his right and casually turned the power to eleven. He was infused with energy left over from pushing so much into Gerry, but the man deserved the chance to go out as he was in life.

A protector.

Michael aimed at a window on the third floor and shot once. The window cracked and he felt the life of the one behind it evaporate. He kept walking forward, watching and listening to those around. Allowing Gerry to have the ability he had been missing these last years. The power and strength to return the injustice back to those who hurt others.

With justice at the end of his claws, and his teeth.

The first wolf jumped at Gerry's neck and received a size fifteen or twenty clawed foot to its chest, cracking its rib cage and booting it the thirty five feet back to the building. Its back cracking as it slammed into the stone siding, it slid down to land in a hump at the bottom, unmoving.

Michael raised an eyebrow, apparently Gerry was seriously

pissed. A Pricolici's power often had to do with how angry it was. The eight-foot tall werewolf of legend was screaming obscenities during the decimation of all who came between him and the Alpha, Joshua.

Michael pivoted and shot twice at the warehouse. One into the opened door where a gun was coming out and once into the metal door next to the opening.

Two more lives snuffed out.

One of the wolves, perhaps believing that the vampire behind Gerry was an easier target, had run around Gerry and was now racing towards him. Michael smiled, his fangs growing. "Idiots," Michael said. "You know not who your injustice has called out to." Michael, hands blazing with speed, holstered his gun and tossed his sword into the air. He reached forward as the wolf jumped at him, jaws gaping huge, teeth ready to tear into him.

"You should be happy..." Michael told the wolf when he blocked the teeth with a quick arm under its throat, then punched it hard before the claws could do anything. With a bark it flew back, rolling over three or four times across the torn up concrete street, before changing back to a human male. One who clutched at his chest, coughing up blood, "...that I'm in a good mood," Michael finished.

Michael put out his hand to catch the sword, then he continued walking. He casually cut off one of the Were's arms. "Regrow that," he told the now screaming male as he walked on, "and stay out of the rest of this fight," he suggested back over his shoulder.

—

Gerry felt the power coursing through him, the animal inside of him released, merging his abilities and his anger and he felt like God himself had given him the opportunity to bring justice to those who had harmed his daughter, his baby girl.

This was it, and he knew what Michael had done. This was his last battle, his last chance and he would be forever grateful to the vampire for allowing this father to bring such violence to those who had dared hurt his daughter.

He went through those who would stand between him and the Alpha in a destructive orgy of mayhem and pain. Both delivered and occasionally felt, his body regenerating.

Then Joshua was in front of him, the gunshots hitting him…

The bastard was shooting him with silver!

—

"DIE MOTHERFUCKER!" Joshua yelled, unloading his pistol with the silver ammo. "You think I'm not prepared to protect my people? NOT PREPARED TO FIGHT?" he screamed at the Pricolici as his gun unloaded into the chest of the eight-foot-tall monster.

CLICK CLICK CLICK.

Joshua looked down in surprise when his pistol refused to fire any more bullets.

"Iii Wonnnnn'tt waassstte worrdds ooonnnnn yyyouooo!" The Pricolici spit, his long legs bringing him to Joshua, who aimed the gun again.

CLICK CLICK CLICK.

"Motherfucker!" Joshua screamed, but then his mouth lost the ability to speak when the clawed hand wrapped around his throat. He grabbed a silver knife but the creature batted it away with its other hand.

Joshua changed to his wolf form, and the hand still held his wolf throat. But now he had claws and he pulled them up to try and mutilate the beast's chest.

"You cocksucking motherfucking asshole!" Joshua heard a woman yell as the silver knife entered his side. "DIE YOURSELF, MOTHERFUCKER, AND LEAVE *MY FATHER* ALONE!"

The excruciating pain of the silver knife, fully twelve inches long, was too much. His eyes, closing, never noticed he turned human again when the monster reached forward and stuck claws under his jaw to rip his head from his body.

—

"Have you seen that shit?" Izzy asked, peeking out at the fight going on, "that shit ain't normal!"

Hank bit his tongue and looked behind them. "He has to dodge the light, right?"

The other two shrugged.

"He can't be this strong in daytime. Fall back and we'll do this right."

The three humans stepped back into the shadows, waiting for the sun to become their ally.

—

Jacqueline cried out when the monster dropped first to one knee, then the other as the blood seeped out of the bullet holes. The beast was now short enough to look into her eyes one more time. She reached out, and enveloped the monster. Hugging it regardless of the blood and gore between them, her tears washing down the face of the beast.

Who changed to become her father one last time.

"Jacqueline," he coughed out, "my precious, precious daughter…"

"Father, forgive me, I never believed you," she cried, rubbing his head. "I never…"

"Shhhh," he told her. "Shhhh baby." He held her tight, the silver in his chest poisoning his system.

They heard the crunch of Michael's boots as he stopped beside them, scanning the surroundings.

"Michael," Gerry turned to look up at him. "I give you my daughter, to protect, to teach, will you accept this charge?"

Michael weighed the commission. "Gerry, where I go there is only danger, there is only death. Justice is the demon inside me."

"Then, if she agrees, she will be living in Honor, and she will be Justice's Vengeance and it will be what it needs to be." Gerry agreed, his voice soft, his pain evident.

Michael turned to the young woman. "I don't live a blessed life, Jacqueline."

Her eyes widened. "Oh my God," she turned back to her father. "Him?"

Her father nodded as she cradled his head. "It's himmmm...." his voice weakened.

"NOOOO!" she cried out. "Can't you do something?" she begged Michael, rocking back and forth, holding her dad.

"I have, Jacqueline," Michael answered, softly. "I gave him his heart's desire and it became more than I thought possible." Michael turned and looked at the building. "I have unfinished business."

Her shoulders jerking as she sobbed, Jacqueline held on tightly as Gerry's arms went limp around her. "Father, why did I not believe you?" she cried, stroking his hair over and over again.

Michael pursed his lips. He would have to wait here until she was finished grieving. He would not, could not, leave her behind and she wasn't ready to leave her father.

Michael allowed his eyes to glow, his fangs to shine in the night.

It was a warning to any looking in his direction to stay the hell away, or suffer. He was curious if any would be stupid enough to ignore the only warning he would give.

13

The sky was breaking from black to gray as Michael laid the last piece of rock he had ripped out of the street onto the cairn for Gerry. Rock being a relative term. In the city, he was actually ripping up huge chunks of concrete.

Jacqueline had tried to help but realized quickly that her rocks, while huge for humans, didn't touch the massive rocks Michael was ripping out of the ground, the street or the walls.

To get the materials he needed, he would crack apart or widen existing cracks in the concrete. Using pipes, hammers and the occasional shot from his pistol he loosened the material to the point that he could grab it.

The show of strength wasn't lost on those who were watching. Once Michael had asked Jacqueline to hold his coat and shirt, his muscular shoulders and six-pack stomach weren't lost on a few, either.

"Thank you," she said when he placed the last rock on the top. He dusted his hands off and reached for his clothes. His shirt first, he carefully buttoned it before accepting his coat. He had never allowed his pistols to be out of his reach.

He had allowed her to hold the sword.

"My future is among the stars, Jacqueline," he said as he reached for the sword, which she handed back to him. Then, he turned his head just a bit and handed it back. "These assholes are just stepping on my last nerve."

She looked back at him, confused.

"You know how to use that, right?" he pressed. She nodded. "Good, take it out. It's silver laced, but our problems are human at the moment."

Michael listened as he checked his pistols, turning them down to seven, he didn't want to possibly hurt others if the loads slammed into walls.

"Big bald fuck out there isn't getting out of the way, can't be so smart as all that," a male voice chuckled.

Michael ran a tongue around his teeth, trying to contain his temper.

He looked back over his shoulder to the east, noticing the sun cracking the morning sky and shook his head. They thought the sun would do what, weaken him?

Michael turned back and noticed Jacqueline, her face nervous, her lower lip in between her teeth.

He nodded toward the building. "It's three humans. They're some sort of vampire hunters that believe I'm the mother lode," he explained.

Her eyes flicked towards the building. "Blood hounds?" Michael shook his head, not comprehending. "I thought them rumor. Humans who grab vampires to drain and drink their blood. For medicine and... stuff," she finally stopped.

Michael's eyes narrowed. "Blood bags?" He turned towards the building and started walking, outrage plain on his face.

"More like Human Forsaken," he spat out.

—

"Ah, Hank?" Calvin called out, "Looks like we got cue ball's attention."

Hank brought his AR-15 around from the quick-sling. "Okay,

the sun is rising, let's see if we can get him to stay out there for a few more minutes."

Calvin yelled through the glass broken sometime during last night's fight. "Hey!"

The vampire stopped in the middle of the street, his arms by his side, staring at the doorway. The three men were behind half-walls or super large planters whose greenery had died decades before, leaving behind the concrete behemoths.

The man smiled. "Yes?"

"Just curious who you might be, seeing how it's obvious we aren't going to be friends and all," Hank called out.

Izzy snickered behind him.

"Not sure you're going to know the name, stranger. But, I'll play with you three for a few seconds longer," the vampire agreed.

"Oh my God!" Calvin whispered, "Jackhole's intelligence must be affected by the sun!"

"Please, oh please," Izzy added, "let him monologue, that would be priceless!"

Calvin turned to his friend. "What the hell is a monologue?"

Hank interrupted, "It's in books, Calvin. The bad guy lays out his plan so the heroes can foil it, now shut up you two!"

Michael slowed down, pushing out the feeling of contentment, the feeling there was nothing to worry about. From the sound of their discussion, it was working.

Good to know.

It was time to go back to old faithful as his eyes blazed red.

—

Izzy bit down on his tongue. The fear he suddenly experienced as the eyes of the man in the street started to glow red while he simultaneously grew a set of fangs, was too much! "Hangth!" He called out, his ability to control his muscles compromised. "I juth bit my tongth."

"Shut up and fire!" Hank shouted, pressing the trigger on his own gun. All three of them shot through the door.

Not that far away, Jacqueline was forced to duck down behind her father's cairn, a few bullets ricocheting off the stones. She peeked around the corner, but Michael wasn't anywhere to be seen.

She noticed that the window on the second floor above the door was shot out. She gripped her sword and looked around. For now, she needed to keep her head, but soon enough she vowed, she would know enough that she wasn't just baggage to him. She wouldn't be someone who needed to be kept safe when he went out and dealt justice.

"I promise you, Father," she whispered, her eyes looking around her. "On your grave, I'll make you proud." She wiped a tear tracking down her face. "No more, the time for crying is passed. Gerry's daughter has grown up!" A bullet pinged off a wall near her, causing her to duck quickly. "And developed a healthy respect for cover," she added.

—

Michael crashed through the remaining pieces of the window as the asshats below fired at shadows. Their ability to resist his fear was annoying, but frankly, it wouldn't matter in the end. He found the stairs down and opened the staircase door, jumping over the rail to drop to the floor below. His knees bent on landing, then he stood and grabbed the door handle and pulled it open to peek through.

"Cease fire, cease fire!" Hank called out, still struggling with the impulse to fight or flee. And fleeing seemed a better choice all the time.

What had Izzy said earlier? Better to be alive than to be profitable? This seemed like it was going to be one of those fights.

"Where the fuck is he?" Calvin asked, looking around.

I'm everywhere, a voice spoke into their heads.

The men turned around, looking behind them and then to

both sides. Hank grabbed Izzy's attention, pointing to his own eyes and then pointing outside. Izzy nodded and moved forward to get the best view outside he could.

Hank got Calvin's attention. Hank pointed a finger up, and Calvin nodded. The men headed towards the back of the lobby, for the door to the stairs.

—

Jacqueline peeked around the rocks once the bullets stopped flying. She stayed where she was, keeping an eye on the front of the building some forty yards away.

—

Calvin licked his lips and reached for the doorknob. With his enhanced reaction speed from drinking the vampire blood, he was able to block his face with his arm when the whole door erupted out of the doorway and slammed into him, passing Hank who had been to the side, his gun at the ready. Finally, Calvin landed, hard. The door continued past him to BANG into the wall behind him.

Hank pulled the trigger of the shotgun just a moment after Calvin, and the door, had shot past him into the lobby area.

He racked another shell into the barrel and looked around the corner, quickly.

Nothing there.

"You okay?" Hank called back to the moaning and groaning Calvin.

"Yeah," Calvin coughed out. "Be good in about twenty days or so." he rolled over and spit blood on the floor.

"Well, get the fuck up and over here!" Hank hissed. "I'm not sticking my head in there while…"

Hank never saw the pistol that unexpectedly appeared around the corner and fired. He never finished his sentence as his body crumpled, his shotgun firing when his hand hit the floor, blowing off his foot.

—

Izzy heard the bang, the shot, and the guys yelling... then, he heard Calvin as he started screaming in fear. Two separate shots from Calvin's rifle before it went full auto and the screaming kept going until his magazine was empty.

Then Calvin's screaming stopped.

Izzy looked around, then started backing out of the building. He stumbled over a dead body as he was walking backward. His arms flailed for a second, but he kept his eyes up, looking into the shadows inside the building.

"Izzy..." a male voice called from inside.

"Leave me alone!" he screamed back.

"But why, Izzy?" the voice mocked him. "Didn't you want my blood, Izzy?"

"Leave me alone, Demon!" Izzy screamed as he tried to back up faster. "I swear to God I'll kick your ass!"

The laughing coming from the building didn't do anything to settle Izzy's nerves.

Finally, some hundred feet from the entrance the stranger with no hair could be seen in the building's doorway. "I'm right here, Izzy!" the man said, holding his hands out. "Come kick my ass, Izzy!"

"I'll do it!" Izzy licked his lips and kept the man in his sight. "Believe me!"

"No," The stranger shook his head. "No you won't, Izzy."

"What makes you think I won't?" Izzy screamed back.

As he finished his question, a sword entered his back beneath his protective jacket and a woman's voice hissed in his ear.

"Because Justice is waiting to send you to Hell!" she spat.

Jacqueline pulled the sword out of the man after his gun clattered to the ground. His body was falling, while one hand grasped at his wound, the other trying to stop his fall. Jacqueline didn't see an easy way to slice his neck, he had some sort of metal around it.

"Fuck it!" She grabbed the Wakizashi and turned it down,

using her enhanced strength and anger to drive it through the protective gear and into the man's back. He spasmed, in even greater pain. She put a foot on his back, pressing him into the concrete.

Michael walked up beside her. "Next time," he said in a normal, conversational voice, "you can slice through the vein under the arm to bleed him out. It isn't as satisfying, but it saves having to sharpen the sword later."

She watched the man squirm, still in pain, before finally lying still. She looked up at him. "Next time?"

Michael shrugged and looked around. The sun was higher in the morning sky, but some rays were still blocked by the husks of the old buildings. "It seems this world has more dishonorable things happening as normal now than I could have ever believed." He paused to look at her. "And that's saying a lot."

"Come," he said. "Clean your sword and let's go. We have supplies to pick up and places to be."

Jacqueline pushed her foot down on the body as she yanked the sword back out and turned to jog back to where she had placed the scabbard. She stopped, kissed her fingers and put it on one of the rocks. "I'll never forget, Father. You were ever my rock, and will be the rest of my life."

After a moment of silence, she turned and jogged back, wiping the blood off the sword on the dead man's pants before scabbarding it and catching up to the vampire. "So, can I call you Mike?"

"No," he said.

The two of them walked out through the open gate. Someone must have run off during the night, leaving the way open.

"How about…" she had started before Michael cut her off.

"You have the choice of Michael or Michael," he said. "Of course, there's always Master," he added a moment later.

The voices, carrying back into the pack's encampment,

floated on the morning wind. "I think I'll stick with calling you Michael." A moment later, "Where are we going?"

Michael rattled off an address.

"Why there?"

"We're following clues, Jacqueline." Any further answers, if there were any, were lost to the wind.

EUROPE

THE OLDER VAMPIRE pointed to a section on the map. "There are people in North America who understand about us, the UnknownWorld. You do not need to be hidden, as we still are here. Soon, we will have the power we need and we will pull it from the Fallen Lands, taking over the City-States here in Europe. Then, we'll consolidate our power across the Atlantic before invading more lands."

He turned to Donovan and said in a dry tone, "No need to duplicate Napoleon's mistakes."

"What will be my command?" Donovan asked.

The Duke patted Donovan on his shoulder. "Sufficient, have faith. We are pulling assets out of my cities here to support you for this. We have acquired multiple zeppelins for your invasion of the New York City-State. You will need to have enough of our kind to keep the Nosferatu controlled. If you don't, then they could consume those on the ships."

Donovan nodded his understanding.

The Nosferatu would kill those running the ship, and then they would lose the ship, the supplies, and the Nosferatu which were their primary weapons.

"Then that is my constraint," Donovan mused, and the Duke simply smiled in agreement.

Michael was discovering a side of Jacqueline he had yet to experience.

Chatterbox.

Actually, he considered, he should upgrade her to *inquisitive* chatterbox.

They headed across the city, encountering groups of people on two occasions. Both times, as soon as they recognized the black coated man with no hair, they turned the corner, or turned around and headed back down the street.

And then, turned the corner.

"Why is everyone dodging us?" Jacqueline asked. "Joshua said something about you killing Kraven. So, is everyone thinking Kraven's goons are after you?"

"I doubt it," Michael replied matter-of-factly, his eyes constantly sweeping the area, his senses pushed out far.

"Why not? I mean, I would expect the humans to have a power vacuum. My dad would tell me stories of the old North American Pack Council and the politics that went on. Why wouldn't the humans do the same?"

Michael maintained his pace, allowing the young woman to

keep talking as a way to, hopefully, work through her grief. Perhaps she just needed to hear her own voice.

"Well? Would they?" she pressed.

Apparently she needed more interaction.

"Jacqueline, you are my charge until such time that you are capable of standing on your own two feet. In order to make decisions and answer questions, I will provide the information you need."

"Information from before the apocalypse? That would be nice. My dad only provided old pack and UnknownWorld information. He was pretty sparse with the old history."

"Why do you think that is?" Michael asked.

"He says the old world had its own problems, and we wouldn't benefit from trying to romanticize it. So, he wouldn't say too much. Oh, don't get me wrong," she went on as they crossed a street, "he told me some of the big stuff."

Michael stopped and looked around, his frustration coloring his voice. "Finding this address is a little harder than I expected with so many of the signs missing."

Jacqueline looked around. "What's the address?" Michael told her. "Okay, be right back." She started jogging down a side street, but called back over her shoulder, "Find somewhere to hide!"

Michael turned back and walked towards an old building entrance that had an overhang and stepped into the small sheltered space. He leaned up against the wall, his hands in his pockets, watching her run. She jogged four blocks before slowing down to hail a couple of people that had been walking the other direction. After a moment, they pointed back towards Michael and then the guy on the right jerked his hand to his left.

Jacqueline was soon moving back and Michael watched the couple behind her. The woman made some comment to the man, and he shook his head in the negative. The woman pointed emphatically at Jacqueline. The man seemed indecisive, so

Michael stepped out of the little niche and started walking towards Jacqueline who smiled at him.

The woman behind Jacqueline grabbed the man's arm and turned him, they started walking away quickly.

Moments later, Jacqueline arrived, noticing Michael's eyes watching behind her. "Yeah, I know, they were arguing if they should have tried harder to hit on me."

"Hit you?" Michael asked, his eyes narrowing.

"No! Hit on me, you know... see if I was interested in sex," she told him as she turned around to watch the couple turn a corner. "Well, I guess taking you to a party is out of the question. I'll never get anyone interested in me."

"Indeed," Michael answered.

—

"Oh my God, the stench!" Jacqueline murmured after Michael opened the locked door to the warehouse's basement.

"Come along, and hold the light steady," Michael said. "Fire isn't the friendliest way to light things. I find it hard to believe how far the world has fallen."

"They have electricity up above, why not down here?" she asked as they descended the stairs. Michael was the first to see the dead man.

"They did," he answered, pointing to a corner. "They have a power cord running to that device."

"Oh," she was quiet as she saw the dead husk lying on the table.

Michael walked over. "Please bring the light."

"One second," she said. Michael turned to see why she wasn't immediately obeying and saw she was lighting a lamp on the wall, one that lit the room well. He turned back to the youth and considered where they had stuck the needles into his body.

Jacqueline's voice was a whisper. "This is the way they take the blood?" she asked. She gently reached out and moved a bit of the dead youth's hair. "What did he ever do to them?"

"Nothing," Michael answered. "They took his blood to sell it. Perhaps keeping him alive as they took more and more. Eventually, the nanocytes were insufficient, or they didn't feed him well enough, and he died." Michael paused and finished, "They weren't doing it very well."

Jacqueline's voice raised an octave, aghast at his comment. "You're complaining they're doing a bad job of it?" she looked from his face to the youth and back again.

"Shhh, Jacqueline," Michael commanded. "Seek to understand before you need salt to go with your foot."

"What's that supposed to mean?" she asked, realizing the man was trying to teach her, but she didn't understand his English at all.

"The whole phrase is 'put your foot in your mouth,'" he replied. "It means to say something that gets you in trouble. Usually, because you didn't think carefully before you said it." He paused before adding, "Or doing something. It isn't always speaking," he amended.

Michael went to study the device. Jacqueline jumped when a CRASH resounded, and she saw Michael, breaking the device with his elbow. Now he was casually pulling it apart to see inside.

"Why doesn't your jacket show damage?" she asked him.

Michael answered, most of his attention on the inside of the machine which he had turned to catch the light better. "It has some unique polymers and frankly, other technical stuff I don't understand, sewn into it that makes it very tough."

"Polymers?" she asked, looking around the room. Anything to help her to ignore the dead body.

"Describes the molecular structure of the materials. Usually synthetic plastics and resins," he muttered.

"Technology!"

Her voice had a life Michael hadn't heard yet, so he pulled his head out of the machine to look at her. "Yes?"

She was animated, at least more than usual. "The past, technology, the power to do so much! That was what my group and I had come into the Fallen Lands to find. If we can figure out the secrets to some of the technology, we could start it up again." Jacqueline walked to him. "If someone could turn on a town again, it would instantly become somewhere people would want to be. Something good again."

He raised an eyebrow when he looked at her. "How are you protecting it?" he asked.

Jacqueline stared at him a moment. Michael's return stare wasn't judging, just patient.

She finally spoke, a frown on her face. "I guess I'm still a little naive, even after everything I've gone through." She turned to her left, pulled out a small chair and wiped the dust off of it before sitting down. "I promised my father I'd do him proud, and the first chance I hear of technology, I want to go chasing the rainbow again."

Michael considered pushing happy thoughts out, but if he did that both of them would get hooked. Her to the feelings like a drug covering her pain, and him for the same reason.

It would mean he didn't have to deal with helping her through this problem.

"Jacqueline," he called out to get her attention. She turned her head to him. "We are who we are, you, me, everyone." He pointed out to the city around them. "Good, bad, selfish, giving, powerful, weak, loving, hateful, it doesn't matter. Just because you have decided on a new course, doesn't mean that new course is without challenges."

He stepped around the table to stand near her with his arms crossed. "There were jets, large planes during my time. Do you have them here?"

She shook her head. "We have large blimps, using lighter than air gasses and anti-gravity for lift and propulsion. But I've read enough to know what jets were."

Michael returned her stare for a moment, wondering why it

seemed for every step this present Earth moved forward, they took two… or, it seemed, twenty steps back?

"Okay," he continued. "So these jets were very automated. They could fly across this land and all the pilots did was to enter information in the autopilot where they wanted it to land. The pilots were there to confirm everything was working as it needed to be and they actually had to land some of the older planes. Now, the interesting aspect is that those planes were rarely on course."

"Wait, how can that be?" she asked. "If they aren't on course, they wouldn't land, and obviously they did, or no one would have flown that way."

"They were off course because of winds, the planet rotating underneath it, occasionally due to storms they needed to fly around. What I am pointing out is they always adjusted throughout the whole trip. So while they were never exactly on course, they were close, and always self-correcting, and eventually you would get close enough to see the airport, and fly it in."

"So, you're telling me my path, my course, is always going to be self-correcting?" she asked, chewing on her lip.

"Yes, and now in the beginning with so much change going on, there is more correction required, after…" he said, walking towards the stairs. "Let's go."

Jacqueline got up from the chair and followed Michael. "After what?" she called out. "What about the lamp?"

"Leave the lamp on," he said from the stairway as he walked up, "It will be used after we check out the rest of this place."

"Okay, but after what?" she tried again.

"Your training." he said, his voice brooking no argument.

She didn't want to tell him she had run away from home partially to get away from the training her father had made her go through. Running from Michael, she thought, wasn't an option.

She pressed her lips together as she thought.

Never again, Father. I won't run again.

—

Michael found a cache of weapons, money and some clothes. A few maps and a couple of books. He gave them to Jacqueline to carry.

They were reviewing the contents of a suitcase when a loud banging started on the door of the warehouse. Jacqueline looked at him, and he shrugged his shoulders. "Stay here, I'll answer the door," he said.

He was halfway across the open space when the door cracked open a little and two tall, muscular guys stuck their heads in the door. "Hank?" the front one called out.

The second said, "Told you they died back in the pack encampment, Lamont."

The leading man's head turned, and he spied Michael and stopped his forward momentum. The second man bumped into him. "Dammit, Lamont! What the hell…" his words died when he turned and saw who was standing twenty feet away, arms crossed in front of him.

Michael could smell the Were on them. He assumed these were the two Weres that had been Kraven's thugs.

"I'm busy, come back tomorrow," he said to them.

Lamont started pushing backward, bumping into his partner behind him. "Yeah, tomorrow's good," he replied, shutting the door behind them.

Michael listened to see if they whispered anything to each other. The only thing he got was they would come back tomorrow after lunch.

He would be gone in a few hours, so that worked for him.

—

Jacqueline looked up as Michael returned to the room. She had stuff packed in three different bags. "Why did you tell them to come back tomorrow?"

Michael picked up each bag, checking the weight. "Because

we're leaving in the next hour or so, and that oil lamp downstairs is going to have an unfortunate accident."

"You're going to burn the place down?" She looked up at him.

Michael's eyes bore into hers. "There are some places where evil has occurred, that need to be sanitized. This is one of them."

She nodded her understanding.

Two hours later, Lamont spoke to his partner as they watched the warehouse go up in flames. "Now we know why he said tomorrow," he commented as he ran a hand through his hair.

His partner shrugged and turned to him. "You upset we didn't try to take him?"

Lamont shook his head. "Hell no."

—

"Seven days?" Michael asked, and Jacqueline confirmed.

There were seven days before the next dirigible would arrive that would take them over to Chicago, and then on to New York.

"Okay, let's get the tickets we need and get out of town."

"Great," she muttered under her breath as she turned to go back to the small office that sold the dirigible tickets. "More training."

—

They had traveled half a day to the north-northwest, skirting a couple of old, dilapidated, small towns and finally found enough wilderness that Michael was satisfied they would probably be left alone.

Michael first put her through stamina and limberness checks. Her Were nanocytes, as Michael explained, helped her regenerative powers, but if she was in better physical condition, they wouldn't have to do as much work. Her time while she was blind hadn't helped her stay in shape.

Michael would often run with her, and it annoyed her that he never sweated. That hairless top of his, she thought, should at least perspire.

Shouldn't it?

She decided she was more annoyed that she didn't understand why he didn't sweat than she was that he was in much better condition than her. Although she was pretty sure she caught him breathing a little hard the third time she collapsed in a nice area of grassy ground, grabbing a cramping stomach in pain.

He would always wait patiently, scanning the surroundings. Finally, she got the hint and started to do likewise as they continued their exercise.

"Where is the blue grosbeak?" Michael asked her on their third day as they jogged along.

"The what?" Jacqueline panted back, looking around.

"The blue bird with the orange in its feathers," he replied.

"Hell if I know?" By this time, she was looking all over the place as she ran, including up in the air for the damned bird.

"We've passed three of them. Stop!" he ordered.

Jacqueline slowed then stopped running, but she did walk in a small circle for her muscles. Michael nodded off to the side. "See that tree, the tall one on the left? Yes, now look up two-thirds to the top and then to the left, there is a blue bird with orange on its wings."

Jacqueline, following his directions, caught sight of the bird. "It's pretty."

"Yes, it is. Now, when we're running, I will tell you every time you miss one. You will get one three-mile circuit to learn. Then, each time you miss one, you'll drop and give me twenty pushups."

Jacqueline was in sheer pain the next morning, even with her enhanced healing. She had been doing pushups all damned day.

Now, her muscles were stiff, and she was trying to limber up, making an attempt to get her body back into a semblance of looseness before the wonderful day of pain ahead of her.

That afternoon, after her second lap without missing one of the birds, Michael added two more types.

The bastard, she thought.

The next day, Michael would start hiding from her. If she

didn't call out where he was by pointing, he would attack her, and it hurt like hell. Her previous hand-to-hand skills were sufficient against humans and some Weres. Now she knew some muscles she hadn't realized existed could be used during fights. And frankly, wished she had never found out.

Finally, he started randomly attacking her with slaps when she was near him, testing her reaction speed.

Finally, she broke.

He slapped at her, which she blocked, but turned her motion around to a kick and followed it up with two more punches, which he deflected.

He taunted her, pushed her and cajoled her as she honed her focus. Just once, she thought, just once she wanted to land a punch on that goddamned perfect face of his.

Just... *once*.

He called a halt as she finally worked her way out of her anger into a state of burning muscles. She pointed at his shirt collar. "I DID IT!" she screamed, tossing her hands in the air and prancing around in a circle. "I did it, I FINALLY did it!"

"I AM THE CHAMPION!" she screamed.

She stopped jogging and put her hands on her knees, her head hanging down. "Oh GOD... I think I'm going to puke." She started spitting on the ground, trying to get the excess saliva out of her mouth.

Michael was checking his collar. "Sweat?" he asked, finally able to see what she had been pointing to.

"Yeah," she answered, nauseated. "I might die in two minutes, but I'll be happy when I die..." She stood up and put her hands on her back, arching backward to stretch it. "In pain, but happy."

Michael shook his head, sometimes he wished he could figure out what motivated a person sooner.

He would have stopped using the Etheric to cool his body down if he had known.

Another day of training and he gave her half a day off before they packed and headed back. They spent the night not that far out of town, arriving the next morning.

She had told him life would be easier if he would leave the coat behind and he explained, in no uncertain terms, that wasn't going to happen.

"Why?" she asked.

"Because," he said. "I made a promise to a woman that I would be back. This coat offers a level of protection her closest friends made especially for me, hoping that someday I might be able to use it. I'm not going to wish I hadn't."

"It makes you stand out, Michael," she pointed out.

He turned to look Jacqueline in the eyes. "Like my lack of hair doesn't?"

15

On the Dirigible Onslaught, En Route from Denver to Chicago via Des Moines

PAUL MULLINS PRIDED himself on excellent table manners. It was something his family, the Mullins from Chicago, had kept as part of their heritage from before the Apocalypse. That attention to detail, his mother told him, was what helped them create the Pods of today.

He had come out to Des Moines on business, tracking down some raw materials and jumped at the chance to go back on the Airship Onslaught.

It wasn't strictly a passenger ship. It was designed for transportation of materials, but it had some berths and nice amenities on it as well. That suited him fine. His family made their money from commerce, and he enjoyed the commercial flights as much as, or sometimes more than, the pure passenger ships with all of their exquisite finery.

"Your beverage, sir?" A polite finger tapped him on the shoulder. Commercial or not, they still offered the level of service he expected.

Paul looked up to see the waiter had a small carafe of orange juice and a morning paper. The country had been able to manage to create paper, of a sort, and now printed the basics every morning.

He had additional information delivered to him from his family's empire, such as it was.

As one of the biggest employers in the Chicago-Great Lakes City-State, Mullins Transportation, he had access to information not shared among the general populace. As one of the richest families in the City-State, he had information on the best of everything.

The best locations to procure old technology, and who to speak with to get it working again.

The best types of foods and foodstuff to produce and the methods to grow year round, putting food on his family's table.

And, the best medicine available, whether legal or not.

Often, the masters of commerce held much of the power, while those that ran for office helped grease the progress of civilization and helped keep it all on track. Generally speaking, those in commerce needed a populace to purchase and use their products. Further, continued businesses growth required an educated populace. Therefore, those in power worked to support the country's infrastructure towards the goal of creating future customers, and civilization was growing...

So were the ways to live beyond a normal lifespan.

Paul Mullins set the local newspaper aside and reached into his bag to pull out the updates his people had filed.

Taking a sip of his orange juice, Paul read the first article about the weather and the expectations of how long the heat was going to affect the region around Des Moines. His R&D group had discussed moving the solar electricity producing infrastructure they had found in old Merriam, Kansas to a Des

Moines farm that still had working water pumps. It looked to be a two-year project, maybe half a year if Paul would supply the transportation. Then the local government would have another large swath of land under cultivation within twenty-four months.

More food meant their population would grow.

Paul considered the farm investment and what monopolies he should negotiate with the local government for risking his capital and resources to help them.

Government, some people never understood, had always been at its core a business, and whether it was able to provide services or not usually determined how effective it was.

Want safety? Need a local police force? Use the power of government to create a monopoly and call it something generic that the locals believed belonged to the city. Like, for example, the Des Moines Police Department.

This company could be incorporated in the Chicago City-State. In order to generate income to run itself, the local government would lease the rights to issue tickets and use deadly force with significant protections against legal retribution.

Monopolies, if run efficiently, could be very profitable.

The second report caused him to set his orange juice down. It was a discussion of recent violence in Denver. About ninety-seven people had been killed in town, and another fifty, they believed, killed west of the town in a small, unincorporated location.

By one man, the stories said. Or, a couple of others suggested he had the help of a woman.

Paul reached out and grabbed a piece of toast, but he didn't realize he was eating it dry as he continued reading the report. Kraven, the local mayor, had been brutally hunted down and killed by the assailant, as well as at least sixty more of Kraven's support staff throughout his building.

Paul could read between the lines. His support staff would have been muscle at a minimum, fighters more likely.

"How the hell," Paul said under his breath.

Then he read a piece that caused chills to go up and down his spine. In the list of the dead, he found Hank, Izzy and Calvin's names. What the hell had they been doing that had allowed one, maybe two people to kill them? They should have easily been able to handle one man, even a vampire.

It was their damned profession, after all. Not to mention they had his investment money and the blood.

He continued reading and then swallowed hard as he realized they had a vampire and his extraction machine with them. The blood drained out of Paul's face, and he lost his desire to eat.

That was when there was another tap on his shoulder, except this time it wasn't the waiter.

EUROPE

IT WAS JUST after ten at night and Donovan smiled in the darkness. He had over a dozen dirigibles loading supplies.

When the Duke decided he wanted to invade a major City-State like New York, he wasn't going to do it with half measures.

"Make sure you seed fear, Donovan," the Duke commanded.

"Don't worry, Father." Donovan replied, looking at the large airships. "With hundreds of Nosferatu and over forty vampires, how can we fail to subjugate the human cattle?"

"I would say pride goes before the fall." The Duke smirked in the firelight. "But we both know that it isn't pride when you speak the truth."

The two men had shared a laugh and a bottle of wine before the Duke left, heading for Frankfurt.

Donovan and the rest of the crew had the airships loaded and were safely in the blacked out holds before the sun cracked the sky in the east.

ON THE DIRIGIBLE ONSLAUGHT

PAUL MULLINS LOOKED up from his breakfast to see a grinning woman staring down at him. "God, you startled me, Kerri," he said as his hand went to his heart. "You know this old ticker could give up any moment."

He pointed to the chair on the other side of his table. "Join me?"

"Of course, you old scoundrel," she agreed, smiling.

He stood to get her chair and admire her figure, but she went around the table to pull out her chair herself. "I'll get it. I never know if I'll get a bill from your company sometime where pulling out chair is a line-item."

They shared a laugh.

She pulled her chair up as Paul sat back down. He caught the waiter's attention and called him over. "I'd like some more toast, and whatever the lady here would like."

Kerri nodded to the man. "My figure needs to stay as nice as it is, to keep young men like Mr. Morris here trying to get my chair. I'll just take a glass of apple juice and some oatmeal, thank you." The waiter dipped his head and left them alone.

She turned to him. "You don't look a day older than when I met you twenty-two years ago, Paul, so don't pat your heart like it's about to fail you now."

He shrugged. "Good genes, Kerri."

"Yes, well, you Mullins mostly have good genes. Even your great-grandfather seemed pretty young when he passed away ten years ago."

Paul smiled but said nothing. The rumors about his family in Chicago were many. Some were created by his family to offset those that were closer to the truth than they cared to admit. They had, in fact, found the elixir of youth.

You just had to be willing to drink the blood of demons to do it. The heavy hitters in the blood trade were based on the East Coast. Paul figured he could make a nice profit and worked to hire away an experienced team and start his own business. Then, he invested a damned pretty penny for the machine to pull the blood out safely from the little demon shits.

Now, his team and most likely, his machine were gone. A serious financial and business setback.

"Are you going to make me carry this whole conversation?" she asked as the waiter came back, laying the oatmeal in front of her with milk and honey, and a glass of apple juice beside it. She nodded, and the waiter left.

"No, just allowing you to get the words out so when it comes time to eating, you don't have problems deciding whether to talk or swallow." He smiled.

"Darling," she drawled. "I always know when to swallow, and when to... talk." She winked at him and took a bite of her oatmeal.

Dammit, she was up two to one, now.

"I, uh, if you say so," he agreed and took a bite of the old toast. "Did you get on the ship back in Des Moines?" he asked, realizing she might have some more information for him.

"No," she put some honey on her oatmeal. "I was in Denver and let me tell you, it was a very unsettling experience."

"Oh?" he said and then reached out to accept the toast from the waiter. "Thank you." He put the toast on his table, using his own honey to flavor it.

She looked at him in confusion. "Yes, you don't know?"

He shook his head and took a bite of his toast. Those that spoke first, lost.

"Someone or someones laid waste to the scoundrel that was the local government there. Totally went through his people, shooting them all and then went to the top. Killed a bunch of men up top, then chased Kraven down the fire escape. And killed him at the bottom."

"What time of the day was this?" Paul asked.

She stopped her spoon halfway to her mouth. "Mid-afternoon?"

Paul's brow furrowed, that couldn't be a vampire. So, who the hell could it be?

She swallowed and used her spoon to point at him. "He went to some sort of religious group that stayed together a few miles from Kraven's. He went and killed the leader and some people over there, too." She twirled her empty spoon in the air for a moment, "People are still trying to figure it out."

"Sounds dangerous, glad I rarely go to Denver," Paul commented.

Nodding, she added some milk to what was left of her oatmeal. "Yes, they had a large warehouse fire north of Kraven's, too. Went up in smoke." She made a motion with her hand. "Poof!"

Paul bit down to keep from cursing. Mother wouldn't have approved of cursing at all. Paul couldn't be sure, but he suspected there went his machine.

"Anyway," Kerri finished, "the rumor is..." she leaned forward and looked around the dining room before bringing her eyes to rest on Jacob's. "He's called the Dark Messiah."

Paul's eyebrow raised up, a small smile on his face. "That's not ominous or anything."

She shrugged and spooned the last of her oatmeal, the spoon scraping the bottom with a noise that irritated Paul's teeth before popping it in her mouth. "Don't know who he would be a Dark Messiah for," she said. "It's not like we both don't know Kraven was a selfish puffed up bastard who was trying to make a little Kraven Kingdom out of Denver."

Paul pursed his lips. "He was known for trying to push up

Denver's level of importance, that's true." He took another bite of his toast.

The mirth in Kerri's eyes, surprisingly, was guileless. "You know, if I didn't know for a fact that you were born in Chicago, I'd swear your humor was from England, very dry."

He chuckled. "They have to have dry humor, to offset how much it rains over there."

"Yes, and it rains money around the Mullins, so dry humor for you, as well," she nodded, thinking the saying apt.

He shrugged. "Work hard, help others build. That's what we do and helping others has been very profitable." He smiled. "Not going to apologize for making money helping people have good lives, Kerri."

She stood up and batted her eyes at him. "Why do you think we women find you so attractive, Paul? It isn't just your dreamy good looks, although those help." She patted him on the shoulder. "Thank you for breakfast, Paul. I'll see you in Chicago sometime."

He said goodbye and watched her walk from the room. She was right, she was taking care of her figure, and he had wanted that figure fifteen years ago. But unfortunately, she had a rather annoying personality defect.

She was too ethical.

He knew there was no way she would support finding, capturing and draining the demons of their blood for medicinal purposes. So there was no chance she would become Mrs. Paul Mullins and her ethics precluded some fun romps in the hay.

He sighed and turned back around. He might as well read the rest of his reports, what could possibly be worse news than he had already received?

Behind him, Kerri slipped out of the dining room and walked down to the berths, the rooms and finally to the suites and knocked on the last one. This dirigible was set up with the general rooms in the center and the berths down opposite sides. Paul, she was sure, was on the other side with the elite rooms.

Her berth was halfway back down the hallway. But she hadn't missed her room when she had walked past it going to the last. The door she knocked on opened. "Please come in, Kerri." His smile damn near melted her heart. Which was weird.

She had never been attracted to bald men before.

Outside the old TQB Base - West of Old Denver, Colorado (United States Post-Apoc)

The darkness in the mountains was offset by the beautiful view of the vibrant stars. The Moon was pleasant this evening, half-full, radiating contentment one might say.

Had you been there, you might have seen a few of the stars twinkle, and twice in one night, shooting stars lit up the sky.

What you wouldn't have noticed was the black Pod that silently came down through the evening, its kind not having visited this location in years upon years.

It circled the area three times, confirming what the communication with the local E.I. was telling them.

No humans were in the area.

Setting down outside of Storage Location D.D.2, the deadly looking ship's top lifted up, revealing three figures.

"Eve, I swear if you don't go on a diet, I'm not bringing you on these trips anymore." A young looking Japanese woman helped the rather short human out of the Pod. The male, keeping his smile to himself, easily jumped out and turned to grab his sword before pushing his senses out across the land.

Nothing he could feel.

He turned to see Eve sliding off of the Pod's side to the ground, landing gently before she started walking around. "If you would make me a seat," said the young girl's voice, "I wouldn't have to sit on your lap."

"I don't make you a seat," Yuko replied, easily jumping out of the craft herself and rubbing her thighs, "because I'm not allowing anyone to possibly destroy one of our Pods."

Yuko looked up at the large building, the normal-sized door about twenty feet away. She walked towards it.

She looked around at the worn down base. "This place creeps me out, Akio," she said. "Just thinking this is where Michael died is bad enough. Having to come check on some sort of possible malfunction just makes this all the sadder."

Akio connected through the Etheric to give the authorization to open the door for Yuko.

The door's lock clicked open for the first time in over a hundred and fifty years.

"We have our orders, Yuko," he replied.

"Some day," she said, grabbing the door handle, "I want to grow up and be a person who doesn't bitch about serving our Queen in a hopeless effort to help her love. I mean, it's romantic and all, and I know she swears he's alive, but I don't want to count how many times," she said as she opened the door and walked into the room, her muffled voice coming from the other side, "we have chased false leads."

Akio was watching the forest when he could feel her emotions emanating from inside the room.

Moments later, she called him, "Akio?"

He turned towards the door. "Yes, Yuko?"

"Would you please come in here?" she asked, her voice subdued.

Akio stepped towards the door and entered, sending the command to the Pod to go up a thousand feet. He walked into the huge hangar.

"How do we see in here?" she asked him, her voice cracking.

Akio looked around. "What is wrong?"

"Please... just, please. I don't want to be mistaken. How can we get more light in here?"

Akio said, "E.I. Denver Base, this is Queen's Bitch Akio, authorize light inside this room."

The room was bathed in LED lighting, kept in working order by the E.I.'s robots.

Akio heard Yuko's intake of breath and saw her finger, pointing to the middle of the room.

The coat was gone.

Akio walked over to the coat display next to the table. He noticed the full-length Katana was still here, but a Wakizashi was missing. The bag, some clothes, Jean's guns and the coat.

All gone.

"Akio," Yuko whispered, tears dripping from her face. "He came *back*."

16

On the Dirigible Onslaught, En Route from Denver to Chicago via Des Moines

PAUL PLAYED the conversation with Kerri over in his mind as he walked back to his suite. He nodded to the staff that stopped those who hadn't paid for the nicer rooms. He caught the man's attention. "Please, no interruptions unless necessary?" He turned the request into a question, and the man nodded his understanding.

Heading towards the last suite, he used his key and unlocked the door, making sure to see if the few strands of hair he had used to gauge if anyone had been inside his room were still in the doorjamb before he opened the door.

They were.

Satisfied, he continued into his room, turning to close and lock the door before laying his papers, except for one folder, on the bed. He took off his jacket and placed it on the coat stand. Walking to the desk, he laid the folder down and unbuttoned his sleeves, rolling them up.

Opening the folder, he pulled out the chair and sat down, deciding what to do about...

Knock Knock.

Paul turned around and grimaced. He had just finished telling the staff to keep the interruptions down to a minimum. He walked over to the door, cracking it open, expecting to find someone from the ship's staff.

"Yes?" he asked, allowing his annoyance to color his tone so this person would know he was very unhappy.

His eyes grew large. The man standing in the hallway raised an eyebrow. "I see you have heard about me already, Paul. Won't you invite me in?"

Paul shook his head and tried to shut the door, but the man had his foot in the doorway. "Ah," the man, his voice like silk over steel continued, "I *insist* you invite me in, Paul."

Paul, his mind gibbering in fear, heard his mouth saying, "Won't you come in?"

The man smiled. "Yes, we would very much like to come in, Paul Mullins."

Paul stepped back, and his surprise was obvious as two more people, women, came in after the man dressed in the black coat.

The man with no hair.

He didn't know the first woman, but the second was smiling at him like she was the cat who had just eaten the canary.

"Kerri?" he stammered, his surprise evident when he could talk. If he could talk, he could yell and maybe he could...

"No," the man told him, his voice echoing in his head. "You will not in any way try to escape or yell for help, Paul Mullins."

Kerri took the door from his limp hand. "Here Paul, let me close this for you." Kerri closed the door and grabbed him by the arm to take him to the bed, sitting down right next to him.

Like he was on trial.

The other woman was busy looking around the room but kept her own counsel.

"Paul," she said, one arm wrapped around his arm, the other gesturing to the man. "Let me introduce you to the Dark Messiah."

Outside, Paul was calm and collected, his eyes going from the man to Kerri and back to the man again. Inside he was screaming in fear.

"I'm not one for small talk, Paul Mullins," he said, "and you may call me Michael." He glanced at Kerri, before back to Paul. "Typically, my version of small talk is killing you."

Paul's blood drained from his face, but his mouth betrayed him, "What is a conversation for you?"

Michael smiled. "Torture, of course." Then, he made a little face. "But I'm trying to be better than that, so let's discuss you, and your options."

Paul's head turned, glancing between the three standing there. "Options?" This conversation was not going in ways he was familiar with. Usually, he spoke, and people not only listened, but they also did everything he wanted and said 'yes, sir' and 'no, sir' every time.

The man in front of him matched the description of the...

Michael smiled. "Oh, I'm him." Michael's eyes grew red, fangs coming out of his mouth. "I'm the one to fear the most, Paul Mullins. Your life, and death," he opened his arms, palms up, "are within my hands."

"Kerri?" Paul whispered, trying to gain any understanding she could give.

"Paul," Kerri patted him on the arm. "You've done some inexcusable things. It seems you have been trying to drain people of their blood, which is why you are so young." Her eyes flashed yellow, just for a second.

Or had they?

She continued explaining, "You see, I've been away from Chicago because there was an Alpha in Denver who was detaining me. Imagine my surprise when I'm released from my captivity by the ones responsible for killing Kraven. Only later to have my saviors ask for help to get on this ship without being noticed."

She leaned into him, breathing on his ear. "I owe them everything." She leaned back, her hand still protectively holding onto his arm. "Now, you have two options, Paul."

The other female, her eyes dark brown, stared at Paul with disgust. "I still vote to toss his useless ass off the airship so I can hear him scream in the night."

Paul shook his head vigorously at that idea.

Michael glanced over at Jacqueline. "Justice will be satisfied, Jacqueline." She looked down and nodded her understanding.

And accepting his chastisement.

Paul swallowed, trying to take control of the conversation. "If you kill me, there will be hundreds of people after your head, for the bounty my family will put on you."

Michael grinned back at the man pursing his lips. "Don't tempt me, that might be fun." This time, Kerri looked over at him, surprise on her face. Michael answered her question, "I don't have to justify deaths to my love if they attack me first."

Kerri tightened her grip on Paul's arm just a little more. Her initial hot infatuation with Michael was cooling, quickly.

"I'm not threatening, I am merely going to explain," Michael looked from Paul to Kerri, "to both of you." She swallowed.

Now she was beginning to understand, to remember. The bedtime stories from eighty years ago when her parents told her about the days before the fall. When the strictures were in place. When Michael, the ArchAngel he was called, was walking the Earth.

Paul noticed her grip tightened, and it was starting to hurt. The woman was strong. He turned to look at her and this time, he noticed a little fear in her own eyes to match his.

"Kerri, you will change," Michael commanded her.

"Change what?" Paul asked, looking back and forth as she

nodded and stood up, starting to take off her shirt. "What the hell?"

Paul had wanted to see her naked, but his present situation was such that he wasn't going to enjoy this. His manners, however, did stiffen his spine enough to argue, "Now, is this truly necessary? I'm sure I can…"

Kerri put a hand on his shoulder. "No you can't, Paul." She turned to Michael. "I guess you can tell me to break any rules you want to, can't you?" She folded her shirt and put it on the bed. She unzipped her skirt to take it off.

"Bethany Anne already rescinded those rules, but if you two are going to change Chicago, Paul needs to understand," he said.

Soon, Paul realized the clothes had seriously hidden the perfection of her body a lot more than he had realized.

She was *flawless*.

Then, there was a large ebony wolf with white feet staring at him, the intelligence in her eyes shining brightly.

Then, she growled, and the size of her teeth shocked him. He backed up on the bed. "Oh shit!" he cried, never taking his eyes off of the wolf.

Michael put his hands in his pockets. "Paul Mullins, you are familiar with the UnknownWorld. There are many more of those that are humans with abilities than you know. We are not demons. We are not devils. We are merely enhanced."

He looked over at the wolf and tipped his head in her direction. "Kerri is older than you, and will probably live longer than you as well. But she is stronger, and more deadly, than you ever thought possible. Should she want to, she could kill most of this ship. That she chooses not to is a civilized decision."

Michael turned to face him. "Unlike yours."

He paused before continuing, "Every drop of vampire blood you drink didn't come from demons, it came from people. People killed for the selfishness of those with power and money."

"My, my grandfather?" he asked, staring at Kerri.

"What about him?" Michael asked.

"He died looking young," Paul explained.

"Probably killed, or received a bad batch of blood. Or," he considered the possibilities. "Someone switched out a batch with Were blood and he drank it."

"What?" Paul looked back at Michael, pointing to Kerri. "Her blood can kill me?"

Michael shook his head. "Only if you continue to consume vampire blood would anything happen to you if you drank Were blood. However, once your blood is cleaned of the nanocytes, and most have exited your system, there is a possibility that Kerri could provide you with her bite. Making you a Were."

"She could do that?" he asked.

Michael shrugged. "I would wait a couple of years, and then I would make sure that it is something you both talk about, often." he said. "I've known couples to do that, but it is dangerous."

"I still vote to toss him out," Jacqueline commented. This time, Paul threw her a dark look. She merely returned it, raising an eyebrow. "What? Your partners killed a poor young man, I saw his body, gaunt on a table."

"He was a demon... a demon...a..." he faltered when Kerri changed back to a woman and walked over to him, her bare body catching his attention.

The animal in her was drawn to him like it had been for oh so long already.

The problem with Paul, Kerri had explained to Michael back in his suite, was he had great ambition but few inhibitions. He wasn't immoral, just amoral. She argued that he could be redeemed. Michael gave her the option, save his life with her own, or not. Paul would not be allowed to leave this ship without his sins being paid for.

She agreed, she would be the one to save it, with her life if necessary.

"Am I a demon, Paul?" she asked, reaching up to push some of his hair out of the way.

"What?" Paul asked, trying to understand how everything was changing so fast. One minute, he was trying to figure out how to not be killed, now Kerri was sitting next to him, nude, playing with his hair. "What are you doing?" he finally asked, staring into Kerri's eyes.

"I'm trying to save you, Paul Mullins," she said, allowing a little of her animal to show in her eyes. "Michael isn't a savior for everyone. I made a deal with him. You can only leave this ship if I make a promise on my life you won't do this again and I go with you."

"You would do that?" he asked, confused.

She nodded.

"What happens if you make a promise for me, and I get off this ship and leave you behind?" he asked her, but Michael answered from behind her.

"She dies in your place," he said.

"No!" Paul reached out and pulled Kerri to him, into his protection. He turned his head to Michael, anger flashing in his eyes. "I may not have thought all things through, but this is someone I know." He turned to her again. "Well, I thought I knew." His head slowly lowered until he was touching her forehead with his. "You can't do this for me, Kerri. I don't know what promise I could give that anyone would believe. I may focus on the outcome, but I won't *do* this." A small smile played at his lips. "My mother would come back from the grave, and I'd never hear the end of it."

"Dammit," Jacqueline hissed.

"Indeed," Michael agreed, watching them. Michael had read Paul's mind and his intent. He was honest. He would not give up Kerri's life to save his own. Even when he had seen she wasn't entirely human, but something else.

Something he might have thought as demonic.

"Marry me?" she whispered, so quietly Paul had trouble understanding before his eyes softened. She was making a promise to him so he could live.

There was no doubt in Paul's mind that Michael, or even the other woman, would kill him and not lose a wink of sleep at night.

Paul's smile was gentle. "No," he answered, and her shoulders dropped just a little as he let go of her. "This isn't the way it is done, Kerri." She looked up and watched as he slid off the bed and onto one knee, holding her hands.

"What are you doing?" Kerri asked, letting go of one of his hands to wipe a tear off of her face.

"I'm doing what needs to be done. I'm offering the promise that's needed. Trust me, while I may be a lot of things, I understand trust. I don't care about people I can't see. I didn't care about someone else's ethics when they stopped me from gaining what I thought was the elixir of life."

He paused, thinking back over the years, the decisions that benefitted people, while still filling the bank accounts of his family. "Yet, you are willing to die for me, to believe in me for something that has absolutely nothing to do with my money. That is love that I'm not worthy of, but I'm not stupid enough to throw away." He looked over at Michael. "Would you kill her?"

"Justice must have blood, or Justice won't be served," he replied.

Paul dipped his head and turned it back to Kerri. "I'm a bastard, I get that. But I'm not such a bastard I'm willing to run from my mistakes and let you hang for them." He smiled. "Even if you do turn into a wolf."

"Is that because I'm sitting here naked in front of you?" she asked.

"Well, to be honest, it is a bit distracting," Paul admitted. "But at the end of the day, Kerri, you never hated me for anything I did. You've always been nice to me, and… well… if it weren't for the elixir, the blood, and your damned ethics, I would have tried to get into your pants fifteen years ago."

"So," he looked into her eyes, "you have the option to say no, and if you should say no, I'll take the punishment. My father might have taught me business, but my mother taught me with manners." He paused. "Kerri, will you marry me?"

Kerri, shoulders shaking with her silent sobs, just nodded and pulled him into an embrace, her tears falling onto his hair.

Neither one of them noticed the man and woman stepping out of the suite.

Twenty paces down the hall, Jacqueline said, "Still think I should have tossed his ass out."

"And, if he had been dishonest, you would have been able to," Michael replied.

"Would you have really taken her life in his place?" she asked as they walked towards the door to the dining rooms.

"Justice would have been appeased, Jacqueline," he said.

After they had finished passing through the dining rooms out into the hallway leading to their suite, Jacqueline continue, "Michael, that didn't answer my question."

He looked down at her before looking ahead again. "Yes, it did. Consider what Justice would want, and go from there, young one."

Even when she went to sleep, Jacqueline couldn't figure out a solution that satisfied her.

Michael had Jacqueline use the bed in the suite while he sat in the parlor. Alone in the dark with his thoughts, he occasionally pushed his ability to connect with Kerri to confirm the authenticity of Paul's decision.

Kerri might have a hard choice ahead, but she had taken it on willingly. Should Paul Mullins ever decide to stray from the path, she would kill him herself.

Or, the Dark Messiah would visit again, and it would be her

pack that paid the penalty. She had seen the deaths in Denver and didn't doubt for a moment he could, and would, make good on his promise.

17

Dirigible Pittsburgh, En Route from Chicago to New York City-State

JACQUELINE, after packing all her stuff and setting her bags next to Michael's, locked and left the suite.

She was headed towards the observation deck.

She passed numerous berths where she could hear people packing, arguing or occasionally making love as she walked down the hall. On her way through the dining rooms, she didn't find many people. A couple was drinking coffee, and she shared a smile with the lady she had spoken with the previous morning.

It was nighttime, and the lights of New York City-State shone brightly, the cacophony of the colors along with the lights blazing into the night sky, trying to attract revelers on the ground. It had the effect of making it very easy to find the City-State from a distance.

She found Michael, hands clasped behind his back, looking out at the city. His reflection shimmered in the window, his expression blank.

Michael might often know what others were thinking, but Jacqueline always found it difficult to understand his thoughts, unless he was angry. That emotion was all too easy to judge.

The glowing red eyes tended to be a dead giveaway.

She walked up and stood next to him. He glanced at her reflection in the window before returning to the scene below.

"Different?" she asked.

"Yes," he replied as he started pointing. "All of this area should be lit up. You could see the whole East Coast of the United States from space, it had so many lights. Now, there are little clumps, like campfires, and then the blazing bonfire that is New York City. After the absence of power in so many towns and cities we have passed, to see it wasted here in New York seems like a mockery."

"That's because you didn't see Chicago at night," Jacqueline said. "It isn't quite this bad, but it is lit up pretty well. The Chicago City-State has more ground lit up, but it doesn't have the buildings that New York does. Plus, New York has a wall."

Michael turned to her. "A what?"

She pointed down. "Look near the water. They've built a wall they can raise and lower. There are a lot of crazies that get attracted to New York." Pulling her hand back, she continued, "We've even had a few Weres that seem to start talking about seeing things or feeling a buzz, and then nothing. Bright colors affecting their vision, something we don't see standing right next to them. They don't seem to be living in our world, at times."

Michael pursed his lips, taking the information in, but not sure what to do with it.

"There are a couple of buildings I don't recognize," he admitted, "and I see floating police vehicles down there."

Jacqueline shrugged. "New York is a tough town. Harder to live, but I understand there's a lot of money to be had. Lots of people all living in this small of an area. But, the infrastructure from before makes it easy to stay supplied with parts. The nuclear power they've run from a reactor up north is almost overkill. So, they expect to continue growing. Their manufacturing is good as is their ability to procure food from the sea."

"Which is good, if you like seafood," Michael said.

She looked up at him. "You don't?" she asked.

"Oh, I'll eat it, if I have to," he said.

"Wait, I've never seen you eat. I'm always eating."

"You," he said, "are a Were. Your metabolism requires you to eat more. My nanocytes are powered differently."

"That must be nice," she mused. "No worry about dealing with food anymore."

Michael pursed his lips. "True, I don't have to worry about it like you do, except to keep normal body functions from degenerating. I do eat, if nothing else, to keep some vitamins and minerals in me. I just don't do it very often," he finished.

Try never, she thought to herself.

The airship turned, taking them further south of the city before it turned due north. Michael noticed the tall towers that had locations to hook up the airships and elevators to offload passengers. He looked down.

Not enough ground space to let everyone land.

—

After retrieving their bags, the two passengers joined the line of those waiting to disembark. Walking with Michael, Jacqueline realized, was a pleasant exercise. Just like on the observation deck, people seemed to naturally give him space.

Or, she supposed, it could be his bald head making him look fierce.

"Where are we going?" she asked as they made it out of the elevator at the bottom, the bright lights of the city some blocks away. Michael looked around and started walking towards the lights. There were a few taxis lined up to carry people, something that wasn't available in Denver. Michael also noticed two police cars and a few men up at the top of buildings holding rifles.

That was a new development.

He turned to look at Jacqueline. "We're going to get you some new clothes."

She looked down. "Why?" She rubbed at a spot that she couldn't get clean on her shirt. "Not that I'm complaining too much, because... girl here. But, these are still in good shape," she said as she tried to catch a view of herself in a passing window.

"You stick out because the fashion you're wearing," he explained. "Look around."

Jacqueline surreptitiously glanced at the others on the street and realized her more rustic clothing style wasn't similar to the general populace. "Hey," she pointed with her head to two men who seemed to be trying to chat up a woman across the street. "I see people that look like pirates, what's wrong with this?" she finished by pointing at herself.

Michael paid attention as those on the top of the roofs kept watch, not only eyeing the people coming off the airship but those on the streets around them as well. "Those men are trying to be noticed, Jacqueline. Are you?"

Jacqueline didn't answer before a bearded portly fellow yelled, "If you are NEW to the city, make sure you REGISTER! If you are NEW to the city, make SURE you register!" His booming voice caught everyone's attention. Many of those from the ship went over to him and accepted one of the papers he was handing out.

"No," Michael told Jacqueline before she got the question past her lips. "We're not registering."

"You know," she grumped, "that mind reading gets annoying."

Michael smiled. "It wasn't mind reading," he replied, his mind trying to match up what he could see of this city with his memories of New York when he lived here.

"Then what do you call it?" she asked as she jogged to catch up with him.

He blew out a breath, sounding weary as he answered, "Being around people for a thousand years."

Jacqueline didn't have a good response to that. She spent the better part of the next four blocks keeping an eye out for anything strange or concerning until she noticed the jewelry shop window. She paused in front, looking through the glass at the rings and bracelets, some of them sparkling from the lights aimed down on them.

"Ohhhh," she murmured, wanting to reach through the glass and pick one up. The brilliance of the reflections made her heart giddy with joy. She would look at one piece, and then go to the next. She tried to understand why certain stones seemed to reflect more than others, not realizing she had stopped paying attention to her surroundings until she was interrupted.

"Looks like we have a new recruit," a deep voice said behind her. She glanced up to the reflections in the window and saw four guys standing behind her. One was looking out towards the way Michael had continued walking. "Are you coming along with us passively, or are you going to make us rough you up, sister?"

She could smell the Were scent coming from them.

Shit, she closed her eyes. *Way to fucking go, meathead!* When she opened her eyes, her look of fascination was replaced with a focused determination that didn't look like it understood the word *passively*.

Michael had beaten that out of her back in Denver, and he hadn't let up on the airship. She might not beat four of these Weres, but there was no way she was accepting any recruiting offer from them.

And besides, Michael was out there somewhere, right?

As the first to speak stepped towards her to grab her shoulder. She kicked back and caught him in the kneecap, pushing his leg in a direction it wasn't supposed to bend.

It snapped. "You fucking bitch!" he screamed, going down to the sidewalk in a spasm of pain.

She twisted in place, leaning to the side to allow the club used by the second to miss her, smashing against the window. "It will heal, asshole," she told him as she backhanded the second in the nose with her right knuckles. She grabbed his right hand, the one with the club, twisted the wrist up, taking control of the club as his scream alerted the fourth that the fight behind him wasn't going the way it was planned.

"Listen, you cunt!" the first yelled, "The Enforcers are going to…"

"Not have a fucking clue I was here," she replied, cutting short his conversation with a solid swing of the club to his forehead.

She dodged the second backhanded swing from her opponent but failed to dodge another club aimed at her head from the third guy. The blow caused stars in her eyes. She threw herself to the side to get some space, and a little time to get her focus back.

Unfortunately, the two remaining Weres weren't idiots, and now Jacqueline was on the defensive, dodging a swing from one club while blocking the other with hers. She was constantly being pushed backward and then jackass number three came at her from another angle. She dodged his attack and found herself in an alley.

Oh, for fuck's sake!

"We got your ass now, sweetheart," the fourth spoke for the first time. "Might as well give up, cause our beat down is only going to be more painful for every bit of pain you cause us," he finished.

Wonderful, she was now sixty feet back in the alley. It was dark, it was smelly, and these three didn't have any reason to play nice.

"You know," the fourth guy grinned and stepped back out of her reach and put a hand under his jacket. Now, all three of them started grinning like they were in on some grand joke. "We've only been playing with you, pussycat."

The rod he brought out started arcing up and down with electricity, an eerie blue light causing shadows to play along the stone walls. "This baby is called the persuader because it will encourage you to do anything we ask just to stop the pain."

"Kiss my ass!" Jacqueline said, spitting at his feet. "Shock me or not, I'll never do anything for you."

"Oh Johnny," the second spoke in a high voice putting both hands up to his face, "she isn't going to do anything for us, whatever shall we do?" he asked and then laughed at his own joke.

"Well, I guess we need to... *persuade*... her to listen to us, don't we guys?" he said as the two of them stepped aside so he could get in front of them. Jacqueline looked around, and she was blocked in. There wasn't an exit and changing to a wolf wasn't going to help much against three other Weres.

Johnny's voice became soft, almost loving. "You are going to join the Enforcers, little one, or die." His laughter, such a contrast to his previous tone, seemed maniacal.

At the far end of the alley, a figure, eyes glowing faintly red, dragged a body into the alley. He tossed it away. The body hit a wall, sliding down to lay in a heap.

All life gone.

Jacqueline considered pointing out the death standing behind them, but then gritted her teeth. She was safe enough, but she wasn't finished here.

Jacqueline darted forward, raising her club to block the first swing of the electrical rod and kicked out, connecting with his stomach, causing him to bend over, but also causing him to swing widely, catching the edge of her right leg with the...

"Holy fuckazoid!" she screamed, the pain racing up and down her leg.

"You..." the guy said, grabbing his stomach and trying to catch his breath, "have only tasted a little." He slowly stood back up. "That was a lucky shot, bitch."

Jacqueline flexed her leg, trying to get full movement back.

"That was just the tiniest taste, sweet cheeks." His grin made her feel dirty. He stood back up and waved the club around. "No Mr. Nice guy, this time."

"So, you want me to call you Mr. what now?" she asked him.

"You don't have to call me anything, except perhaps master," his grin became feral, his eyes slowly looking her up and down. "And you look good enough to..."

Her scream split the night. The three men stepped back as her eyes flared yellow, the humiliation, fear and despair she had felt while she was blind rose up in her mind like three demons and the guys in front of her afforded the opportunity to release the pent up fury.

The pent up *rage*.

She forgot about the electricity, the three to one odds, the pain in her leg. She ran into the middle guy with the electric rod and slammed her club at his head, making him use his for defense. She kicked out at the one on her right, nailing him in the crotch and Were or no Were, a man doesn't heal quickly from that punishment.

She ducked under the return swing, the electricity humming over her hair and used her momentum to lift the club up from the ground, slamming into the last guy's head. She used her momentum to pivot outside of the middle guy's easy swing range. She blocked the second strike from the glowing blue weapon and kicked out, breaking his leg as she swung her club in an arc, trying to deliver a smashing hit to the back of his head.

Unfortunately, her club didn't beat his stab and the two hit each other at the same moment. He went down, the back of his skull fractured and she screamed as her body spasmed against her will, the rod's electric charge coursing through her. She slammed into the concrete, her eyes open, but her body trembling violently, taking away any ability to control her movements.

The last guy standing, the one she kicked in the nuts, walked carefully over and reached down to pick up the arc rod. His eyes were cruel in the faint light as he spoke. "Well, that was a hell of a fight, I'll give you that," he said. Jacqueline was barely able to follow him with her eyes.

He turned the club to show her a switch on it. "See this?" He knelt down so she could see. "Here, it's kind of dark, even for our kind. Now," he looked annoyed and slapped Jacqueline, "pay attention!" Jacqueline tried to get her eyes to focus back on the asshole, trying hard to move, to get out of the way of the pain that was so close to her, the electricity arcing.

"Now, we have it on half power, thinking a small little female like you... Oh, sorry, looks like Johnny moved it to two-thirds power." He looked over at her, impressed. "That drops a two hundred and fifty-pound Werebear, you got some big ovaries. But," he continued, "I'm going to move it on up to max because my nuts hurt like a son of a bitch." He shrugged. "And they really want a little payback."

Jacqueline could only stare in horror as the man looked down at her. Then, another voice cut in.

"I think not," Michael said from her left. Jacqueline could see the Were turn in surprise, not realizing another party had been there in the alley with them.

"Who the hell are you?" he said gruffly. "We're part of the Enforcers, we're taking this person in for questioning..."

"No, you will not," Michael said. "In fact," Jacqueline heard a bit of noise, then a sudden CRACK, loud and moist. A neck being broken.

"What the hell!" the Were's eyes were surprised, and then he backed up a step, and Jacqueline could see Michael's legs.

He swung the electrified rod at Michael who merely caught it, the electricity buzzing loudly in her ears, the electricity arcing into his hand. He yanked the club out of the Were's hand and grabbed it by the bottom.

"That tickles," he said to the stupefied man.

"Perhaps it might be malfunctioning?" he asked. In a flash,

Michael was touching the Were with it. He was blown backward to land some ten feet away.

Jacqueline could just see his feet twitching.

"Guess not," Michael said, and the buzzing and humming stopped. He stepped back to her left, out of her vision. She heard another loud CRACK and then Michael walked into her line of vision and past the last man's feet, and a final crack and that person's feet stopped quivering.

Michael came back to her and bent down. Then she felt him pick her up, gently. "Let's go, Jacqueline, I think you've had enough therapy for this evening."

She felt a calmness overcome her, and her eyes closed to darkness.

18

Michael made sure to walk outside of lower Manhattan. Away from all of the lights and activity, he could see. He carried Jacqueline, keeping to the darker streets. A lot of the buildings and homes seemed to have electricity, but not all of them had people.

He pushed a little fear out into the night, enough to cause people to shy away and leave the two of them alone as he considered what he knew.

Michael had noticed Jacqueline's interest in the jewelry and stepped across to the other side of the street and watched from a corner.

The four Weres had been walking by, noticing her figure until one caught her scent and then it became business to them. Apparently, these Enforcers needed more Weres.

Michael had pulled the information out of their heads. Their jobs were to hunt other Weres and vampires.

Especially vampires. His eyes had narrowed at that. He had seen enough of what was going on. While he wasn't very supportive of vampires that were Forsaken, who was leading them to the right path in this day and age?

Jacqueline started moaning, her eyes started fluttering, and her heartbeat changed. He stopped at the next block and laid her down on a soft patch of ground. While he waited, he looked around.

So much had changed. The buildings, in general, were in a state of neglect. Brick and concrete either broken off or cracking. More than one building had the foundation broken.

And yet others looked in good repair.

Obviously, they had people with skills to build, to mend and to design here. But the dichotomy between the haves and the have-nots, from what he could tell near the airship port, seemed substantial. It was as bad as before the fall, if not worse. The large tower that rose into the night, he figured, was where the elite lived and worked.

Jacqueline lamented, "God, my head hurts." She rolled over to her side, clutching the side of her head. "Can you just kill me now?"

"Time to get up, work yourself through it," Michael told her, his voice calm. "Or I will be forced to give you something worse to worry about."

Jacqueline turned to look over her shoulder at him, rolled her eyes and started pushing off the ground, knocking some of the grass off of herself while she stood. Looking around, she asked, "Where are we now?"

"A few minutes from my old home," he answered.

"You think it still exists?" she pressed, looking to him for confirmation.

"Oh yes," he said, "it still exists."

—

The police car's red and blue lights flashed in the dark street, the light's colors highlighting the buildings around it. A few who lived nearby looked out of their windows and figured someone had tried unsuccessfully to break into the jewelry store.

The store's front window was cracked.

Odd, one man thought, the police car was in front of the alley half a block from the store. He let his drapes drop back and went to sleep. Life these days was hard enough; he didn't need to get involved in any police action.

He mumbled as he pulled the covers over his shoulders, "I ain't heard nothin, I ain't seen nothin … I was asleep."

And, soon enough, he was.

—

Michael could hear the two heartbeats in the trees ahead of them. He had decided to take the shortcut through old Gramercy Park South, which in his day had been a private park. Now, it looked like it was near the North Wall. Michael wasn't sure why they put up a wall, but he could see the horizontal line a few blocks from here.

"Seriously?" Jacqueline murmured low enough so that Michael could hear. "This is bullshit. Chicago isn't this much of a pain in the ass to walk around in." She started walking faster down the path, heading towards the two people that had moved into positions behind trees ahead of them.

Michael wasn't convinced that Chicago was any safer. He wondered if possibly Jacqueline just knew which locations were dangerous and avoided them. He shook his head at her behavior and then stepped off the path into the shadows of the trees and disappeared.

—

Jacqueline was pissed. Angry that she had been attacked. Pissed she had lost her situational awareness. Pissed that she had been shocked and laying helpless in the street, requiring Michael to save her. And finally, pissed he hadn't been there in the first place.

He could have stopped her from making a painful mistake. What had happened was a blow, both physically and to her ego.

This time, it was one guy and one girl that stepped out of the shadows. He had a gun pointed at her. "Far enough, toss me your money and any food you have."

The girl was brandishing a knife, her eyes glittering in the moonlight.

"What, are you just going to steal from me?" she asked, her anger boiling over quickly. There was something funny about the way they only focused on her... Jacqueline turned to look behind her and noticed Michael was nowhere to be seen.

Again.

"You motherfucker," she whispered before turning back around to face the two.

"Hey," he snarled. "I'm talking to you!"

"Well," she replied, "I wasn't talking to you. I was upset with my companion that was with me." She jerked a thumb over her shoulder. Both looked back down the path, but their grins suggested they thought she was lying.

The girl waved her knife. "This isn't stealing, consider it a toll to get through our park."

Jacqueline crossed her arms, annoyance with Michael coloring her tone. "That's a steep toll and I have no money, nor any food. The guy I was with had both."

"Well, I guess that leaves shooting you, or cutting you," the girl pronounced. Jacqueline looked closer and noticed that the gleam in her eye seemed off-balance. She had naturally assumed the guy with the gun was the most immediate threat. But, sexism aside, she was now thinking crazy bitch here was the more dangerous of the two.

"You couldn't cut me with that little knife if you tried, sister. So, screw you," she turned and pointed at the guy. "And if you shoot me, I swear, I'll rip your throat out."

Crazy bitch took a step forward, waving her knife. "Big words for a little-too-stupid-to-live slut like you."

"Dammit!" Jacqueline threw her hands up. "I. Am. Not. A. Slut!" She ignored the woman in front of her for a second and yelled into the trees, "You hear that Michael? I AM NOT A SLUT! I have been with two guys, two!" She paused and thought about her words for a second before yelling again, "NOT AT ONE TIME!" She stomped on the ground. "Just because this body is amazing doesn't mean it's always open for business."

"Here," the woman started walking towards the paranoid delusional woman "Let me cut up your pretty face and you won't have as many problems with guys hitting on you."

"You crazy-assed bitch," Jacqueline spit out when the woman tried to slash her face. The second time she took a swing at her, Jacqueline pivoted and struck. She caught the wrist with the knife and bent it. The woman shrieked when a bone cracked in her wrist, and Jacqueline took her knife away. The loud BANG caused her to release the woman's arm and roll to the side, coming up with the knife prepared to throw.

Not that there was any need to throw anything. The guy was struggling, his feet dangling off the ground, Michael holding him up by his wrist, the pistol pointing up in the air. "Now that," Michael hissed, "would have been unfair."

He turned in Jacqueline's direction and raised an eyebrow. "Kill them or let them live?" he asked.

Jacqueline pressed her lips together. "She needs medical attention." she nodded to the guy Michael was holding. "His arm is probably out of its socket." Michael jerked up real quick, the guy screamed in pain, interrupting her response.

Michael said, "Now it is."

Jacqueline swallowed, "So, uh, let's take their weapons and let them go." Michael dropped the guy, who collapsed to the ground. Reaching down he picked up the pistol and casually checked for rounds.

"Pity, only one shot left," he commented, then put the weapon inside his coat.

"Go get medical help," Jacqueline told them, looking from one to the other, "and don't make this park your home, or next time I smell you both, I won't be so stupid as to confront you. I'll just sneak up and kill you myself."

The guy helped the crazy girl up, and they staggered down the path, back towards the entrance that Michael and Jacqueline had used to enter the park.

Michael ignored Jacqueline's stare and turned towards a large building on the other side of the park and pointed. "My place."

CHICAGO CITY-STATE, (United States Post Apoc)

BRICK JESSIMS WAS A BIG GUY. He wasn't stupid but not entirely smart. He went about his business, knowing that what he carried was gold in his pockets. It was getting close to dark, and he was annoyed. One of his best customers, Paul Mullins, had sent him a message that he didn't want any more product.

Well, that wasn't good enough. One doesn't just quit using his product. Not without a withdrawal period. Almost everybody that ever had more than a few hits of the blood could never stop. It was a bad situation if they lost their income and couldn't afford it anymore.

He had watched a withdrawal once, and it cured him of ever getting addicted to the product.

He needed to talk to Paul in person, probably would sell him three times the quantity he normally would because of his convulsions from the withdrawals and then he would hit Paul with a ten percent restocking and continued distribution fee.

Send a letter telling Brick to stop coming around? Fat-ass chance of that happening.

It wasn't until he was eating over at Jerry's bar and someone mentioned Paul getting engaged did Brick understand why Paul would try to quit. Damned females could create all sorts of problems for a man. Stop one from enjoying a night out with the guys, drinking when they wanted to, and the occasional hit of the elixir of life.

Usually, they weren't sure why the elixir was bad. But, with it looking like blood, women really didn't like it. Hell, he had been with a girlfriend who told him he needed to find a new business because she didn't like the way the product smelled.

"No," he told her, "I just need to find some new pussy," and tossed her out of his apartment with a threat that if she ever spoke about him, he would knife her in the night.

Fortunately for him, the next guy she hooked up with killed her during an argument. His hands, and conscience, were clean.

The trees were thick on this side of Mullins' land. Brick knew the back way in, it wasn't like Paul ever wanted anyone to see Brick arriving and doing the deal. He sent a message ahead that he wanted to speak with him, just to make sure he understood the situation correctly. That he would leave him alone if that was what he wanted.

He smiled, they might not want to be seen with him, but they always wanted to meet with him. He received a message that Paul would be home. Brick didn't pay attention to the handwriting that looked more feminine than Paul's.

He was about two hundred yards from the house when a low growl caused him to stop in his tracks and look around, his heart pumping faster.

Two glowing yellow eyes were staring at him from the darkness under the trees.

—

Paul was rolling around in his bed. He was sweating profusely, and hadn't been out of his room for three days.

Kerri had promised she would help him through this, and after she had cleaned up the second time he threw up without making it to the bathroom, he had to admit she was a woman of her word.

He would have ditched his own ass if he could have.

Early that morning, Kerri had come into the room with a letter and asked him who Brick was? Paul explained the man was his blood dealer. The one who made sure he had the product he needed and the one, he promised her, he had told he was done with the blood.

She held his hand, dabbed the sweat off of his forehead and bent down, kissing him and then made sure he was comfortable.

Had he seen her eyes flash yellow? In this fevered state, he couldn't be sure if he had even talked with her.

Later that evening, he heard the chilling howl of a wolf, not that far from the house.

In his dreams, he imagined Brick had been killed by the wolf who had howled and his fever broke.

In the morning, Kerri brought him breakfast in bed, and her smile warmed his heart.

NEW YORK CITY-STATE

THE POLICE LIGHTS continued to strobe into the alley. Three police officers and one coroner worked the scene, but it was easy to figure out what happened. Four punks had met up with someone very strong and had a fight.

Four punks had lost.

The problem, at least from Ralph Kornicki's point of view, was these guys worked with the Enforcers. He walked over to his police vehicle and reached inside to grab the radio handset. "Control."

A male voice came back immediately, "This is control."

"This is Kornicki, I'm over at the call about a dead guy in the alley. Seems we don't have one dead guy, we got four. All with broken necks."

"Understood, do you need backup?"

"No," he replied looking back towards the alley. "This fight happened sometime earlier. I need you to patch me through to Enforcer Control."

"Why the hell do you want to talk with them, Kornicki? You itching to have a bad night?" the guy on the other end of the line asked.

Ralph clicked his handset. "No, but these four guys worked for them."

—

Michael kicked, and the door slammed open, dust falling from the inside and a chunk of the ceiling in the living room crashed to the floor.

Jacqueline peeked into the building. "If your house is the big one down the street," she asked. "Why are we going into this one?"

"Because," Michael answered, working on his patience, "vampires always have multiple exits from their resting places."

Jacqueline walked into the old, dilapidated home behind Michael and looked around. The dim light from the city street lamp barely helped her see. "I feel like something is going to jump out and bite me," she said.

Michael continued walking around to the back of the house, causing Jacqueline to, once again, catch up. "Not much for sightseeing, are you?"

"Forgive me," Michael said as he opened a closet that was next to the kitchen. He started tapping in the upper right-hand corner until the sound changed. Then, making a fist, he punched through the wood. Grabbing some pieces, he tossed them out behind him.

She noticed a faint light coming from inside the closet, so she stepped up and looked around the door. Her jaw dropped. "Your hand is glowing. How is your hand glowing?" She looked from his hand to his face and back again.

"Etheric energy, pulled into our dimension, released as light," he replied as he reached into the hole and grabbed something metal that needed oil, badly. Next, he started pulling, his face actually showing some strain. The four-inch iron ring and chain came out about a foot before she heard multiple clicks.

"That was probably scientifically correct, and I didn't understand a bit of it," she grumped. "Why can you do these things and I've never heard of any Wechselbalg able to do them?"

"I practice, something you should consider doing more of," he replied, "and because the nanocytes in vampires come from one group of Kurtherians. The ones that work in Wechselbalg to change you to a wolf, or the Pricolici form, are from a different Kurtherian group."

Her voice got softer. "Like my father changed."

There was a loud chunk and Michael pushed back on the wall; it slid out of the way. He turned to Jacqueline. "Your father never had the ability to change to that form in the past, that I'm aware of. His love and concern for you allowed him to attain the most dangerous form. Don't ever doubt, Jacqueline." He turned and reached inside, flicking a switch. Tiny red lights lit up the hall. He stood, looking at the lights for a moment. "I'm surprised. I wasn't sure the batteries would hold this long. The LED lights don't suck much wattage, but let's be going," he turned to her. "Unless rats crawling over your feet in the dark don't bother you?" He smirked.

Jacqueline wiped a tear and pushed on Michael's back. "Let's go, DM."

Michael gave her room to get inside, and then shut the door to the closet, then the secret door to his exit. He closed and locked the door.

"What's going to stop the next person from pulling it out?" Jacqueline asked.

Michael stepped around her in the tiny hallway and answered, "Fifteen hundred pounds."

Her eyes widened, and she asked him as she scooted forward, "Pulleys?"

"None, otherwise what's the point of making one lift fifteen hundred pounds?" he asked.

Then, as they walked, the quiet surrounded Jacqueline, and she looked ahead, determined that her father wouldn't be ashamed of her.

She wouldn't squeal should anything jump at her. She was a werewolf.

By the time Michael took her into the lower sewer system, back over to another entrance and through two more trapdoors, Gerry would have been very proud of his daughter.

She hadn't squealed once.

Denver, Colorado (United States Post-Apoc)

IT WAS close to three o'clock in the morning when the silent, small black aircraft descended from space and landed a couple of miles out of town.

This time, only one person, a male, exited the vehicle.

He reached back into the Pod and pulled out a bag and slung it over his shoulder.

When he finished, he sent a short message to the E.I. he was using for this operation, and the Pod lifted silently back into the night sky. It would go up and stay in orbit over his location.

The Asian man confirmed all of his weapons were where they needed to be, including his own Jean Dukes' special. He set off towards the town in a ground-eating jog. On his arm was a faded patch.

It had a white fanged skull on a red background.

Akio was a Queen's Bitch, and he had a task given him over a hundred and fifty years before. He was to wait. Wait until her love came back and then find him, and give him whatever support he required until such a time that she came back.

Because, if there was one thing Akio was comfortable believing on faith? It was that Bethany Anne would be back.

NEW YORK CITY-STATE

JACQUELINE WAS impatient as Michael made them wait for fifteen or so minutes before entering his home, his lair. He told her the air needed to be recycled.

"Oh my God..." Jacqueline looked around the room that the final door opened into and was shocked. "How big is this place?"

"Three stories deep. This room is over twelve hundred square feet. There are four bedrooms besides mine, you may choose any of them on the second floor. There is a kitchen, restrooms, showers and we have our own power if necessary. Although I'm plugged into four different power trunks, so one or more of them should work." He reached over and hit a light switch, and the lights started warming up. His lips pressed together as he looked at the lights, his annoyance showing. "Two are burned out."

The room, approximately thirty feet by forty feet, had three separate areas that Jacqueline could see. There was one that was designed for watching television, one for reading, with most of one of the forty foot walls lined with bookshelves and books. Plus, one for... "What's that?" she asked as she pointed. The bamboo flooring was different than the stained concrete throughout the rest of the room.

"Stretching and practice," he replied, and he dropped the bags on the floor near the chair he had last used for reading a very, very long time ago.

"Of course it is," she mumbled. Then, she bowed her head and closed her eyes. When she opened them again, she looked over and called to him, "May I use it?"

Michael turned to view her, one eyebrow raised. "First, let me show you around. This home was as close to hermetically sealed as I could make it, with one small hole the size of a straw to allow exit."

"How does one get out through a straw sized hole?" she asked him, catching up.

"I plan on showing you, little one," he said. "I will figure out my problem, of that you can be assured. And when I do, a demonstration will answer your question."

He showed her the bedrooms, and she decided she liked the deep green room. Michael had built this personal home planning that at some point, he might have a family, or friends, or at least compatriots that he would like to offer protection.

It had never happened.

Instead, over the years, the decades and the centuries, he had gotten tired. That was before he was almost destroyed by a nuclear bomb.

That was before the woman named Bethany Anne changed his future.

They were walking up the stairs to the first level, where the kitchen and dining areas were when Jacqueline asked about a set of double doors.

Michael stopped, turned and smiled. He stepped back to the double doors and spoke, "Door?"

It took a few seconds and Michael had just about decided to call out a second time when an electronic voice responded, "Door is listening."

"Open arms locker. Permission granted by Michael Nacht."

"Code word?" the voice requested.

"ArchAngel," he replied.

A large CLUNK sounded, and Michael pushed open the double doors. Several lights turned on.

"Dammit," Michael was annoyed, another three lights weren't working.

"Holy shit," Jacqueline whispered.

Denver, Colorado (United States Post-Apoc)

Akio walked into town, and more than a few people there looked at him funny. Apparently, he mused, not too many with Japanese blood running around here.

Once she and Akio had realized that Michael was back, they needed to figure out where he had gone. They used all sorts of advanced methods to try and track him, but it was the simplest that finally worked.

Where had a lot of people died recently by abnormally violent means? Moving out from the base, he could track a disturbance to nine days before. Now, he just needed to find out which direction Michael was headed and Akio would also head in that direction.

As he walked through town, he got more glances. Some people were fearful, some were worried, and a few were people who seemed like they wanted to test him. But Akio assumed testing a stranger wasn't considered a good idea at the moment.

He followed the general movement of people and found most of them heading towards a twenty story building surrounded by walls.

There was a gate, but it was open and unguarded. Akio strode through and moved off to the side. He could still smell death in the air as he watched the people coming and going. There was a group of people arguing just outside the building entrance, so he headed that direction.

They were talking politics. After a few moments, he understood a massive reduction in the local political infrastructure had taken place.

He walked away from that group and located a corner where he could lean against the wall in peace. He opened a communication channel. *"Eve."*

"Here, Akio."

"Michael's definitely been here," he subvocalized.

"What are the parameters for my next search?"

Akio shook his head and looked around the area at the people. *"Unknown."*

Eve replied like she always did when she calculated Akio wasn't delivering the information he could. "Why unknown? Can you not derive some characteristics?"

Akio snorted. *"Yes, seventy people died due to an outbreak of gun and sword wounds."*

Eve processed his answer. "Ah, no other characteristics?"

"Not at this time," Akio said and noticed two large men were looking in his direction. One popped the other on the chest and pointed directly at Akio.

"Okay, need to go, I've got company." Akio terminated communications and waited for the men to approach. Their swagger and aura of self-importance seemed abnormal compared to most of the rest of the people around here. At about twenty feet away, he understood what he was facing.

Were.

Akio nodded to them. One of them noticed his patch. "Hey Lamont, look."

The other man glanced at Akio's patch and then back at Akio, then back to the patch and licked his lips. "No fucking way, not two."

"Not two what?" Akio asked.

Lamont looked around him and then shrugged. "Can we come closer?" he asked. Suddenly, the belligerence in his eyes was replaced with respect.

Maybe Michael had the right idea, Akio thought. It sure seemed to calm people down.

Akio nodded. "Names, Wechselbalg?"

Lamont chewed on his lip and looked at his friend. "Well, that tears it, Jake."

"God damn and steal my girlfriend," Jake hissed, looking around before turning back to Akio. "Are you here to kill half the town, too?"

The men walked forward, careful to keep their hands in plain sight.

"Half the town?" Akio asked as they came close enough that the three made a small circle.

"No, not really, just fucked up the last political boss here. We used to work for him but were out on a project when the Dark Messiah came through," Darren corrected.

"What did he do?" Akio asked. "And why?"

"He fucked up people left and right. Then, he went over to the local pack's encampment and fucked up another group, including the local vampire hunters, with a Pricolici and…"

"Vampire hunters?" Akio interrupted.

"Well, yeah," Lamont answered. "People trying to find your kind and extract your blood."

Akio considered what he was learning when Jake asked, "How come you can handle the sun, like the other one?"

Akio dodged the question. "He is more powerful than you guys can understand. If he had wanted to, he could have destroyed this town."

Jake started to laugh, but Lamont was silent. "You're talking about one of the old ones, aren't you?" Akio nodded. "Then I'm sure glad we didn't push him."

"You saw him?" Akio asked, and started reaching into his jacket. Both Weres tensed as Akio brought out a small tablet. "Don't worry, if you don't offer me violence, I won't cut off your legs and allow the ants to consume you out in the desert." He turned the tablet around. "Is this him?"

Both men puzzled over the picture. "Is that a tablet?" asked Jake.

Lamont rubbed his face. "Could be, but he has too much hair."

Akio's eyebrows drew together and turned the tablet back so he could see the picture. It was one of the pictures that the paparazzi had taken of Michael and Bethany Anne. "Where?"

"His head," Kerry answered. "He was wearing this all black coat and his head was shaved clean. Not a spit of hair on him."

Akio put up a finger and connected to communications again. "Eve."

"Yes?"

"Give me a picture of Michael with a bald head, no hair, and add the black coat the Bitches left him."

"Eyebrows?"

Akio asked them, "Did he have eyebrows?" Lamont nodded. "Yes, eyebrows."

"Sent."

"Thank you, goodbye." Akio turned the tablet with the new picture, and both men agreed.

"Oh yeah," Lamont said. "That's him."

"Where did he go from here?" Akio asked.

"The pack encampment, then the vampire hunter's warehouse," Lamont answered.

"Which he then burnt down," Jake added.

"Then?" Akio asked.

Both men shrugged their shoulders. "Beats us," Lamont answered. "He left, and we didn't see him again. Half the town wanted to find him and lynch him. The other half wanted to put him up on their shoulders as a savior from Kraven."

Akio weighed what he should do.

"Any transportation out of here?" he finally asked.

Lamont answered, "Sure! The dirigible, Onslaught. Runs from here to Des Moines and then Chicago."

"But," Jake interrupted, "fifteen people were trying to see if he got on that ship. He didn't."

"He didn't, or no one saw him?" Akio asked.

"Well, no one saw him," Lamont admitted.

"Well, then they missed him," Akio said. "Thank you both, I'll be leaving."

The two men watched the small Asian man walk out the gate and then they walked back to the building

"Aren't you two supposed to be our sheriffs now, Lamont?" an older woman asked him as they came to stand where they had been before they saw Akio.

"Yes ma'am," he said.

"Then why are you talking to that man, was he trouble? Should you have been running him out of town a bit quicker, maybe walking him to the city limits or just kicking his ass right here?" she pressed.

"Ma'am," he looked down at the old woman. "We took care of the problem the absolute best way possible."

"Says you!" she grumped and turned around. The possible chance to see another fight lost, she stomped away.

"Yeah, says us," Jake muttered. "And that's who is going to be making the decisions anytime a damned daywalking vampire shows the fuck up."

"Amen, preach it," Lamont added as they started watching the people around the little business square.

New York City-State

Jacqueline stared at the display in front of her.

She sprang into the room. "Where are these weapons from?"

She walked up to a suit of armor, displayed as if a man was wearing it and ran her fingers across it.

"Different centuries, of course," Michael answered. "That set of armor you're looking at was worn for battle. The style is called the Maximilian, and I had it made towards the end of the fifteenth century."

"This is over five hundred years old?" she asked, looking around the large room and the different sets of armor, weapons, swords, and forms of battle dress.

"Yes," he said. "I didn't collect too many things over the years except companies and my weapons."

She turned to him. "No frilly things from the ladies... uh... damn." she saw his stern expression. "Sorry, I'm a little bit of a romantic."

"No, you are a lot of a romantic. Unfortunately, you aren't doing too well on your goal of protecting yourself. You keep getting distracted by things."

"Like what?"

"Rings and bracelets," he said.

"Oh come on!" She threw her hands up. "Did you see how beautiful those stones were? It's like you have no idea how they affect women."

He raised his eyebrow and she pointed at him. "Reading their minds is not the same as knowing how it affects them."

He pressed his lips together. "Jacqueline, you seem to think that being strong and kicking ass is the opposite of being a woman."

"Well, it sort of is, isn't it?" she replied. "All the he-man beating of breasts, shouting and kicking, punching and biting and all the blood."

Michael paused. "Let me ask you a question," he said. "What would you do if someone had your child and threatened them?"

"Well, I'd rip the head off, and..." she stopped for a moment.

"Okay, I'd shout and kick and punch and bite until my child was safe."

"Are you any less of a woman doing that?" he said.

"No, of course not," she said. "I'm more of a woman because I was protecting my child."

Michael continued his questioning, "Does it have to be your child?"

"Well," she looked around the room to organize her thoughts. "If I say no, then the next question you will ask is what? Does it have to be someone that I know?"

"Something like that," he agreed. "The desire to protect is often innate; it is in most of us. The difference, for some people, is they like violence and the connection to protecting someone is nonexistent. One of the most fascinating women I know is happiest in a shoe store and at her most dangerous when protecting this world from outside threats. If one should try to hurt someone she loves? She wouldn't hesitate to kill them, and she'd still sleep like a baby at night."

"Isn't that barbaric?" Jacqueline asked. "That she can sleep like a baby after killing someone's child? I mean, even if they're thirty, they're someone's baby."

"Based on that logic, a killer should always be allowed to go free," he replied.

"That's not what I'm saying," she looked around. "Can we go somewhere that doesn't have a bunch of armor, swords, and guns staring at me?"

Michael waved her to the door. "You were the one who asked to come in here."

"Yes," she said, walking through the double doors and watching Michael as he locked it back up. "But I wasn't expecting to have to deal with killing people and going to sleep."

"Not being able to kill someone is not a weakness," Michael said. "Nor is it a strength, it just is. At some level, there is a value associated with everyone." He started walking towards the stairway. "We'll need to get food, but for now we can use what's in the bags."

You still don't eat, she thought, *but then again I'm starving and if he's offering, who am I to say no?*

"Why did your father not go after Joshua when you were first stuck in the pack encampment in Denver?" Michael asked as they went down a set of stairs to go back to the bag with the food.

"He couldn't take him at that time," she replied. "He went to go find you to help."

"Okay, why should I care about you?" Michael asked as he handed her the food from the bag.

"Well," she opened the bag and took a bite of some jerky and used it to point at him. "You saved me back in the town, and you knew my father."

Michael crossed his arms but used one of his fingers to point. "True, but I know a lot of people, or have anyway. I've saved dozens or hundreds now in the last week or two. Do I owe them all?"

"Well, no," she chewed slowly. "Otherwise every time you save someone, they're your responsibility, and that would make no one want to help anyone after a while."

Michael walked to the spot in the large room that reminded Jacqueline of a library and sat down on a nice chair that allowed him to lean back and put his feet up. She wondered how many hours he'd spent in that chair, reading the books in this room. She sat down on a brown leather chair, the cushion comfortable and well broken in.

He put his hands behind his head and stared up at the ceiling. "Who was ultimately responsible for your life when you went into the pack enclosure?"

"Well, Joshua was the Alpha," she answered, then thought about it for a moment as he stared at her, waiting for the next part of her answer. "But, he was ready to kill me. So, if he didn't care about me, it falls back on me to be responsible for my life."

MICHAEL ANDERLE

"Not your mom?" Michael asked.

Her eyes scrunched together. "My mom? She's been dead a while so there's no way it could be her responsibility. Really, when I left home the responsibility became mine."

"So, why help anyone?" Michael asked. "What about the young man that was on the table, dead?" Jacqueline's face clouded up, and her anger was just under the surface as he said, "If you had known about him fifteen minutes before they killed him, what would you have done?"

"Kicked their asses and ripped their fucking heads off their shoulders. I would have ripped one arm off and used it to beat the shit out of the next guy, and then I would have..." her voice trailed off. Realization dawned on her face. "I didn't know him."

"No, no you didn't." Michael agreed. "But you were ready to throw Paul Mullins off the airship and listen to him scream in the night as he fell to his death."

"All because of one guy I never knew," she whispered and looked over at him. "I still see his face, Michael. I still imagine the torture he must have felt, lying there with no one coming to save him. Who was he? Does he have family that's wondering if he's okay, not knowing if he's alive or dead? No closure for them because we have no way to tell them?" A tear escaped her eye and slid down her face before she reached up and wiped it away. "How many more people are there like him out there?"

"I suspect dozens, perhaps more," Michael guessed. "And it isn't just who's out there now. There could be hundreds or thousands in the future that might suffer if I do nothing. The tree of Justice must be refreshed from time to time using the blood of those who practice injustice, and the souls of those willing to fight for it."

She looked at him, a little awe in her eyes.

Michael smiled. "It's a bastardization of a Thomas Jefferson quote, way before your time," he explained.

"How do we find them?"

"Those that are being sucked dry?" he asked, and she nodded. "We find the wealthy and follow the clues. Then to get rid of it, we locate others who are willing to fight for Justice and Honor. Those willing to make sure we stop the selfish who use excuses to attack those different than them for personal benefit."

"And then what?" she asked.

"Kill them?" Michael answered. When her eyes narrowed, he chuckled. "Not all of them. But, I've found killing to be a really good deterrent. Unfortunately, my love suggests I not use that as my first response."

"What's your first response now?" Jacqueline asked.

"I say 'Please,'" Michael answered.

"That isn't going to work!" she barked. "No fucking way!"

"Why do you think killing them is now my second response?" he asked, a smirk on his face.

"You really are a Dark Messiah, aren't you?" she whispered.

"I can be the darkest, Jacqueline," he said his voice growing cold. "Never mistake compassion for inability to proactively remove a threat. Take out the dishonorable, and problems in the future are *significantly* fewer."

She sat there thinking about everything he had just told her, and her mind was arguing with itself.

He stood up and looked down at her, not unkindly, and then started towards the bookshelves. "The young man on the table's name was Daniel." Michael didn't interrupt as she stood up and walked out, heading towards her own room. Now, Injustice had a name to go along with the face for her.

And the name was a man who had died in a nowhere warehouse in old Denver.

Jacqueline stared at the ceiling as she lay in bed thinking back on her life. The selfishness, the pride, the ego, and pain, and the humiliation. She thought about using the knife to stab the pack Alpha her father had in his hands.

Her father.

"God, Father, why did you die for me?" she whispered into the darkness. "I'm not worth your life." Tears fell, soaking the covers. With the home sealed, most of the furnishings had lasted through the decades and centuries.

Except for the food. There was no way they were trusting that.

She wiped her red eyes and sniffed. Her confusion, her pride, her reluctance were battling inside her mind. She didn't want to be her father's daughter, helping others and not having time for his family. Even when she had been young, he had been pulled away for meetings where others wanted him to intercede, provide guidance and judgment, and others took him away from her.

So, she ran away with her friends, and he had followed her. Only to die at the end, protecting her, to give her another chance.

She had promised, on his cairn, to make him proud. She didn't feel like that was accomplished, not yet. "Why is this so hard?" she asked the room, but it offered no answer.

"Daniel," she spoke aloud, thinking of the face, the emaciated body as he had lain there. "I didn't have your back when they took you, handcuffed you and locked you away. I never knew you, now… I never will. I'm not a vampire, I have no idea what your life was like, what you had to do just to survive." She wiped away more tears. "I would have come for you if I had only known. What happened to you is bullshit, on so many levels I can't even begin to comprehend."

More tears.

Her head was in her hands, her shoulders heaving as the tears flowed down her face. "Be with me Daniel, I beg you, be my totem, my reason for doing this. I can't go back to being the selfish one, the indecisive one… but I'm scared Daniel, *I'm so, so scared.*"

—

Michael retired to his own room, the one he hadn't visited in so long. He opened the dark brown stained box with the linen cover that rested there and smiled.

His collection of watches sat arrayed like a row of cars in a garage, each waiting to be matched with the suit of the evening.

Which watch, he wondered, would be appropriate to go with an apocalypse?

He could feel the turmoil emanating from Jacqueline's room but left her feelings and thoughts private. He shouldn't get back into the habit of reading everyone around him. Well, perhaps not his friends. Which, in this city, meant only Jacqueline.

Existential ethical crisis averted for now.

He closed the watch box lid and slid the coat off and walked to his closet. He had clothes, all from a hundred plus years ago. He wondered what they would do above if he went out in this fashion? Was it normal on the street?

He hung up the coat and sighed. He needed to figure out this problem with his ability to Myst. Which meant he needed to delve deep into the memories of his... what... death? He had been dodging this problem for too long. It wasn't like him to do that, but then the pain he tried to block wasn't fun, either.

He pulled off the holsters and set them on a shelf, and laid the sword he had pulled from his armory beside them. He stripped and walked into his bathroom to test the water. It took about half a minute of choking sounds coming from his pipes, and then some incredibly disgusting brown water spat out before it cleared up enough that he had hoped he would get a chance to wash up.

He tested the water with his hand and frowned, hot water was a no go.

—

The soft pitter-patter of her feet going down the steps were the only noises she could hear. The occasional light in the halls or the stairways impressed her as the technology, even with it not working at a hundred percent, was still so far in advance of what she was familiar with. It made her want to search the rest of the house.

But she felt a presence. Maybe it was just a construct of her brain, but she chose to decide it wasn't and it encouraged her to start her changes early.

Right then.

Jacqueline found the light switch on the wall and flipped it. The large room lit up, and she started walking towards the area that was for stretching and practice. She stepped onto the bamboo floor and stopped, thinking about what she was doing and then stepped back off.

She got down on her knees and closed her eyes. This was the place Michael, the Patriarch of Vampires, the ArchAngel, the Dark Messiah himself used for untold years and she *would* change her attitude. Respect would be given to him, to her father, to those who had died before she grew the hell up and stopped sulking about poor, selfish her.

Jacqueline stood up and stepped back on the bamboo floor and felt right, centered. She stilled her face, erasing any emotion, and put her feet shoulder width apart and knelt. Michael had been teaching her, and she had been learning. But, it wasn't with all of her focus, because it had lacked all of her heart.

She listened to the beating inside her chest, to her breathing. Her balance, when off, she corrected and noted why she thought she had been off. She took in the sounds of the building, the heartbeat of the concrete, as subtle as it was, and in time, she believed she could recognize Michael's heartbeat.

Standing, she went through the first kata, as he had called them. She paid attention to power, to efficiency in movement, to the joy of teaching muscles the right way to accomplish an act. Not so she could produce the most pain or destruction.

But rather, so she would be prepared to protect the next Daniel.

—

Michael reached back in his memories. To the time before the age of silence, to the time of pain.

Unfathomable pain.

He felt it. He felt the fire in his nerves as he soaked under the cold water, his hands pressed against the ceramic tile wall of his walk-in shower.

His head hanging, his face a mask of agony.

The destruction coming from behind him, devouring even the insubstantial form of his Myst. His mental scream of terror, of loss and...

Dishonor.

Failing to honor his promise. That wouldn't, couldn't, he remembered thinking, be allowed.

He would NOT fail her in this.

Then the darkness. Darkness in his heart, his mind, until at some point, consciousness returned. Over time, he had figured out he was in the Etheric, Bethany Anne's realm. Not his.

Not *his*.

The Myst was his realm, his to own, to be, the area he had owned for hundreds of years. Until the time Myst and pain were intertwined in his psyche. The association of Myst with failure. The form he had been in when he had failed to return to Bethany Anne.

Until now.

Michael's eyes turned red, his teeth started elongating, and then the water stopped hitting his head and dropping to the floor below.

Because there was no body there anymore.

—

When it happened, she felt it, knew it. Michael wasn't there anymore. She didn't allow it to affect her next punch nor the pivot and kick that followed. It was just information, awareness... BLOCK PUNCH KICK! Jacqueline performed the roundhouse kick and dropped to the proper block before continuing with the kata.

She never noticed her own perspiration, she never felt Michael leave the house through his little straw-sized hole.

Nor did she feel him come back a few minutes later until he reappeared in his room, just another bit of awareness and information as she continued her practice, ignoring the pain in her muscles.

Michael cut off the water in his shower and walked back into his closet.

"Fucking clothes," he said. While annoyance colored his voice, his eyes were serene.

He could switch to Myst again.

—

Morning, according to Michael's internal clock, had arrived. He got up and dressed in clean clothes, added his weapons, his black jacket and slid on one of his watches. He was able to get about two-thirds of his watches to wind up and work again. The one he grabbed both worked and went with his outfit.

He stepped out of his room and locked it. Some things should be sacrosanct, and while Jacqueline was welcome here, there would only be one other female allowed in his room.

Jacqueline wasn't in her room, so he went downstairs and found her in the practice area. She was sitting in a lotus position, facing towards the chamber. This was not something that he had taught her.

"Good morning," she said, without opening her eyes, nor moving her hands from where she had them near her knees.

Michael raised an eyebrow and looked behind him, before turning back to her. "I'm sorry, who am I speaking with this morning?"

She did not open her eyes, and her voice was calm, reflective, assured. This did not seem like the woman that had attacked the two punks the previous night. That woman had been boisterous, angry, headstrong and rambunctious... undecided on how to proceed.

The one in front of him seemed calm, reflective and in touch with her inner self. Whether that continued when put into the flame, he would soon find out. "We need to go."

She unfolded and stood up with smooth grace and stepped off the bamboo. He raised an eyebrow when it looked like she bowed her head for a split second before turning, eyes alight, and jogged towards the steps. Michael's head swiveled on his neck as he watched her hit the steps and disappear.

"Thirteen hundred years later," he whispered to himself, "and they are just as confusing as the first time you met one." Two minutes later, she returned with her sword in its scabbard and a smile on her face.

"Clothes?" she asked, excited.

Michael grinned. "Yes, clothes."

"Great!" she turned towards the door and started walking. "Out the way we came in?" she asked.

Michael's body disappeared, and he flew over to her. This time, she also disappeared, and he turned them around, heading towards his special exit that no one but himself, as far as he knew, could get in.

—

HOLY SHIT! Jacqueline mentally screamed. *WHAT THE HELL IS HAPPENING?*

Well, your calmness seems to have evaporated, Michael's voice rang in Jacqueline's head.

That's not all that's evaporated! she said. But Michael could feel her working to calm her response. *Where are we and how did this happen?*

One of my skills, he replied when he felt her flinch as they went into the pipe. Anyone in the Myst with him could see around, they just couldn't control anything. Moments later, they were up in the city outside. Michael swooped over to the park they had walked through in the dark and then they rematerialized when he got close to the ground.

Jacqueline stood, her feet apart and her arms outstretched like she was working to keep her balance. Looking around, she checked her clothes. "You might have warned me," she said. Not in an angry tone, but very matter of fact.

"Yes," he agreed and started walking past her. "I could have."

Enforcer HQ

Billy "The Bomb" Wattson stood a hair's breadth under six and a half feet tall. His ebony skin matched his black enforcer's uniform.

He was a vampire hunter, or if you knew the right term, he was a Nacht hunter.

There were no special emblems on his uniform except a badge he could put on or take off depending on his job for the day. When it was time to go in for a takedown, well he would take it off. No need to have a bright shiny target bouncing around.

He nodded to the riot team as he passed through the operations room and kept going to the back to slide out into his group's area.

Here, they didn't talk about crime or criminals, here they talked about taking down vampires and Weres that had run amok.

Or, refused to work with them.

Billy needed Weres to help locate the damned vampires. Then the vampires were either killed or moved into medical research. Basically, their blood helped pump money into the coffers of the Enforcers and those who helped fund them in the beginning. He was here at the beginning, and he owned a very small cut of the overall income.

And even a small cut was enough to make his life very good indeed.

Billy grabbed his pistol and a stun gun, then he grabbed the arc rod he'd made special. It was two arc rods put together with an extra foot of metal rod in the middle. Normally, arc rods were sufficient to cover anyone who knew what they were. Vampires almost always assumed they could dodge the rods or survive the shock. It wasn't until he and his partner, Vince, had run into a small nest of the bastards that Billy had decided to use two arcs.

Then, they met a vampire that knew how to use a quarterstaff, and that was the night he'd lost Vince. Even with two arc rods, and his training, he couldn't get inside the quarterstaff's reach. The vampire had blocked an overhead slash by Billy, twisted, and stabbed out with his staff and hit Vince in his face shield, cracking through the visor and into his skull.

Billy had seen the fatal blow, saw his friend and partner collapse, and he lost it. He attacked the vampire with a ferocity born of anger and retribution. He had been hit twice before he got a good shock to the vampire, which had retreated to a back room and out a window into an alley. Billy wasn't small enough to fit through the window to follow him, and he would be gone before Billy made it out of the house.

Which meant that Billy had to go back and face his fallen partner, and apologize for failing him.

Now, Billy had his own upgraded staff and had practiced for months after he made it. He had taken out six vampires with it so far. One he had killed from shocking him too much. Billy didn't care, the vampire shouldn't have mouthed off to him.

Like he cared what a creature like that said. They might speak like a human, look like a human, but they drank blood, and that made them inhuman.

And inhuman deserved no compassion from Billy.

He slammed his locker shut and smiled at his four teammates. "Tonight's going to be good guys, we got us another lead."

"HELL YEAH!" they cheered.

Another night, another Nacht to capture and hook up to the machines.

——

Michael and Jacqueline came out of the grocery store, two packages each between them. "This stuff costs as much as the clothes!" she commented as the two of them walked down the street.

"That's because you asked for lamb," he replied. "The chicken was cheap enough."

"Oh my God!" her eyes lit up. "Have you ever had lamb?" She looked over at Michael. "Wait, of course, you have." She stuck her nose in the bag with the meats. "I'm sorry, I kinda feel bad," her voice was muffled until she brought it back out of the bag. "But LAMB!"

Michael smiled. He paid attention to the coinage, and it looked like they were using old coins for money. He wasn't sure how they were dealing with artificial inflation if someone found a treasure trove, like what he had as spare change in his home. For now, he had enough money in a few jars in his closet. The woman had looked at the dates and how clean they were, but she winked at him and then gave him an extra half-pound of lamb.

They walked back to the park, and this time no one accosted them. He waited until she stuck her face back in the bag of meat. "Are we clear?" he asked her.

With her face still in the package, she pointed forward and up. "Two birds up there, blue and gray. I don't know their names. And," she pulled her head back out of the package, "there are two rabbits behind us my wolf was whining about chasing down."

Michael grinned. "Well done, let's go."

"Let's go whe…" she started.

Michael disappeared first, she disappeared immediately after.

Somewhere Over the Atlantic

Donovan walked out of the captain's quarters onto the deck. The holds of the ships had at least sixty Nosferatu, their insatiable hunger appeased from time to time by tossing in human cattle.

The screaming entertained him.

Twice he had women offer sexual favors if he would just save them. He took particular delight in stringing them along as his men opened the doors to the pit below. He would pick them up and kiss them, then bodily throw them in to hear their delightful screams as they realized they had been betrayed. One had actually had the strength of mind to call him a bastard before the Nosferatu ripped her throat out.

His hunger, his anticipation, was growing. He would be able to invade the New York City-State and unleash the beasts below. The delightful screams would rush up into the heavens and be a magnificent offering to his ears as he watched the carnage below.

He could see most of the ships in the night. One had fallen behind and occasionally they would get a call on their radio to let them know they were still back there.

When they finished this first invasion, he would personally kill that captain. Incompetence couldn't be allowed.

Like his sister, the little bungler who couldn't even be entrusted to attack a small village without getting emotional.

Not Donovan. Emotion wasn't an issue for him.

"Sir!" one of his men called. He turned from looking over the side and raised an eyebrow. "We are about to feed the Nosferatu sir, and you asked when it was the blonde's turn."

Donovan put his hands behind his back and strode off the forecastle towards the feeding area.

Blondes were always more fun.

New York City-State

MICHAEL LEFT Jacqueline in his kitchen. He was able to get the stove to work after locating and flipping the breakers. He hoped no one tried to track down where the extra electricity was being used. Because that would be annoying.

If someone shut off his power, there would be hell to pay.

Not knowing what to expect out in the city, he also showed her how to get out the main exit going up the stairs to the home above his personal quarters. There was a group of people living in the upstairs house, it had been modified to be an elite living space in the past, but had seen hard times. But if she had to exit that way, she could.

He needed more information, and she needed personal time with her lamb.

Jacqueline thought his black coat was too bland, so she bought some fabric and had him wear it as a red sash. She explained the red would capture people's attention, and maybe they wouldn't notice any discerning features.

Like, she remarked, his bald head.

That didn't help, but he did wear the red sash, it fit his mood.

He Mysted back out of the living quarters and halfway to lower Manhattan before rematerializing. It had started to sprinkle, and he could see lightning playing amid the clouds in the distance. As he drew closer to the center of town, the buildings used more and more lights externally. It looked like an old time circus had come to town.

Except, this time, they stayed.

There were no cars on the streets, so he chose to walk right up the middle. As he got close, he saw an elevated walkway running between buildings. It looked like maybe public transportation might run along it as well. He couldn't be sure. There were cop cars, their red and blue lights flashing down the side of the vehicles, the big letters spelling POLICE easy to see.

The largest, tallest buildings were in front of him. He wondered about the engineering that allowed them to be built so high. Further, how did these cars fly? Was this TQB technology or something else? If it was TQB technology and not the old Nazi technology, then he suspected they had stolen it somehow. He doubted Bethany Anne would have given the technology herself.

Too little information, and too little to be seen down here. He turned left and walked into the darkness of an alley and turned to Myst. He floated to the top of a three-story building and solidified. Walking to the edge, he stood there and observed, listening to the random thoughts of people below him.

Twenty minutes later, he disappeared from that rooftop and moved seven blocks closer to the largest building and found a spot to reappear. The building one over was two stories shorter, but it also had an Enforcer on the roof, rifle in hand.

Michael crossed his arms, studying the man who was walking back and forth, his eyes focused on those in the street.

It seemed it was never the police that held the guns on the rooftops. He was tasting the different minds, watching the

Enforcer when he encountered one that was screaming in fear and pain.

One that was running this way in the darkness, down an alley two blocks behind him. Michael turned and started walking across the rooftop while he searched for the reason the person was running. His eyes narrowed, the person was a vampire, a nanocyte infected human. He could feel three... no, four minds that were working to corral the man. Michael switched to Myst, glided over to the next building and reappeared in a corner. Walking to the edge, he looked down the four floors to the streets below.

A large black man was waiting in the middle of the alley exit.

—

Mark was sprinting for all he was worth! He knew that if he was caught, he was a goner. Enough rumors about the Enforcers had floated around that even he, as little as he went out, had heard enough to believe that they either killed vampires or did something worse.

Right now, he was running for his life. How the bastards had found him at his sister's home, or even knew about him, he could only guess.

He had been taking care of her. She had contracted the flu and was barely able to make it back and forth to the bathroom. So he promised that he would come take care of her after he got off work at night.

In the dark.

She had asked him one day, while he fed her soup, "Where do you work?"

Mark smiled. "Sis, can't tell you that, super-secret hush-hush. I'll get in trouble if I do." He fed her another spoonful of the chicken soup to try and keep her questions at bay. Unfortunately, it didn't work. Over the next four nights, more and more questions came. He had been starving himself around her, and at one point, his canines had come out at the sight of her sleeping, her neck right there, waiting for just a small bite, enough for him to satiate the hunger and craving within.

The next night was when the banging on the door started. He was almost to the front when the door exploded open, two men in Enforcer uniforms rushing through the doorway together.

"Shit!" he yelled.

Mark didn't wait to figure out what they wanted. He turned, ran up the stairs and dodged left as he heard two shots fired at his rapidly disappearing figure.

He ran into a bedroom door, shoulder first, slamming it open and then continued right out of the room, crashing through the second story window, falling to the front lawn below. Rolling, he got up and sprinted away,

He had taken three turns and now was stuck in this alley, running but not seeing any good way out. He saw the large man at the end of the alley, a block away. His lips compressed and he hoped he didn't hurt this man too much, but...

That was when the dark figure turned on the arcing rods on each end of his staff, and Mark quickly came to a stop, jerking his head to look behind him. Three other men were behind him, and all of them had pulled out arc rods as well. Mark looked both ways and felt despair.

He couldn't even tell them he was a lover not a fighter because he didn't have a girlfriend. He studied their faces. No pithy quips were going to get him out of this shit.

—

"What's it going to be?" Billy yelled. "You going to try your odds against three," he beat his chest with one hand, "or just one?"

This wasn't even going to be a challenge, Billy thought. It's obvious this skinny little runt vampire wasn't in shape. Which was a shame, really. Billy hadn't had a good fight in over a month.

—

Dodds grinned. "We got the little pecker this time," he whispered, clutching his arc rod. "The question is whether he takes on Billy, or us."

Fitzsimmons, about six foot one and the second biggest guy on the team spat, "I'm voting Billy," he said. "My big ass and you two scrawny sidekicks make us seem too harsh. I told Billy we should make it two and two…"

"And how," Walarand interjected, "are we supposed to do that? Have one of us walk up there and ask him politely to step aside, 'I need to join the other guy?'"

"Fuck that," Dodds replied, "and you too, Fitzsimmons. I'm like ten pounds lighter than you and bench twenty more. My weight to strength ratio kicks your ass, you puss. Second, Wally, we don't ask a little twatwaffle anything. It either obeys, or it dies."

Fitzsimmons said, "Oh, it's going to die soon enough. Either on the other side with Billy…"

"You think he's got that feeling tonight?" interrupted Walarand.

"Yeah, it's been a year tonight since his partner bought it. He's probably still pissed. If this joker goes to Billy, he's dead," Dodd's confirmed.

"Well, shit. That means if he comes our way," Fitzsimmons turned on his arc rod, followed quickly by the others, "we have to go easy on him."

The vampire turned his head in their direction.

Fitzsimmons smirked, whispering, "Come to Poppa, you little shit."

—

Mark felt hopelessness, he wasn't going to survive, and as he looked back towards the three, he had to consider if his sister had set him up. He heard the middle man behind him talk about how the single guy ahead of him would kill him.

For what? What had he done to anyone? He was trying his damnedest to take as little blood as necessary. He enjoyed technology for fuck's sake. *HE WAS A VIRGIN* he screamed in his mind.

Stay where you are, a comforting voice filled his mind, *deliverance is at hand.*

His eyes opened in wonder and looked around in the night. Mark quickly stepped to the side of the alley, putting the wall at his back. He noticed the three men had stopped looking at him, and turned to face something coming from the other direction.

That was when the screaming started.

—

The blue electricity arced up and down their rods, their clubs. Fitzsimmons' smile grew at the thought of the violence to come.

I've not come to bring peace, said a voice in their minds. They turned to each other.

"Did you hear that?" Dodds asked.

"Hell yeah," Walarand answered, licking his lips, his eyes searching.

"Pull your panties up, Wally," Fitzsimmons smirked. "You're always the scared one."

"Try careful, Fitz," Walarand said. "Your ass wasn't attacked two months ago."

...But to bring Judgment, the voice concluded in their minds.

—

Jacqueline cleaned up the kitchen and the memories as she washed the plate brought back ugly feelings, feelings of despair.

"I'm not that woman anymore," she murmured as she put away the last plate. She was full, her stomach hadn't had this much food in it for years, she thought, and she wanted to sleep.

"Sleeping," she said aloud as she walked out of the kitchen to the stairs. "Never helped people get ahead." She continued down the stairs to the bottom level and heading left, she stopped before the bamboo floor, slipped off her new shoes and pulled off her socks, setting them to the side.

Michael had taught her a new kata before he had left, and she was going have her muscles learn it.

Even if she fell asleep on her feet.

—

Wally turned around, and his jaw dropped open. Not twenty feet behind them stood a man, a black trench coat hanging down, the faint light from their arcs and the surrounding alley reflecting off of his skin.

And his eyes were glowing red.

Someone was screaming, and Wally thought that was very appropriate. Screw being a man. Wait, it was him!

He shut his mouth.

Fitzsimmons and Dodds got the message already. "I've got a package of little girl pink panties for you, wuss boy," Fitzsimmons ground out as he turned around and looked at the new player. "Oh, boy. We got us a live one, boys!"

Fitzsimmons saw the new bastard and had to admit, he was a little concerned. This wasn't going to be easy, and few of the previous sacks of shit had massively glowing red eyes.

"You know what they say, guys," he said, "you turn up the arcs to ten and they fall even harder."

The thing started walking towards him, his hands behind his back, his eyes narrowing as Fitzsimmons set himself to deliver the painmaker. An overhand swing to both club and electrify at the same time. He was proud of the painmaker. He had coined the term and used the move as often as possible. Dodds had stepped up beside him on his right to make sure he started the attack, allowing Fitzsimmons the luxury of using his height and strength for a fast takedown.

Wally, Fitzsimmons noted, had finally stepped up. "Maybe I'll give you the yellows for swallowing your balls and putting them back in their sack where they belong," he snickered.

"Fuck you, Fitz." Wally answered, "and your momma who I rode last night."

Fitzsimmons chuckled, Wally was back in action.

—

Michael didn't need to read the three men to see how they wanted to play this. The two on the edges would attack, the middle would deliver either a stab or a crushing blow from above. He voted for the attack from the top. The man looked like he preferred to induce physical pain, although the quick jab would be smarter using the electric stun.

Either way, it wasn't Michael's responsibility to explain how to use the arc rods.

Michael had already read the youth's mind and not only was he happy to save the young man, but he could also help Michael.

This young man understood technology.

Michael stepped into the circle, and the attack started.

—

"What is he doing?" Mark murmured as he watched the red-eyed man walk straight towards the Enforcers, seeming to have no cares in the world.

Didn't he know the power of the clubs the Enforcers used?

Mark looked back at the single Enforcer, but he was looking down the alley as well. Mark turned back. He wasn't only closer, but his eyesight was much better than big-and-brainless over behind him.

And what he was watching was confusing as hell.

—

Don't run away scared, Billy, a malevolent voice spoke in his head. Billy's eyes narrowed, no one called him scared and lived.

The yells from the men down the alley reached his ears, and he gritted his teeth. The three lit up their arc rods and set up for an attack.

—

Dodds pushed off his back foot, stabbing forward with his stick. The man never blocked his attack. The hissing blue tip nailed the bastard right in the ribs and delivered the top amount of power possible. With a feral grin, he started yelling, "Take this shit, you blood fucker!"

The man shot his right hand out and Wally's head, just as close as Dodds' to the vampire, exploded in gore. Wally's rod fell.

Dodds watched in horror as the beast grabbed Fitzsimmons' club, stopping it on the way down to strike him as if Fitzsimmons' strength was a baby's, not a grown-assed man. "The fuck?" Fitzsimmons got out as he watched the arcs at the tip of his rod get sucked into the man's hand, his fangs reflecting the light in the night.

"The 'fuck' as you call it," the man's dark voice said, "is beyond your wildest horrors, Fitzsimmons." He put out his left hand just a foot from Dodds' face and blue arcs of electricity reached Dodds, who screamed in pain as the little blue monsters ate at his eyes and reached around through his ears to electrify his brain.

His smoking body fell to the ground.

"Now, it's just you, and me." The malevolent eyes regarded him. "And soon, *it will just be me.*"

"The hell it will!" Fitzsimmons reached for his gun, but couldn't finish. The beast was suddenly right in front of him, red eyes just a foot from his.

"Hell is for children, Fitzsimmons," he whispered, "but Justice is *here.*" Fitzsimmons looked down to see a hand, with nails grown to knives, had stabbed his chest. He felt blood disgorge from his mouth.

"Fuck... fuck you... demon..." Fitzsimmons tried to spit at the man whose face wasn't angry but composed, watching him die.

"Not a demon, Fitzsimmons, a man... one who knows what honor truly is, and compassion. Although compassion..." he shrugged his shoulders as he clenched his hand, those nails piercing Fitzsimmons' heart, cutting it apart, "...was taught a bit more recently, and I have trouble backsliding to my old habits from time to time."

Michael pulled the arc rod out of Fitzsimmons' hand and

turned it around and pressed it to his chest, blowing the man back off his arm, leaving his nails dripping blood. Michael made the sign of the cross with the arc. "Go with God."

He turned the arc rod off and picked up the other two, turning them off as he added them to his collection.

Michael stared down the alley and sent out the mental thought, *Scared, Billy?*

—

Billy gripped his arc rod and considered what to do. The Nacht group was the elite, but something had taken out...

Scared, Billy? The voice entered his mind once more. *You don't mind scaring others. Are you just a bully, Billy?*

"Go fuck yourself!" Billy called out, his voice reverberating down the alley. The vampire they had cornered started jogging towards the figure.

BULLSHIT! Billy started running down the alley. He wasn't sure what had happened to his teammates. It was too dark, but he wasn't allowing this bloodsucker to eat his friends.

—

Mark watched as the final Enforcer attacking the other vampire died. *Come this way, Mark.* He turned to look at the remaining attacker before running towards the unknown man. He didn't know what this new person promised, but he absolutely knew what the other meant to do to him.

There was no contest.

His savior was ahead of him and he was running for all he was worth again. But this time, towards someone, and something, not away.

—

Billy wasn't going to make it to the new challenge before the skinny little fuck was safe. So, Billy would just take care of him now by shooting him in the back.

Billy pulled out a pistol and started aiming at the skinny one when blue arcs of electricity blasted forth from the stranger's outstretched hand to his gun.

"Shiiiit!" he yelled as the weapon was painfully electro-shocked out of his hand to clatter off to the side of the alley.

Billy felt his sweat suddenly go cold.

The new man had walked past the bodies, but Billy could see them. The three of them dead. Wally's head had disappeared, Dodd's was black, and Fitzsimmons' chest was bloody, caved in near his heart with arc burns on his chest.

Billy's eyes narrowed. "Killed my partners," he spit out. "You're going down, you bastard."

"No, I'm just getting started, Billy. Justice is rising like the sun in the east," the vampire replied calmly.

Billy slowed down and put out his quarterstaff, tips blue, the electricity arcing. "Over my dead body."

"Well, that was the plan," the malevolent voice said as the demon shrugged. "But since you insist, I now have absolution." The eyes narrowed. "How nice of you to deliver that."

"Fuck…" Billy held the quarterstaff in the middle with his left hand and one-quarter of the way down towards the end with his right. He twisted, pushing out the longer edge to deliver a slam to his opponent's head, expecting him to duck, "…you!"

Billy's eyes widened when the man just slapped the tip away, causing Billy's arm to go numb in pain and shock. It was like he had hit a concrete building. Billy turned the violent redirection of his quarterstaff and twisted backward. He adjusted to holding his staff like a bat, bringing it back around with all the power his six-and-a-half-foot body could muster.

But there was nothing there to hit, and he continued twisting and fell down as the momentum tangled up his feet. He rolled to the side and got himself back up, holding his quarterstaff at the ready.

You know, the voice spoke into his mind. Billy's eyes tracked everywhere, turning around continuously to make sure no one could sneak up on him. *The Ulfberht is a very special sword. You can tell them often by the "+VLFBERHT+" engraved on them. I'm rather fond of this one, myself. I own three, all in as perfect condition as when I had them first made for me. The other two I took off of enemies. Enemies who thought their swords were more impressive than mine.*

But, the voice continued as Billy looked around, *it isn't the sword that makes the man, but rather the wielder that allows the sword to do what it was designed to do. A lot of these swords,* Billy's eyes started darting around, frantically, *were made in the Rhineland area of Germany. Ever heard of Germany, Billy?*

"How the fuck do you know my name?" the Enforcer snarled.

Billy, does it matter? The bigger concern should be what your sins are? Killing people?

This time, his voice cracked, just a little. "They were monsters!"

What, because they were different from you? It isn't the external, or internal differences that make us a man or a monster, Billy.

Billy cried out in pain as a sword erupted out of his chest. The man's voice whispered in his ear. He could feel the air coming out of his mouth. "But what is in your heart that judges you!" His hand squeezed Billy's shoulder, pushing the sword to the hilt and wiggling it, causing more spasms of pain throughout Billy's body.

Billy coughed up blood, his quarterstaff clattering to the concrete. He dropped to his knees, the sword sliding back out of his body as he fell, slicing God only knew what, Billy thought, as his muscles ignored his commands.

"Your judgment has come too late for far too many, Billy." The man making the sign of the cross was the last thing Billy witnessed before his eyes closed for the last time.

New York City-State

MARK STARED at the stranger who saved him. The man made the sign of the cross over the Enforcer who had slid off of his sword blade to crumple, dying, at his feet.

Then, those red eyes turned towards him and the glow disappeared, the fangs retracted, and he bent down to use the body to clean his sword. Which then disappeared under his coat.

Damn, this man was so badass! "Can I get a coat like that?" he stammered. Mark's cheeks flamed, he wanted to slap himself. He tried again, "Ah, thank you for saving me. Sorry, sometimes I can't control my thoughts from polluting my mouth. It's like I take a fistful of stupid pills every time I walk out of the house."

The man looked at Mark, raised an eyebrow and smirked. "In my experience, Mark, the smartest technology geeks I've ever known always had poor communication skills."

Mark was surprised, first that this man knew other people who loved technology, and the second, that he shared anything with them. "They do?"

"Yes," he said and walked towards Mark. "Come with me, I'll tell you about a female geek named Tabitha."

"A female tech-head, really?" Mark asked as he joined the man, never considering if he should follow him or not. His request wasn't a command.

It just... felt right.

"Oh yes," he agreed. "Really."

"Not to be too guy and all," Mark's voice carried on the wind as they turned left at the end of the alley, leaving the four dead Enforcers behind them. "But, was she hot?"

Michael's laughter echoed down the street.

—

"OH MY GOD THAT WAS AWESOME!" a strange male voice assailed Jacqueline's ears as she moved slowly through the latest extension in her kata, both arms in tight syncopation. She finished the move, attempting to keep her eyes closed and reach out with her Were senses, sniffing the air, working to see if she could feel vibrations regardless how much she wanted to look.

She could hear two sets of footsteps coming down the stairs, one of them stopping and the second pair, Michael's, coming towards her. "Oh, wow..." the first, younger male, said quietly, perhaps not realizing Jacqueline could hear him. "*Hot.*"

She missed a step slightly and grimaced. She knew Michael was watching and wasn't pleased the guy had made her mess up. She finished her kata and opened her eyes. Michael's face was unreadable as he chewed on his lip, his head cocked slightly. "You favor your right leg. See if you can figure out how to do the kata starting with the left leg, and work to make it as smooth as what I just witnessed. It typically takes at least a week for most acolytes to attain the level of control you have at the moment."

Externally, Jacqueline's face was as calm as Michael's, internally, her wolf was howling in glee. Michael turned and motioned for the young man to join them. He quickly came forward, smiling at Jacqueline and putting out his hand to shake hers.

"Mark, I would like to introduce you to..." Michael was pointing to Jacqueline when Mark, his eyes glittering in happiness blurted out.

"Tabitha!"

Jacqueline's eyes narrowed.

"No Mark, Jacqueline." Michael finished.

"What?" Mark asked, turning his head to Michael in confusion, with his hand still held out. He surreptitiously sniffed and realized he was shaking hands with a Were.

"Jacqueline," the beautiful young woman took his hand. "Sorry to burst your bubble."

Mark turned back to the girl. "Sorry! I didn't mean anything by it, but Michael said he knew another vampire female that was into tech and was... ahh... umm..." His face, stricken, looked at Michael who merely looked back at him, not offering him an out.

"Hot?" Jacqueline suggested.

Mark's blood drained from his face, and his chin hit his chest. He groaned, "Another round of stupid pills, please." Jacqueline decided that maybe she wasn't meeting a complete idiot.

Just a social idiot.

But Michael *had* mentioned Tabitha, so she knew who he was speaking about. She knew of Tabitha as well as Bethany Anne, Gabrielle, Ecaterina and a host of other females. Why it annoyed her to be mistaken for Tabitha, she wasn't sure. But it did.

Michael continued, "Now that the two of you have been introduced, would you please show Mark around the house and show him where to get something to eat?" Mark looked up at Michael after dropping the handshake with Jacqueline. His eyes looked away. "What is it?" Michael asked.

"Um," Mark turned his mouth away from Jacqueline and whispered, "Blood?"

"Ah, first lesson, young one." Michael chose to leave Jacqueline involved in the discussion. "We," he pointed to Jacqueline, Mark and himself, "are all human. Just different. The differences are science based. We have significant amounts of small medical machines inside our bodies that are called nanocytes. For us," he pointed to Mark and himself, "we energize these nanocytes through the blood which has a connection with the Etheric Dimension. Don't ask me how that works. Science was never my specialty."

"Bet it was Tabitha's," Jacqueline murmured before biting down on her tongue.

Michael turned to her. "No, just computer science. Tabitha couldn't engineer her way off a jungle gym without falling, I don't think. But, get her around a computer interface, and she could work magic."

He turned back to Mark, ignoring the look Jacqueline gave him. "So, these machines are making you want blood, or they will start eating you to drive them and eventually, you will die. You could prolong this by going into a long sleep, substantially reducing the amount of energy they need."

"Is there another way to get this energy?" Mark asked.

"What about mine, is it only food that can drive mine?" Jacqueline asked, deciding to push her personal issues off and hopefully forget about them. She wasn't driven by her emotions anymore, she decided. Whatever feelings they happened to be.

"Yes, Jacqueline," he told her and turned to Mark. "And yes to you as well." He stopped to consider what he had done with Gerry and the Etheric energy he felt he could tap at will. It was an unfathomable amount of energy, and there was probably a huge amount of ability wrapped up in it, but he needed time to study. Even moving into an advanced state of speed, rushing ahead to review and think, try and fail, he could be busy for days, weeks, months or years. Time he didn't have at the moment.

He had made a promise.

He lifted his left arm and used his right to roll back the sleeve on his coat. He took off his watch. Mark's eyes lit up, fascinated. Michael handed the watch to Jacqueline who tried to keep the delight off of her face. Michael looked over at her and raised an eyebrow. She shrugged, pointed at herself and mouthed, "Female!"

Mark had missed it, his eyes strictly on the watch until he noticed Michael's left hand was glowing.

"Whoooaaa!" He whispered, then took a step back when Michael's glowing hand got closer to him. "What? Sorry!" He took a step forward, deciding that trusting had worked for him so far.

The hand pressed against the middle of his chest, and he felt warm. The constant desire to find and feed on blood went away, and then he felt more energy than he had... well, ever before. "What's happening?" he asked, watching little scars he had from his flight out of his sister's broken window heal in front of his eyes.

"That's how it is supposed to work if your nanocytes are functioning properly," Michael told him. "You are a very weak vampire. Probably six or seven generations from the first is my guess."

"Wow, who was the first," he asked, watching a particularly bad cut finish healing, the little scab falling off and the scar going away.

Jacqueline hissed, "Mark!" He looked up to see her using her eyes to point to Michael. When he looked up at Michael, his mouth made a large O. "Uh, another round of stupid pills?" he asked.

"No, more like not thinking it through," Michael said. "It's fine, it can be refreshing not to have everyone know who you are."

"Why's that?" Jacqueline asked.

"Because then they aren't afraid of you right away," Michael answered and turned to her, his hand up. "Care to try?"

She stepped forward so that his hand was pressed to her chest, between her breasts. His hand started glowing, and she could feel a calmness wash through her body, like a constant little annoyance you had grown accustomed to had suddenly stopped. So instead of noticing it happening, you feel its absence.

She stepped back, her eyes glowing faintly yellow. "Oh my," she said, and then turned back to the training area, did a bow—more head dip than a bow—and stepped onto the mat, losing herself in the latest kata. Michael could tell her movements were smoother. She glided from one to the next, her eyes closed.

He would need to introduce the next three katas and then weapons soon.

"Why don't I feel like I need food?" Mark asked him.

Michael patted him on the shoulder and started walking towards the kitchen.

"Come with me. You might not strictly need food, but if our resident Were didn't eat me out of house and home, we have enough for a meal. Food helps the nanocytes keep our bodies running efficiently and have mass for healing other problems."

"Like if we hit our head or something?" Mark asked, going up the stairs.

"No, like if we get shot," Michael replied.

Jacqueline, so engrossed in her movements, didn't hear them leave.

—

Michael left his two charges back at the house, making sure Jacqueline understood she was responsible for the young man. She nodded her understanding, and Michael felt her sense of protection lock in. He wasn't a friend now. He was Daniel personified for her.

At least until Michael got back.

Michael floated through the city, trying to understand just what was making these people tick. It wasn't normal, there were so many levels to the populace. He stopped in a particularly bad area, listening to many of the sick, the indigent and those living here on the street and in the alleys, all talking to themselves. They were muttering, talking about seeing colors.

Like they were drugged, but he could not smell drugs in their body odor. Something he would otherwise have been able to pick up.

He could feel evil coming. He looked to the east, the direction of the storm coming from the sea and something... else.

He Mysted up to a rooftop and listened. Towards evening, he could feel another set of emotions, of Weres and vampires coming out from underground, all heading somewhere. He turned, trying to understand.

There!

Central Park and the large building. It looked like maybe the second largest in the city, a long blue line of lights going up to the top. Rather like the blue stripes he saw on the Enforcers that held the guns on the rooftops pants.

He Mysted over towards that area. Solidifying a couple of buildings away, Michael watched through the darkness as random sets of people all seemed to be converging on one building.

Then two of them broke off, a male police officer and a female in boots, and strode into the building.

Not long after, he noticed two more bodies break off from the buildings in the darkness. The female threw a rock and then both jumped off of a car to go crashing through a second-story window. A grenade, it sounded like, went off shortly after that. All sorts of gunfire and the sound of people fighting and dying broke out.

It seemed possible that New York might have a force fighting for it already.

Michael Mysted around to another side and materialized at street level, inside the entranceway of a closed store. He turned his head, hearing footsteps rushing towards the main building, but sounding like they would pass his location. "Come quick!" a voice called out over a radio. "Enforcer HQ is under attack! Repeat, we have Weres and vampires attacking!"

Michael's eyes flashed red. He reached under his jacket, pulled out his pistols and dialed them up to ten.

He stepped out into the street and turned the corner towards those he could hear running in his direction.

—

"God dammit," Peterson yelled at his men. "Hurry the fuck up. We got people dying back at the base right now!"

The seven men had been enjoying a late dinner when the call came in that their headquarters was under attack, with the code word UnknownWorld tossed into the sentence.

"Fucking Vamps and Weres," another groused behind him. "Knew we shouldn't have trusted those hairy fucks."

"Shut your pie hole and save it for when we get there," Peterson called back. "We have..." he put a hand up. "Hold!" the men behind him all slowed to a stop and spread out to stand on both sides of him.

In front of them stood one man, his eyes red, his teeth marking him a vampire. In each hand he held pistols, faint blue lights glowing on their sides.

"Fire on that fucker!" Peterson screamed, and Michael *moved*. Dodging left, his right gun came up, and he released the first kinetic round, the pellet slamming into the building behind Peterson before his head even partially exploded. Michael had already aimed at the man to his right and fired before the first person cleared his gun from his holster.

Michael killed the next two on the right as he brought his left pistol up and he started on his left and took them out one, two, three, the last person dying before his gun had been brought up twelve inches. His finger spasmed, sending bullets into the concrete, the line passing Michael on his right.

Michael changed to Myst and went up. The evil was getting closer. He could feel a massive amount of Etheric energy coming at them.

Coming here to New York.

23

The rain started falling, the darkness was coming, and the weather was announcing the imminent arrival of those that were evil incarnate.

Michael checked the rounds in his pistols and smiled. One had to love a gun with such a capacity for destruction, and he had two.

He was on top of the building when he first noticed the black airships, lightning outlining them in the distance. He set his foot on a step, stared at them, and waited. He was still waiting when he noticed multiple air cars coming from the Enforcers HQ. The first airships docked on the tall towers in the same manner as the one he and Jacqueline had arrived on.

He aimed a pistol at one of the airships and fired.

Nothing happened. He wasn't sure if it was a miss, or he hit it but the kinetic energy had run out due to the distance. Hell, he might have hit the airship, and the small holes weren't able to do enough damage to harm it. Some of the other dirigibles tossed ropes over the side, uncoiling as much as two hundred feet to the ground below.

Now, Michael could see other vampires going down the sides, and Nosferatu following in their wake, like organic automatons waiting for permission to start feasting on the people of New York.

Another few air pods came flashing by his position. He leaped over the side and Mysted toward where a clump of vampires was congregating below the elevators.

—

Amedaeusz Wassil could feel the ravenous minds of his Nosferatu all begging to be let loose. They could smell the delicious flesh of the humans so close.

So *damned* close.

It was a strain for him to keep all of his Nosferatu in check. Thank God these weren't the ones Donovan had changed, or he would be up shit creek. The more powerful the vampire, the more powerful the Nosferatu created.

Still, to feel like he was the one to release his own version of hell on the world was a feeling he couldn't ignore and he felt ready to crush the planet. He smirked and slammed his hand with Jonathan's. "Going to change the Earth tonight." He laughed. "And it's time the world learns who the real masters are!"

"You hear Donovan's last message?" Jonathan asked, and Amedaeusz shook his head. "He told us maximum carnage!"

"The best kind of carnage, I would think," Amedaeusz agreed. "Can't wait for my little puppies to grab a couple of four-year-olds, they're old enough to really shriek, calling for their mommas who come running out, cursing whoever holds their babies. They run right into the mouth of the beast and get consumed." He put his fingers to his lips and kissed them. "Best trap ever."

Both men laughed and ducked when a lightning strike hit the tower they were standing at. Instead of shunting to the ground, like both expected, it stayed up at the top of the tower, frying the airship connected to it. The gravitic controls shorted out, it started floating away, the cables that kept it docked to the tower snapping. It was losing altitude, and they both could see that it would crash out in the water.

The lightning arced down the tower, and both men started backing up until it jumped off the tower to a point behind them.

Both turned around to see a man standing in the middle of the field, nothing around him for twenty feet, the electricity entering his open hand like he was accepting it into his body.

His eyes glowed red.

"Who the fuck is that?" Amedaeusz asked, but his partner just shook his head.

The new man looked at all of the Nosferatu around him. He clapped his hands together in front of him, and electricity started flowing between his hands, lighting up his face, reflecting off his head, his white fangs clearly outlined against his skin.

His voice, when he spoke, hit both their ears and their brains.

"JUDGED!" his voice rang out, the mental voice causing them to wince. *"FORSAKEN!"*

"Oh god no!" Jonathan hissed, "No no no no no!"

"Who no?" Amedaeusz punched his friend trying to get his attention. "Who is that?" he pointed, yelling over the loud hissing, crackling bolts of energy.

But all Jonathan would do was shake his head in fear.

The stranger threw his right hand out, and electricity arced from his hand to nearby Nosferatu, and spread among them, jumping from body to body as they spasmed, mouths open in silent cries before collapsing to the ground. He tossed his left arm out, and the Nosferatu on that side started jerking, then collapsing as the electricity burned through them

Amedaeusz grabbed his head when his Nosferatu got slammed by the current and dropped down to his knees, screaming in pain. The pain coming through the connection with his Nosferatu threatened to knock him out. He released his hold to them, severing it in a last ditch effort to save his own sanity. He could see Jonathan lying on the ground, his unseeing white pupils staring off into the distance.

Dead.

He glanced up in time to see the figure mere feet in front of him, his sword slicing down at him and then he joined Jonathan.

Dead.

Michael looked around and sheathed his sword, yanking his pistols back out and jacked up his speed.

—

The police were holding the line, shooting over the guys in front of them that were holding up the riot protection gear. They were fighting to stop monsters. Creatures that would grab one of their men and then bite them, tearing them apart, eating the flesh until you killed them.

Best to shoot them in the head, multiple times.

"FUCKING ZOMBIES!" Ted yelled, slamming another magazine in his pistol. "Who the hell are these fuckers?" he asked as he took out a zombie that was reaching for Janine up on the front line.

"Who the hell knows?" Ethan called back. "Make your *damned* shots count!"

Just then, Enforcer air pods flew overhead, and the doors opened. Figures jumped out of the back to attack the back of the same group they were fighting.

"What are those fuckers up to?" Ted asked, shooting two more. "They never gave a shit about us before."

"Don't think they're Enforcers, buddy!" Ethan commented as he pulled a magazine off of Janine's belt.

Janine looked back really quick and winked. "Next time tell me you're copping a feel Ethan, so I can enjoy it more!"

"God damn, Ethan," Ted laughed. "Now's the time you pinch her ass?"

"Don't want to die without feeling that, at least once," Ethan admitted, perhaps putting too much of the truth into his comment when he caught her looking back at him, realization in her eyes.

"Shiiiiiiiit," he mumbled and shot the two in front of her. "Fuck my life."

"You kill these fuckers," she called over her shoulder, "and I'll fuck your brains out!"

"Well, shit then," he winked and reached forward, unsnapped her holster and grabbed her pistol. "Now I got something to live for!" Ethan started pulling triggers as soon as he had a decent shot, keeping the three cops in front of him as safe as he could.

Especially the blond in front of him.

"Why don't you think they're Enforcers?" Ted asked, bringing him back around to the previous conversation.

"Cause I don't think humans turn into wolves in midair," he said. "At least, that's what I think I saw."

Every human in the line flinched when a rocket-propelled grenade slammed into one of the Enforcer cars. There had been a sniper up there, blowing the shit out of the zombies in front of them.

"Motherfuckers!" Janine called out. "That was one of the good ones!"

The police laid down a torrent of gunfire. It allowed them enough time to look around, so that most of them saw someone leap off a car, up into the twirling air pod, then jump back out with another body before the air pod hit the ground, plowing through more of the bastards.

"Who the fuck is that?" Ted yelled, taking out two zombies that tried to attack the end of their line.

"Hell if I know," Ethan said. "I need mags!" Janine bumped his hand with her ass.

"Reach around!" she said. "I've got some up front."

"FUCK!" Ted screamed, laughing. "Shit Janine, if I had known blood, guts and almost dying made you so randy, I'd have shot myself!" Ted added, "Or better yet, shot Ethan. I hate competition."

The line around them burst into laughter as Ethan groped around and grabbed the magazines Janine was talking about.

"Hey!" she said. "That better be a promise. You better not leave me hot and bothered up here."

Ethan pinched her ass. "It's a promise!" he replied and started firing once again.

—

Michael saw the explosion out of the corner of his eye and looked around, seeking more of the vampires. Once more, he had been able to capture a lightning bolt and use it to fry Nosferatu around him. Out of all the limitless power the Etheric offered, he hadn't figured out how to capture it and release it like he had been able to hold and re-release the lightning.

What seemed like just moments later, he caught sight of a female making her way up to the airships, and his eyes opened in surprise.

She carried a righteous anger. She was driven, but not out of vengeance, out of caring.

That vampire, he could *feel*, had honor.

—

"I'm running out of fun, guys!" Janine called out when she felt Ethan grab her last two mags.

"Grab mine," Milton said from her right. "But I'm not going to be as fun as Janine, I'm afraid. Meredith would rip my pecker off in the middle of the night and feed it to me."

"What happens on the front line," Ethan said as he grabbed a couple of extra magazines, "stays on the front line, Milton." They all laughed when Ethan slapped his ass and Milton let out a loud 'whoop!'

"Hey, I got him first Milton," Janine said, using an arc rod someone had passed her to zap a zombie. "Don't make me tell Meredith on you!"

"Dammit, Ethan!" Ted said, firing two more rounds to his left. The constant press of the zombies had lessened a few times. Those in front had been able to be relieved when the opportunity presented itself. "Now you're taking married guys from me, too!"

—

Michael heard the short scream and looked up. He saw the young female vampire falling. He changed to Myst, but she caught a rope before he needed to grab her. She was taking care of herself. He looked around and found one of the stronger vampires running away.

Now that wasn't going to work at all.

Michael dropped back to the ground and ran, catching up to the fleeing man in a block.

—

This was fucked up!

Kelvin couldn't believe the utter destruction occurring. First, the humans were supposed to fall to their Nosferatu, not be able to call upon a massive amount of firepower. In Europe, they didn't have the guns that they did here in the old United States. Apparently, that was a significant oversight of the Duke and Donovan.

Then, who the fuck were the Weres and vampires that joined together to fight against them?

And finally, who the hell was the scary-as-fuck bastard that's throwing around lightning?

Gott Verdammt! Donovan could kiss his ass. Kelvin wasn't sticking around to find out what happened with this clusterfuck. He was getting out while the getting was even remotely possible.

He would find a hole in this city to crawl into and wait. Well, he would grab a human or two to feed on while he let everything else blow over. Eventually, he would be able to come out and figure out a plan. One that included a...

Kelvin turned in time to see the vampire from hell right behind him. He turned back around, looking for a place to dodge and didn't see the sword coming.

The body crumpled to the ground. The head, a look of surprise still on its face, bounced down the street for over a block. By the time it came to a stop, Michael was already heading back to the fight.

—

Michael changed to Myst and went straight up. He had touched the minds up above and could feel the one who had Honor was fighting for her life.

Against her brother.

He flew over the side of the ship as he heard her mental scream 'HELL NO' and charged those who had arrayed against her.

She was charging into her death.

Michael swept her up into his Myst, the bullets flying past, the sword aimed at her chest now missing her.

Michael dropped her out of the Myst and materialized. He drew his sword and decapitated two of her attackers. The one armed with the sword was looking around. He didn't look like he had a damned clue how to use it properly. Michael made a guess. He cut off the hand holding it and tossed the sword towards the woman. He then punched the vampire in the chest, caving it in and throwing the body onto the deck, a bloody mess.

Michael wanted to rip through these dishonorable Forsaken. He wanted to cut into them, tear them apart, hear their screams...

"Enough!" shouted her brother.

He lifted his head, barely in control of his emotions but he would be his own man. He wouldn't do as his anger desired. He would judge, and judge fairly.

The woman to his right whispered, "The Dark Messiah."

Michael touched her mind, her emotions, her thoughts. He turned to her. "That's not distasteful. *You* may call me that." He looked up at the other vampire, his eyes glowing in his frustration, his voice cold in his wrath, "...though most call me *Michael*."

24

The male vampire, Donovan, took a step back. One of the vampires that had been attacking Valerie jumped over the side.

Donovan looked around. "There... there is no Michael! If you're the Michael, that Michael, you've been gone for...?"

Michael thought about it. "Much too long... yes?" While he tried to smile, he doubted it came across as very sincere. Michael threw his arms wide. "And at long last, your Savior has returned!"

"This isn't your fight!" Donovan screamed, reaching towards his waist. Michael moved, reaching Donovan before the powerful vampire could even touch his weapon. Grabbing the struggling man's throat, Michael hoisted him into the air.

Tempting, so tempting, he thought... Just squeeze hard and pop his head right off. Instead of doing that, he hissed, "Then do not make me decide its outcome by your stupidity!"

Michael's eyes flashed red, and he threw the young vampire back to the deck of the ship, where Donovan grasped his throat and coughed, trying to fill his lungs with air again.

"This is not my fight I think. Rather, I believe," he looked first at Donovan, then at Valerie, "that Justice is calling for this battle to occur. Who am I to take Justice away from those who need it? This fight is between the two of you. But I've been watching..." he turned to look at the woman. "Valerie, is it?" he asked, the voice demanding yet gentle when he spoke to her. She nodded. "I find *you* to be honorable," Michael said before turning to regard Donovan. "You, who'd stand behind while your minions attack her? You are *dishonorable*."

"So what, you're some sort of judge, is that it?" Donovan asked, spittle flying in his rage. "I won't have it!"

"You'll have whatever I tell you... boy." Michael crossed his arms over his chest, weighing each of them with a calculating gaze. He could hear the machinations in Donovan's mind. How he planned to shoot her in the back first chance he got.

This one had no Honor. He was irredeemable. "You will fight, fair. To the winner go the spoils," Michael declared.

Donovan's eyes opened wider, then narrowed shrewdly. "Whoever wins, whatever the case, you accept the outcome? You won't kill me if I—"

Strike two, fucktard, Michael thought. "I never promised that. But I won't kill you now. After it's over, if you're still alive? Then we will talk."

As I choke your pitiful life out of you.

Donovan turned to Valerie with a smirk and reached for his pistol a second time.

"If you dare use that," Michael said conversationally, Donovan stopping in mid-draw, "I will cut off your arm myself, and you will then be down to one arm in this fight. That was your only warning." He pointed, "Toss it over the side."

Michael, his mind always scanning, caught the mental image of a vampire shooting him during the fight. Michael started pacing the deck, keeping his eyes on Donovan, but his senses aware of what was around him. When he got close to the scheming vampire, he snatched the man by the throat and stared him in the eyes. "This fight will be fair. No weapons, simply brother to sister. You apparently don't believe in fair?" Michael watched his head nod yes, and his thoughts say no.

Michael shrugged and tossed the vampire over the side of the ship. His screams lasted all the way to the ground.

The female vampire asked, "May we begin?" her voice cracking only slightly. She turned her sword over and struck it into the wooden deck.

Good, he didn't have to tell her the same thing. He liked this one more and more.

Michael lifted one hand in the air, gave them each a look, and brought it down. "Begin!"

The brother and sister charged each other. The other vampires had pushed themselves to the sides to get out of the way of the fight. While they watched the fight, they would sneak glances at Michael. Apparently, they didn't trust that he wouldn't snatch another to toss over the side of the ship.

Donovan had them scared, the Duke had them in awe.

Michael had them feeling abject terror and bone-deep panic.

The brother and sister traded punches, kicks, holds and broken holds. Ribs were fractured, and heads were smashed with vicious elbow jabs.

The rain would ease up, then pour for a minute as they went at it. Michael was impressed. Both fought well, both struggled, knowing life and death were on the line. However, Donovan was fighting for his life, Valerie was fighting for others' lives.

That, he considered, would be the difference. While she was smaller in stature, the woman was insanely strong for her size. Most women didn't survive the change. When they did, they were often stronger than males changed by the same parent.

In the end, Donovan got behind her, squeezing her throat, half his own throat ripped out by her claws. Valerie was close to suffocating before she was able to reach over her shoulders and dig her thumbs into his eyes, destroying them.

She was still being choked, even with half his throat gone and eyes gouged out. She looked at Michael, and he returned the stare, giving no indication of his thoughts.

Valerie was losing. But he was listening to her internal argument and to Donovan's as well. He noted when she decided it was all for her friends, for the people below, for the city.

For *Justice*.

She gave up trying to protect her throat and made a move, grabbing her brother and using the last of her strength to fling them both off their feet, but doing it where she could spin in the air to get his head and twist.

CRACK!

Donovan landed on the deck, his head bent at a wrong angle, unable to move.

Michael nodded to Valerie. "Justice has spoken." She stumbled toward her sword, and he nodded. "For this, the use of your sword is permitted." She moved forward and lifted the sword high in the air, pausing at the apogee before slashing it down, ending Donovan's evil desires.

She dropped to her knees, weak.

—

The total deaths among the New York City Police would be staggering. They had lost a minimum of ten of his fellow policeman that Ted had witnessed himself this night. Dragged in among the zombies and eaten alive.

"What the hell is happening?" Ted asked, as the few zombies still fighting seemed to suddenly lose their ability to think. Like their brains had been reset. The cops didn't wait but took the opportunity to blow as many away as they could. Soon enough, the zombies started moving again, but it was like they went after whoever was closest, instead of the coordinated attack that they had been using before.

"Fuck me!" Ethan roared, exasperated when the zombies started coming at them again.

"After a shower," Janine retorted, arc rod ready. "'Cause zombie guts? Gross!"

—

Michael waited patiently for Valerie to recover, to understand she delivered Justice's punishment, without help.

Without him.

"What... now?" she asked, as the water dripped off of her head.

"You fought bravely, and acted with courage and *Honor*," he replied. Michael walked over to her, his hand glowed, he touched her, pushing Etheric energy into her body, allowing the nanocytes to regain their power to help her. It affected her almost immediately, her exhaustion lessened. Michael wanted to sigh.

Another who knew the myths of him, and thought he was a walking demigod. This needed to stop.

Michael took from her mind the presence of her father, the Duke in Europe and his plans. His lips pressed together.

So many fires, and so few firefighters.

He considered his next actions carefully. He couldn't leave America without support. He was needed in Europe to stop the carnage, and prevent the destruction that the Duke planned to perpetrate.

He would have Valerie drink from him. His blood had been corrected from the faulty programming it carried, repaired on the same alien spaceship where he had originally been injected with the nanocytes. His blood was pure. Now, if he wished, he could share those nanocytes with whomever he desired. With his Etheric connection providing enough energy to the nanocytes, the person he helped didn't require time in the Pod-doc like so many others.

Which was a good thing since he didn't have a medical pod handy.

Valerie caught on that he was reading her mind.

Michael smiled. "You have a quick mind, you may learn to do this," he touched the side of his head, "in time. Though the power I am about to give you manifests in many different ways. One thing it will change. It will allow you to walk in the light, and that is necessary for you to continue your battle here in America."

"Against the hunters?" she asked, still trying to catch up to what was going on.

Michael considered her question, and the ramifications of the fight this night. "Those, yes. And now there are other vampires, Donovan's followers, who you will hunt down."

"But you?" She shook her head, not understanding. "You're here, or returned, now. Certainly, you can do it?"

Michael shook his head. "I've been doing my part because I didn't know I'd have a worthy champion here to do it for me," he said. "But I'm needed in Europe. This Duke you speak of, or rather, think of, you can rest assured he'll be getting a visit from me shortly. Then it's time I cleaned up the rest of Europe." Michael considered what he had pulled out of Donovan's thoughts, and those of the vampires on the ground.

Europe was a damned mess. He wasn't sure which of David's children this would be, but he was almost sure it had to have been David's. He knew of no one named the Duke, but the description sounded like David's son Charles. He had gone missing and presumed dead hundreds of years ago. David would have killed any vampire in Europe for taking a title like the Duke.

David hadn't liked anyone having higher aspirations than himself.

"And what? I'll be like... your enforcer, an enforcer for justice?" Valeria asked, pulling Michael out of his thoughts.

This time, his smile reached his eyes. "Yes, I like the sound of that. Get your friends and put this city back in order. Remove the Peace Enforcers and take on the title for yourself, so it means something true and honorable. You will be the first of my Justice Enforcers." Michael looked down over the side of the ship.

"Though you won't be the last." He turned back to her. "Do you accept my charge, young Valerie?"

She nodded, and so he moved to stand in front of her and held up his wrist. "Then by my blood, on your oath, you are the first of my Justice Enforcers, Valerie." He nodded to his wrist. "Drink."

It seemed almost sacrilegious, wrong on so many levels, but he said it was right, so she trusted him.

On faith.

She leaned in and pressed her lips to his skin, then ecstasy filled her mind as her fangs pierced his skin.

And *oh God*, the way his blood felt as it filled her mouth. Her eyes rolled back as her limbs filled with warmth and her injuries healed. A moan escaped her lips, and she gently pulled his arm to her mouth so she wouldn't miss a drop.

Then he was pulling away, and as she watched his wrist leave with longing, his skin healed.

"Come," he said, taking her by the hand and leading her back to the edge of the ship and pointing down. "The rebuilding must start immediately."

They looked out over the lights of the city, fires scattered about where the fighting had been. There were no signs of Donovan's people, but her fighters, Weres, vampires, and a of couple policemen were gathering below the ship, looking up at her with curiosity.

She turned to him, his bald head reflecting the flames in the night. "Will I really be able to walk in the sunlight? Lay under its warm touch?"

"When the sun rises today, have *faith.*" He sighed and looked at her. "There's a lot for you to learn about our kind, some now, some in days and years to come."

"I'm ready," Valerie whispered into the night.

Michael nodded slowly. "I know you think you are. And as the world rebuilds, you will help it along the way, and when the time is right, I'll tell you all I know. But for now, just realize that we are so much more than the stories would have you and most normals believe. There's a whole other side to this Vamp and Were existence."

He looked around the city. "We are no more evil than our decisions. Is there a Satan? I do not know, but our condition doesn't affect our morality any more than it would a normal man or woman walking the streets down below."

She stared at him, then slowly let her eyes drift up to the heavens.

After a moment of silence, he asked, "Is there anything you want me to tell your father?"

She jerked her head back down. "You're going to him now? Leaving now?"

He nodded. "America has you." He shrugged his shoulders. "Europe needs me."

She thought about his question, then shook her head. "Tell him to change, to join us. And if he doesn't… or let's be honest, when he doesn't, I'll not shed a tear when Justice comes calling for him."

Michael nodded once, slowly. "You have my word." He indicated the dead body of her brother. "I could sense the strength in each of you. There was never a possibility Donovan could have won." He pursed his lips, as if a question was inside his mind and then answered it aloud, "Bethany Anne would approve of you."

With that, Michael was gone.

—

Michael Mysted up to the tallest building in the city and solidified, scaring a couple that had been getting ready to join a special club in the sky.

"Dude!" the man called out when his girlfriend shrieked and pointed behind him, "I'm getting some here!"

Michael turned around and eyed them both. "If you don't want me to explain to Ada you were up here just last Tuesday with Marian, and the Friday before that with Juliana, I'd leave. Or, I can explain that to her, and then help her toss your useless ass over the side."

Michael turned back around to view the city, the loud "CRACK" of Ada's hand across the guy's face confirmed he would be alone soon enough.

It took her less than a minute to leave, as the man stumbled through excuses right behind her. Sometimes, Michael thought, spreading truth and light helped keep things peaceful around him.

Other times? Not so much.

Michael viewed the City-State of New York and considered his next actions. He would need to take the fight to Europe. He sighed, thinking that Bethany Anne had been created to take some burden off of his shoulders, and now, he was back cleaning up another mess.

If he had a chance, he would find the original Kurtherians that had decided that modifying races across the Universe was such a good idea and slap the ever-loving shit out of them.

He needed, he decided, a way to blow off steam.

Maybe he would take up cursing more often, it helped Bethany Anne with her stress. Now that he wasn't just killing those who annoyed him, he had to learn new skills.

The door opened slowly behind him, and he turned around to see Ada peek her head out. "I uh, I just wanted to say thank you," she said.

"You're welcome," Michael answered.

"Uh, you don't want to join the sex in the sky club, do you?" she asked. "I'm kinda hot for guys who are bald."

Michael just stared at her for a moment, confused as hell. "You like bald men?"

She stuck her head out a little further, showing a bare shoulder. "Yeah, is that so weird? Some women like hairy chests or tall guys. I like chrome domes."

Michael answered, "Noooo, although I'm flattered." He smiled. "That might have been the nicest gift you could offer me. Go and enjoy your life, Ada." His voice changed, to a silky smooth over steel tenor. "And forget you ever saw me."

Ada closed the door, and Michael turned back around to look back over the expanse beneath him. The lights rolling out to the darkness. His own house to the north.

If anyone had a telescope and had been watching the top of the building, they would have seen a man diving off. He disappeared two-thirds of the way to the street below.

—

"No! That's not the right way," Jacqueline sighed. "I'm sorry Mark, I'm working on my patience." The two of them were on the practice mat, Jacqueline trying to explain the first kata to Mark.

Mark shrugged. "I think you're more patient than my parents were with me. I'm not very coordinated."

She stood up from the kata position. "I thought all vampires were coordinated?" she asked.

He stood with her. "I was changed by a girl. I thought she liked me and the hickey she was giving was fantastic."

Jacqueline put her hand to her mouth, but she couldn't stop her giggle, then a snort, her eyes alight with amusement. "You're telling me," she finally said, "that you got changed because of a hickey?"

"Well," Mark flushed red. "It wasn't only one hickey. And hell, I thought this was it. I was going to stop being the big V!"

"Vampire?" Jacqueline's face scrunched up. "That doesn't make any sense at all. How was her nibbling on your neck going to help you stop being a vampire? Didn't you just say you were changed because of a hickey?"

Mark's head dropped, and he put both hands over his face. "Not V for vampire, V for *virgin*!"

Jacqueline's eyes opened wide, and she looked at the ceiling. *I am such a dumbass!* she mouthed silently. She looked back at Mark, his face still in his hands. "How many times did she make out with you?"

"Over a four-day weekend, then she left, and I had the worst sickness ever. It lasted over a week, and it was after that I noticed the changes. I'm something of a history geek, and I searched the New York Public Library and there were some books on the paranormal." He shrugged. "It's been hard."

Jacqueline bit back the retort on the tip of her tongue. She doubted he would appreciate a double-entendre right now. She was so damned used to Weres and their lack of body modesty that Mark's troubles were completely outside of her experience.

He was nice enough looking, but she didn't think he would want a pity fuck.

Oh, Michael spoke in her mind, *He certainly would accept one, but that wouldn't make it right or the best thing for him.*

Jacqueline jerked around to look for him, which got Mark's attention. "What is it?"

"Michael is here, somewhere." Her eyes narrowed as she looked around the large room. "Now, how do we find him?"

Mark shrugged. "I imagine by asking him where he is?"

"Good choice," Michael replied from behind them. They swung around to find him standing there. They both leaned forward slowly and sniffed.

"Where have you been?" she asked, her nose wrinkling in distaste.

"Dude, were you fighting?" Mark questioned, noticing the splatters of blood on his clothes.

"Down at the airship port and yes, I've been fighting," he answered and walked around them. "Meeting in the kitchen in ten minutes, I'm going to shower."

25

The two young people were sitting on kitchen barstools, talking to each other.

When Michael arrived in the kitchen, clean and feeling considerably better, he opened the fridge and found enough food to make himself a lamb and cheese sandwich. He closed the door, put the food on the counter and grabbed a plate.

"You DO eat!" Jacqueline called out from behind him.

Michael turned around, eyebrow raised to see the young woman was pointing at him, eyes afire, like she had just proven where Jimmy Hoffa was buried.

Michael smiled. Not that she would know who Jimmy Hoffa was, he thought.

Mark looked at her, confused. "Yeah, he eats. He ate with me."

Jacqueline turned her finger on him. "When!"

Mark's eyes crossed, looking at her finger so close to his face. "When I got here, right after he did the little hand warmy thing and my desire for blood went away." He backed his head up a bit to give himself space. "Why so tense?"

Jacqueline looked at her hand and pulled it back. "Sorry, but I've never seen him eat. I was thinking maybe he was always feeding the fat and happy werewolf and not taking what he needed to eat."

Michael was watching the two of them chat back and forth while he chewed on his sandwich.

Mark, oblivious to how it looked, leaned to the side on his chair to check out Jacqueline's body. "Fat?"

Michael snorted, Jacqueline's eyes darted to him, then back to Mark.

"Yes, fat!" she stated.

"Where?" Mark asked,

Jacqueline's voice went up an octave. "Where?"

Mark looked up at her. "Yes, where. It is a common word to mean 'show me,' 'tell me,' or in some way explain."

Jacqueline rolled her eyes. "I know what 'where' means!" Then her eyes altered and her voice changed, going from annoyed to sounding like how a cat's might alter when it was about to play with a mouse.

"Uh oh!" Michael took another bite of his sandwich. This drama was unfolding in real time. Would Mark realize what was about to happen, or was he too hopelessly naive about werewolves?

"So, you need me to show you the fat, am I getting this right?" Her voice moved just this side of seductive.

"Yeah," Mark agreed. "That was my original question. Where?"

"One second." She stood up from her barstool and patted Mark on the shoulder as she stepped around him. Jacqueline turned the corner, and both guys could hear her step into the bathroom down the hall.

Michael chewed on his sandwich, Mark shrugged his shoulders at him. Michael fought to keep the grin off of his face.

"Mark?" Jacqueline's singsong voice called to him from the hallway.

Mark turned in his chair, leaning out so his voice would be

louder then shook his head at his stupidity... He had a Were here! "Yeah?" he asked.

"Can you come here for a second, I want to show you something."

"Yeah," he stood up. "Sure." Mark walked around the corner. Michael could just imagine what he was about to see.

"Nope," came Mark's voice, very matter of fact. "Beautiful, not an ounce of unwanted or undesired fat anywhere, I completely fail to see it."

"You... fail... to... see... any... fat?" she replied. Michael couldn't tell if she was astonished, annoyed her prank on Mark was failing so miserably, or realizing he really loved her body just the way it was.

It wasn't Michael's place to tell her most guys would gaze all day at her naked body and never get tired. THAT would be inappropriate.

"Okay," she answered contritely. "Uh, thank you." Michael heard her shut the bathroom door softly.

When Mark came around the corner, he winked at Michael and mouthed 'HOT!' Michael smirked at the young man. He had played his cards very well. The older vampire raised the last bite of his sandwich in salute to Mark before he finished it off and started cleaning up the kitchen.

A minute later, Jacqueline joined them, and he turned back around, all business.

"So, I learned some things this evening when a small army of vampires came here from Europe to attack New York..."

"What?" Jacqueline interrupted.

Yeah, she got over her embarrassment very quickly, he thought. "Yes, I'll tell you the full story later. But I need to make plans and want to be gone by the morning if possible. We," he pointed to the three of them in a circle, "need to understand what you two," this time, they were the only ones indicated, "are going to do going forward."

He put up a hand. "You have options, hear me out before you choose."

"Go with you," Jacqueline announced. Michael looked at her and her face colored. "Uh, if that's an option?"

"It is an option," Michael agreed. "But the statement *hear me out before you choose* generally means *hear me out before you choose.*"

"He's got you there," Mark whispered before the resounding *crack* of her slap across his arm put an exclamation mark to the end of his sentence. Mark waited a moment before slowly reaching across with his left hand to rub the spot where she hit him.

She had never turned from looking at Michael.

"Mark, let's start with you," Michael said. "I'll be traveling to Europe, which I haven't visited in over a hundred and fifty years, to locate a powerful vampire who has dozens, if not hundreds of minions, and thousands of soldiers."

"I'm in," Mark announced.

"I'm not done," Michael replied, his voice clipped. "Don't be taking lessons on how to answer too quickly from our resident Were here." He nodded at Jacqueline. "There is a very good chance you could be killed. There is a group of vampires, led by an honorable female who could probably use your technology skills, right here in New York. You can find the protection you need, and help a good group fight in your own town."

Mark shrugged. "I have nothing keeping me here. My parents are dead, my sister turned me into the local Enforcers for what, money? Because she was scared? I was feeding her soup to help her recover from the flu when they crashed down the door. I don't think I need that kind of family in my life."

Jacqueline turned to view Mark. "You were taking care of your sister?" Mark nodded. "God, that sucks." Mark shrugged.

"Besides," Mark worked up a smile. "I'd be working with you, the Dark Messiah himself. Who better to help me figure out how to stop popping the stupid pills?"

"Let me try this one more time," Michael looked straight into the young man's eyes. "You. Could. Die!"

Mark shrugged. "I'm already dead. I died back in that alley. My sister turned me in. You're the only reason I'm still alive! And, if I'm to have any future where I'm not a virgin? It's with you."

Michael tried his damnedest not to snort. Mark would be out of luck if Jacqueline decided to stay. He turned to the young female Were. "And you?"

This time, it was Jacqueline who turned introspective. "I'm just now starting to like the new me. The temptation to fall back into the old me is still there, with you I'll continue to strive to be the person I want to be."

Michael explained it as simply as he could a second time. "You could die."

Jacqueline pulled herself together, sat up in her chair and looked Michael straight in the eyes. "Then I'll die respecting myself, and I'll meet my father with my head held high. This new me?" she motioned at herself up and down, Mark's eyes following her finger. "This new me, I respect. And... more importantly, my father would respect."

Michael shrugged. "So be it. You're both old enough to make your own decisions. Mark, I can use the technological support, so don't think I'm bringing you along just because I'm nice. You will work. Jacqueline, you will train and then train some more. You will be used on operations in the future."

"Now, who knows what we need to use for money, and how we should go about getting it?" Michael asked them.

"Steal it," Mark answered and then noticed both of them looking annoyed with him. He put up his hands. "No! I don't mean take it from good people. I'm suggesting that we go to one of the bars that sell vampire blood to the rich and take it back."

"Oh?" Michael's eyes flashed red. "There's a place people go to buy vampire blood?" Mark swallowed and nodded, Michael's visage had gotten ugly, very quickly. "I'll be happy to visit them," he agreed.

"We need clothes," Jacqueline mentioned, hoping to bring Michael's annoyance back down. *Note to self,* she thought, *Don't talk about people selling vampire blood if you don't want DM to pop up in the middle of a conversation.*

She'd tell Mark the same thing later.

Michael's head pivoted to her, his eyes losing their I-am-going-to-rip-someone's-head-clean-off-their body look, and replaced with a why-do-you-need-more-clothes-now look.

She pointed at Mark. "Do Europeans dress the same way we do? And, does he have what we need to go overseas?"

Michael turned back to Mark who looked at them looking at him, and then looked down at himself. "What? I've got two or three pairs of something back at my place."

"Are they clean?" she asked. When Mark didn't reply, she added, "That's my point."

Mark tried to be sneaky, and sniff his shirt while he turned and faced the other direction.

"Mark will need new clothes," Michael agreed. "But that's because I doubt he will look the same."

"What? Why, am I changing?" Mark asked.

"Yes," Michael answered. "You'll be having your nanocytes modified. I imagine they will change your body a little bit, as well."

"Why?" Mark looked down at himself.

Michael said, "You'll need to be able to walk in the sunlight, and this will accomplish that. The new programming in your nanocytes..."

"Programming?" Mark interjected, excitement on his face.

"Focus," Jacqueline popped him on the arm.

"Yeah, got it, focus!" Mark rubbed his arm again. "Say, could we find a new way to get your point across?"

"Yes, but you can't handle it, trust me," she said, her voice a sexy kitten purr.

Mark looked sideways at her and swallowed. He turned back to Michael. "I'm sorry, nanocytes, sunlight?"

Jacqueline looked positively pleased with herself. Michael wanted to rub his face, he was too old to be a father to two young people, when killing them was the only punishment not permitted.

Michael nodded. "Yes, you will have your nanocytes reprogrammed. First thing in the morning, you two will find a place and acquire clothes for the trip. We will need transportation for the three of us."

"Ah," Mark put up a finger. "The winds have been pretty messed up since you were around a hundred and fifty years ago. The airships might or might not have any trips going back right now."

"Is that so?" Michael asked, and Mark nodded. "Then I'll have a talk with one of the captains that just came across."

Mark shrugged. He didn't know what captains Michael would talk to, but that wasn't his concern at the moment.

"All right, you two get some sleep, I'll get the money and work on passage and then we will be leaving." He turned to Jacqueline. "No dawdling when you shop. Mark, come with me."

Her face was a study in innocence.

Michael walked out of the kitchen, assuming he was going to find that she had pulled a fast one somehow. Mark was screwed, Michael thought, but not in a way Mark was probably hoping for.

—

Lucas Brzezicki, bouncer, eyed the two young women, diamond necklaces working to compete with the short... Lucas looked once more, taking in the very short rhinestone dresses they were wearing. One in white, one in black.

Yin and Yang, Lucas approved. He moved his seven foot tall,

three hundred pound mountain of muscle and reached down to unhook the velvet rope, allowing the two women to cross before reaching back to hook it up again.

Michael Mysted into the club along with the two women.

Like clubs he had been in for centuries, it was dark, it was loud, and it smelled of pheromones, smoke, and alcohol.

The music wasn't anything he recognized, but then he had slept through a few decades so perhaps it was new, something he missed.

He searched for the expected door to the back and noticed a large Russian-looking man in a black suit standing beside a blank wall.

Michael considered his next action and shrugged. He doubted the UnknownWorld was going to be undercover to the general populace for very long after the fight earlier. He made his way around the dance floor. People were still gyrating against each other after midnight. The guard turned towards Michael, taking in the white shirt, dark blue jeans and expensive looking boots he was wearing under his coat.

He leaned over so Michael could speak to him.

Michael looked out over the dance floor, ostensibly to check if anyone was watching them before he turned to the guard. "Who would I speak to regarding the blood?"

"You got the cash?" he asked.

Michael shrugged and pulled the cost of the blood out of the man's head. It was incredible what the value of money had become once they dropped it down to strictly coins. "I've got it." He pulled out a handful of change to show him.

The guard looked down and nodded. He reached over to the wall and pushed on it. Michael heard a click, and it opened up a few inches. He nodded to the guard and walked in.

Inside, the hallway was poorly lit and the carpet was worn. While the club had seemed in good shape, back here was a mess.

There were four doors in the hallway, the first on his left was open. He could hear a man talking, so Michael waited and listened. They were talking about the fight earlier.

"I don't care, Wyznoski!" he was saying. "There were fucking vampires all over down there. What kind of shit is going on?" Michael heard a few taps of a pen. "Look, screw this. I'm done. No, you said this was a few vampires selling their blood for some money. I heard the rumors, you guys in Enforcement are sucking them dry. Now, those that you were preying on are running around killing your asses."

There was a pause before he came back on. "Yeah? You think I'm concerned about you coming over here? No, you guys have lost it. You're going to be running and gunning now for a while. Yeah, well, I'll have the guys show you in, and we can talk. But before you come over, why don't you see if you can get your building back." The phone slammed down before the man spat, "Jackass!"

Michael took two steps and turned left into the doorway. The balding older man noticed him coming in his office. "What the hell do you..." His eyes opened wide, taking in his black trench coat and bald head. "Oh shit. You're him!"

Michael raised an eyebrow. "Which 'him' are we speaking about?"

The bald man put his hands up. "Look, I don't want any problems with you guys. I thought this blood stuff was all legit, or I wouldn't have done it."

Michael stepped further into the office and sat on his desk. "Louis, isn't it?" he asked, and the man nodded. "I heard your side of the conversation a minute ago, so I understand your side. So, two questions." He received another nod. "What do you get for money from Europe?"

"Mostly same as here, coin. Although, if you have any Euros, they might work as a single. Doesn't matter the denomination, though."

Well, that explained some of the inflation trade-offs.

"Where does one get this coin?"

Louis shrugged. "We get it from time to time, but it sits here. It's easier to take it and keep the customers happy. If any of my people go to Europe, we spot them."

"Money exchange?" Michael asked.

"Usually you get half face value because it's such a pain," he said.

"I see." Michael stood up. "Your blood is going down the drain."

"What, tonight?" Louis asked in alarm, noticing Michael's annoyance. "Yeah, sure, tonight. That bastard Wyznoski would probably confiscate it anyway, he'll just think I'm doing this and rough up the place. I'll hide the good liquor."

Michael's smile turned malicious. "How bad do you want to keep them from damaging your club, Louis?"

The next day, Wyznoski showed up to take back the blood. After seeing the bandages, the black eyes and the sutures, Wyznoski believed Louis's story that the Dark Messiah had been there.

After visiting two other clubs, Wyznoski decided that maybe he should get out of the blood trade as well. It wasn't looking like it would remain a profitable operation.

Or good for his health.

—

Michael arrived back at his house to find the other two getting ready. Michael had shared blood with Mark, then pushed energy into him and sent him to bed earlier. Now, Mark was awake, but he was certainly tired. "I feel like I want to sleep for a month," the younger vampire said while he was pulling on a shirt, talking to Michael who was watching him from the door.

Wearing a shirt that didn't seem to fit him too well, Mark sat on his bed and stared at his arms. The shirt was at least a half-inch too short for him at the moment.

"Well, this is unexpected," Michael said. "Try on your pants."

Mark slipped his pants on. While they fit in the waist, maybe even a bit more loosely than before, the length was going to be a real problem.

Mark looked at his clothes, then up at Michael. "What's going on?"

Michael thought back to his conversations with Bethany Anne and through her, with TOM. "Your genetics."

Mark looked as confused as he must feel. "What's wrong with my genetics?"

"Your genetics must have a better version of you designed in your DNA. The genes that made the original you weren't the best choices apparently."

"So... I'm growing again?" he asked, and Michael nodded.

"When will it stop?" he asked.

Michael shrugged. "Sometimes, people could be in the Pod-doc for a month or more. But, I wasn't expecting you to do anything this drastic, since the Pod-doc can make proactive changes, more radical changes, and my blood shouldn't be able to do anything like this. Frankly, this is surprising."

"That's not good," Mark mumbled, looking down at himself.

Michael smirked. "Oh, it's going to be good long term, trust me."

—

"What happened to you?" Jacqueline asked, stopping in her tracks to take in her shopping partner. "Did your clothes shrink?" She started biting her lip, trying to figure out why he was so different.

He shook his head at her question.

She made a face and stepped closer to him, then grabbed his arm and pulled him next to her. She looked up, her eyes widening. "You've grown!" She grabbed him by his upper arm. "Flex!"

Mark made a muscle and then looked at Michael before returning his gaze to the Were. He hesitated before asking, "Are you purring?"

The purring stopped.

"No!" she replied, letting go of his arm. "Of course not. But you're getting stronger, that means more kata work for you!" She turned quickly and went towards the stairs to go to the street level. "Let's go shopping!" she called out before turning the corner and stepping out of sight.

"I'll drop you two off outside. When you're done, I'll meet you back in the park."

—

Captain Miles O'Banion was stationed ten miles off the New York City-State coast. He had been roped into the damned invasion, and now he had an airship, twenty damned Nosferatu in his hold with no vampires aboard, and fuck-all idea of what to do next.

The trip back to Europe... if he showed up empty handed and the Duke found out, would be a one-way trip... with excruciating pain at the end. Not much of an option, if you asked him. With eighteen other men and women looking to him for leadership, he wanted to ask them what the hell was he supposed to do? He had been pulled out of his home, tossed on the airship and told what to do. That he gave half a flying shit about these people looking to him was a curse, not a damned benefit for him personally.

He wouldn't fly the Jolly Roger, that was out, and he shut up the two guys who even mentioned it. Either of them, he told both emphatically, would take a short hop off the side of the ship if they ever brought it up again.

Miles walked out to the top deck, feeling the wind in his hair. The storms from the previous night could be seen in the west, and another group of clouds could possibly be forming to the east. No one on the radio was coming across right now and talking, so he had no other information to make his decision on whether to go back or stay right here. Until he figured out what to do with those damned Nosferatu, or they died, he couldn't take any freight on with them in the hold.

"Captain O'Banion," a voice called out from behind him. He turned from looking over the side to see a bald man in a black trench coat, his hands behind his back staring at him.

"Aye," he acknowledged. "I am. Who are you an—" The flashbacks to the screaming on the radio last night, the people talking about the Dark Messiah, the man in the black coat, raining lightning down on the Nosferatu. He swallowed. "I mean, yes?"

Michael's smile didn't warm Miles's heart. "That's better, Captain O'Banion. I'm not too happy with the attempt to bring those Nosferatu into New York, be glad I don't just drop this airship into the water below."

Miles made a face and turned to spit over the side, keeping his eyes on the man. "If I knew how to toss them over my side right here, I would have done it already. I didn't hire on to this mess, I was shanghaied if you understand my meaning." He pointed to the few people who had stuck their heads out or were watching this new man, wondering what he was saying to the Captain.

And how the hell had he gotten on the ship?

Michael turned his head slightly. "You're worried about the Duke?"

"Of course," Miles agreed. "Anyone with half a brain worries about a vampire." He narrowed his eyes. "Except you."

Michael's smile reached his eyes. "No, I don't," he said. His smile disappeared.

"But they all worry about *me*," he finished.

—

Michael tossed half the Nosferatu off the ship by simply commanding ten to climb out before he grabbed them and threw them over the side. He could have had them climb over the side and jump, but that wasn't as impressive as physically grabbing a grown human being and throwing them through the air as if they weighed the same as a small rock.

He had the Captain bring everyone out onto the deck when

Michael explained what they would be doing and then explained he would be back.

Then he disappeared.

Unfortunately for the one loudmouth who decided it was past time to push for his idea of turning pirate, Michael hadn't left.

Everyone realized he hadn't left when Michael appeared right behind the wanna-be pirate, eyes flaring red and grabbed him by the neck. "The Captain," Michael told the man as he picked him up and walked to the side of the ship, his legs kicking futilely as he tried to break Michael's grip on his neck, "told you no to turning pirate once already. That was sufficient."

The falling man's screams after Michael tossed him off the ship reinforced the idea that the Captain was in charge. Michael disappeared once more.

This time, no one assumed he was gone.

—

Michael found his two charges in the park, arguing.

"And I'm telling you," her finger stabbed Mark in the chest, "that this looks good and you'll grow into it!"

"I look like a jock!" Mark exclaimed, a look of horror on his face.

"Exactly!" she replied. "*Hot!*"

"How does this," his voice was heated, his hand waving up and down his body, "say hot?"

"Listen," Jacqueline huffed, "for now you have to imagine you packing on another ten pounds of muscle, because when you do, this is going to fill out. It won't look like an oversized sack on you, I promise."

"And if you're wrong," he countered, "how does it get fixed?"

"I can fix it," she assured him.

"Hooooowww?" Mark emphasized his question by drawing it out.

"Needle and thread, easy-peasy," she told him.

Mark stared at her for a moment. "You're going to take in these clothes?"

"If I'm wrong?" She looked at him a second time and put out her hand. "I will!" He reached for her hand, and she jerked it back. "BUT!" she said. "If I'm right, what do I get?"

"What do you want?" he asked.

Jacqueline thought about it for a moment, remembering a story she read when she was young. "You have to say 'as you wish' for one whole day every time I ask you to do something."

Mark squinted at her. "No more than three times," he countered.

She pursed her lips. "Okay, deal," she replied, reached out and the two shook hands.

"Wonderful," Michael said, and they jumped, turning to see him standing five feet away.

—

The sheets were strewn all over the bed, both people gasping for air.

BAM BAM BAM...

The woman spoke between breaths, "Maybe they'll go away?"

BAM BAM BAM...

"No," he answered. "I recognize that banging..."

BAM BAM BAM...

"How can you recognize banging?" she asked, running her hand along his side. His skin reacted, bumps rising.

BAM BAM BAM...

"Oh fuck it," he griped, getting up from the bed. The woman admired his ass as he walked out of the bedroom. She wondered idly if he was going to answer the door naked.

BAM BAM BAM...

"Go away!" he yelled. She heard another male voice yelling, but couldn't tell what he said.

BAM BAM BAM...

Finally, her lover opened the door. "Ted! I said no fucking way are you getting in here, I don't care what time it is, they can all kiss my ass, I'll see you tomorrow." There was a pause before he added, "Nice seeing you too, Milton."

SLAM!

Janine smiled, she liked it when Ethan talked dirty.

—

Captain Miles O'Banion was eyeing a fresh storm brewing on the horizon south of them. It shouldn't come this way, but he'd normally move his ship to keep it a little further away from the turbulence. The extra air required them to run the gravitic generators more, taking a lot of battery power.

No way was he moving at the moment, though. He didn't trust that he and his people weren't being tested right at that very moment. While he appreciated the support of the new owner of the ship, he didn't want to piss him off, either.

Certainly, not a daywalking vampire.

Miles happened to be staring across the deck when three people appeared right in the middle, with luggage.

It was the man in the black coat accompanied by a strong-looking young man and a very attractive brunette with dark eyes.

They made a good looking family, he thought.

He nodded to the man and turned around. He walked into the ship's bridge and picked up the radio mic. "Attention New York Air Control. This is the DMS ArchAngel, we are leaving your zone, headed toward England, then Europe."

"The is NYAC, ArchAngel, understood. Name change complete, heading to England. I imagine you've seen the storm to your south. One other storm reported off the west coast of France but is expected to also head south of your path. Please report all weather you find and pirates you see. Safe voyage, DMS ArchAngel."

Miles clicked his mic. "Understood. Safe times to you and yours. ArchAngel out."

Miles O'Banion stepped out of his bridge and eyed the two

youths. Neither seemed particularly afraid of the man, unlike the Duke back in Europe. In fact, they appeared to smile more than those around the other set of vampires.

He felt a little hope that maybe this time he and his crew would be working for that rarest of mythological creatures.

An Honorable Vampire.

FINIS

THE BLACK POD was silently moving through the upper atmosphere much higher than the storm raging below when the person occupying the front seat received a message.

A moment later, the Pod turned east, heading to the New York City-State.

AUTHOR NOTES - MICHAEL ANDERLE

DECEMBER 22, 2016

As always, can I say with a HUGE amount of appreciation how much it means to me that you not only read this book, but you are reading these notes as well?

Let me get some of the normal stuff out of the way, then I will talk Dark Messiah.

The last time I had my own Author's Note (in a non-collaboration book) was "way back on November 12th, 2016" with **Don't Cross This Line.**

It seems like forever ago that I published that book (It was 6 weeks). Why? Because since that time, I have published and worked on multiple books with multiple authors plus The Dark Messiah...and Thanksgiving was in the middle of that time somewhere.

I'm going to chat a little more about this, but let me talk the books, first.

Three of these books now out include:

JUSTICE IS CALLING (Reclaiming Honor Series) - (December 8th, 2016) Written with Justin Sloan. As of right now, it is still top #1,000 book on Amazon (here are the rankings):

Amazon Best Sellers Rank: #845 Paid in Kindle Store (See Top 100 Paid in Kindle Store)

#1 in Kindle Store > Kindle eBooks > Mystery, Thriller & Suspense > Suspense > Paranormal > **Vampires**

#6 in Kindle Store > Kindle eBooks > Mystery, Thriller & Suspense > Suspense > Paranormal > **Werewolves & Shifters**

#8 in Kindle Store > Kindle eBooks > Science Fiction & Fantasy > Science Fiction > **Genetic Engineering**

NOMAD FOUND (Terry Henry Walton Chronicles) - (December 21st, 2016) Written with Craig Martelle. As of right now, it is a top #1,000 book on Amazon (here are the rankings):

Amazon Best Sellers Rank: #359 Paid in Kindle Store (See Top 100 Paid in Kindle Store)

#1 in Kindle Store > Kindle eBooks > Mystery, Thriller & Suspense > Suspense > Paranormal > **Werewolves & Shifters**

#2 in Books > Science Fiction & Fantasy > Science Fiction > **Post-Apocalyptic**

#3 in Books > Science Fiction & Fantasy > Science Fiction > **Genetic Engineering**

BELLATRIX (Frank Kurns Stories of the UnknownWorld) - (December 22nd, 2016) Written with Natalie Grey. As of right now, we have no ranking as it is too soon to get one. However, here are a few review comments:

"Love the back story on Bellatrix. Hope to see more of her and the puppies in future books (huge dog lover). Bobcat finally gets what he deserves. Alec has lots of potential now the he has been upgraded, looking forward to see where he shows up again."

and

"So I love this so much I was surprised when it ended. I want more. The characters are so entertaining, that I was laughing out loud at times. Great debut, keep them coming."

Working with each of the authors above is a different experience, to be sure. I realized as I was writing the author notes for BELLATRIX that Natalie Grey was the first female author I was collaborating with in The Kurtherian Gambit. I thought that was cool. I hadn't MEANT it to be an all-male club (Paul C. Middleton, Justin Sloan, Criag Martelle, TS (Scott) Paul and Tom Dickerson) but that is what had happened.

However, it won't be the last, I don't think. I've had two (2) other lady authors approach me and one is working on her trilogy collaboration which should be done end of March and then will setup to work inside the Universe. Another is looking to talk again in January for starting her efforts in late February after she does a seminar for author's on building worlds.

Plus, Natalie Grey is doing a Trilogy (first book out January) so we will see a bunch more from her.

THANK GOD that a lot of fans loved the first books coming out from Justin and Craig! It would have ever-loving *SUCKED* if they had bombed. I know that a lot of readers assume that since my name isn't on top, I'm not as involved but that isn't the case (less on Bellatrix - but that is because Stephen Russell picked up the slack).

However, while the authors and I talk beats, and what can and can't happen and maybe emotional tone - THEY write the stories. I might edit the books during my pass, but I rarely change anything even halfway significant (well, ok, I might add a bit more colorful language in there a few times…but I digress).

Except for Paul's…I'm not allowed to add colorful language to the Etheric Academy.

There is one thing that all books share, the core that is The Kurtherian Gambit. The reason for picking up any of these series and raising your fist in the air, or shedding a tear, or laughing out loud and having people look at you funny and that is *emotion*. The sense that Honor is important, Justice is warranted and the opportunity to flip off those who believe otherwise is, at our core, something that makes each of us…you, me, the next TKG fan next to you tick.

Now, we come to The Dark Messiah.

Wow, to say I freaked a little thinking about writing Michael's Return wouldn't be doing justice to my experience. I had a few times where I wanted to chew off my fingernails, thinking about it.

Michael Anderle

Thank you to the following Super Help
    for putting together a SERIES TIMELINE
    Keith Hellis

Michael Anderle Social

Website:
http://kurtherianbooks.com/
Email List:
http://kurtherianbooks.com/email-list/
Facebook Here:
https://facebook.com/TheKurtherianGambitBooks/

Michael Anderle

Kurtherian Gambit Series Titles Include:

First Arc

Death Becomes Her (01) - Queen Bitch (02) - Love Lost (03) -
Bite This (04)
Never Forsaken (05) - Under My Heel (06) - Kneel Or Die (07)

Second Arc

We Will Build (08) - It's Hell To Choose (09) - Release The Dogs
of War (10)
Sued For Peace (11) - We Have Contact (12) - My Ride is a
Bitch (13)
Don't Cross This Line (14)

Third Arc (2017)

Never Submit (15) - Never Surrender (16) - Forever
Defend (17)
Might Makes Right (18) - Ahead Full (19) - Capture Death (20)
Life Goes On (21)

New Series

The Second Dark Ages

The Dark Messiah (01)
The Darkest Night (02)

The Boris Chronicles

STORIES BY MICHAEL ANDERLE

* With Paul C. Middleton *

Evacuation
Retaliation
Revelation
Restitution 2017

Reclaiming Honor
* With JUSTIN SLOAN *

Justice Is Calling (01)
Claimed By Honor (02)
Judgement Has Fallen (03)
Angel of Reckoning (04)
Born Into Flames (05)
Defending The Lost (06)

The Etheric Academy
* With TS PAUL *

ALPHA CLASS (01)
ALPHA CLASS - Engineering (02)
ALPHA CLASS (03) Coming soon

Terry Henry "TH" Walton Chronicles
* With CRAIG MARTELLE *

Nomad Found (01)
Nomad Redeemed (02)
Nomad Unleashed (03)
Nomad Supreme (04)
Nomad's Fury (05)
Nomad's Justice (06)
Nomad Avenged (07)

STORIES BY MICHAEL ANDERLE

Shades of Dark (02)

Storms of Magic
With PT Hylton

Storm Raiders (01)
Storm Callers (02)

Tales of the Feisty Druid
With Candy Crum

The Arcadian Druid (01)
The Undying Illusionist (02)

Path of Heroes
With Brandon Barr

Rogue Mage (01)

The Revelations of Oriceran

The Leira Chronicles
With Martha Carr

Quest for Magic (0)
Waking Magic (1)
Release of Magic (2)

SHORT STORIES

Frank Kurns Stories of the Unknownworld 01 (7.5)
You Don't Touch John's Cousin

Frank Kurns Stories of the Unknownworld 02 (9.5)

Bitch's Night Out

Bellatrix: Frank Kurns Stories of the Unknownworld 03 (13.25)
With Natalie Grey

AudioBooks

CLICK HERE TO SEE ALL LMBPN BOOKS ON AUDIBLE

Available at Audible.com and iTunes

The Kurtherian Gambit

Death Becomes Her - Available Now
Queen Bitch – Available Now
Love Lost – Available Now
Bite This - Available Now
Never Forsaken - Available Now
Under My Heel - Available Now
Kneel or Die - Available Now

Reclaiming Honor Series

Justice Is Calling
Claimed By Honor
Judgment Has Fallen
Angel of Reckoning

Terry Henry "TH" Walton Chronicles

Nomad Found
Nomad Redeemed
Nomad Unleashed

CPSIA information can be obtained
at www.ICGtesting.com
Printed in the USA
LVHW030712061118
595974LV00003B/92/P

9 781642 020175